...'s

...TO ME

"Absolutely first rate—readers will be thrilled and delighted by this new Rizzoli & Isles outing!"
—SHARI LAPENA, *New York Times* bestselling
author of *The Couple Next Door*

"Suspenseful and clever—nobody is who they seem to be in this shocking and fast-paced mystery. Come for Rizzoli & Isles. Stay for an unbeatable read."
—KARIN SLAUGHTER, *New York Times*
and internationally bestselling author

"I loved *Listen to Me*. Only the super-talented Tess Gerritsen can meld multiple storylines so successfully while she keeps the twists coming, the pages turning, and the blood spray arterial. This is her best novel yet. If you haven't read Rizzoli & Isles, this is the one to get!"
—LISA SCOTTOLINE, #1 bestselling
author of *What Happened to the Bennetts*

"Gerritsen walks that high wire between humor and suspense without ever falling off as she plays a great game of bait and switch with her readers."
—LINWOOD BARCLAY, *New York Times* bestselling
author of *Take Your Breath Away*

RIZZOLI & ISLES: LISTEN TO ME

BY TESS GERRITSEN

RIZZOLI & ISLES NOVELS

The Surgeon
The Apprentice
The Sinner
Body Double
Vanish
The Mephisto Club
The Keepsake
Ice Cold
The Silent Girl
Last to Die
Die Again
I Know a Secret
Listen to Me

OTHER NOVELS

Girl Missing
Harvest
Life Support
Bloodstream
Gravity
The Bone Garden
Playing with Fire
The Shape of Night
Choose Me (with Gary Braver)

RIZZOLI & ISLES:

LISTEN TO ME

A NOVEL

TESS GERRITSEN

BALLANTINE BOOKS · NEW YORK

Rizzoli & Isles: Listen to Me is a work of fiction.
Names, characters, places, and incidents are the products
of the author's imagination or are used fictitiously.
Any resemblance to actual events, locales, or persons,
living or dead, is entirely coincidental.

2023 Ballantine Books Mass Market Edition
Copyright © 2022 by Tess Gerritsen

Published in the United States by Ballantine Books,
an imprint of Random House, a division of
Penguin Random House LLC, New York.

BALLANTINE is a registered trademark and the colophon
is a trademark of Penguin Random House LLC.

Originally published in hardcover in the United States
by Ballantine Books, an imprint of Random House, a division of
Penguin Random House LLC, in 2022.

ISBN 9780593497159
Ebook ISBN 9780593497142

Cover design: Regina Flath
Cover images: © Magdalena Russocka/Trevillion Images (window),
Alex Linck/Shutterstock (house), Mario Savoa/Shutterstock (crack)

Printed in the United States of America

randomhousebooks.com

2 4 6 8 9 7 5 3 1

Ballantine Books mass market edition: February 2023

To Josh and Laura

RIZZOLI & ISLES: LISTEN TO ME

ONE

AMY

I SHOULD HAVE WORN MY BOOTS, she thought as she stepped out of Snell Library and saw the fresh layer of sleet and slush covering the campus. When she'd left for school that morning it had been a balmy forty-nine degrees, one in a string of springlike days that made her believe winter was finally over, and she had come to campus wearing blue jeans and a hoodie and brand-new pink flats made of buttery leather. But while she'd been inside all day working on her laptop, outside, winter had come roaring back. Now it was dark, and with this frigid wind sweeping across the courtyard, the pavement would soon be as slick as an ice rink.

With a sigh, she zipped up her hoodie and hauled her backpack, heavy with books and her laptop, onto her shoulders. *There's no way around it. Here we go.* Gingerly she descended the library stairs and landed ankle-deep in slush. Her feet now wet and stinging, she forged ahead down the path between Haydn Hall and Blackman Auditorium. Well, these new shoes were ruined. Stupid, stupid. That's what she got for not checking the forecast this morning. For forgetting that March in Boston could bre'ak a girl's heart.

She reached Eli Hall and suddenly stopped. Turned.

Were those footsteps she'd heard behind her? For a moment she stared at the alley that cut between the two buildings but all she saw was the deserted walkway, glistening beneath the lamplight. Darkness and bad weather had emptied out the campus and she heard no footsteps now, just the rattle of falling sleet and the distant *whish* of cars traveling down Huntington Avenue.

She hugged her hoodie tighter and kept walking.

The campus quadrangle was slick and gleaming with a crust of ice and her sadly inadequate shoes crunched through the rime into puddles, splashing her jeans with ice water. She could no longer feel her toes.

This was all Prof. Harthoorn's fault. He was the reason she'd spent all day in the library, the reason she wasn't at home right now, eating dinner with her parents. But here she was, toes numb with impending frostbite, all because her senior thesis—the thirty-two-page paper she'd been working on for months—was *incomplete,* he'd said. *Inadequate,* he'd said, because she hadn't addressed the pivotal event in Artemisia Gentileschi's life, the life-changing trauma that imbued her paintings with such violent and visceral power: being raped.

As if women were formless lumps of clay, needing to be pummeled and abused to be shaped into something greater. As if what Artemisia needed to become an artist was a good old-fashioned sexual assault.

She felt more and more angry about Harthoorn's comments as she walked across the quad, splashing through slush. What did a dried-up old man like him know about women and all the wearying and infuriating annoyances they had to tolerate? All the helpful advice foisted on them by men with their *I know better* voices.

She reached the crosswalk and stopped at the pedestrian light, which had just turned red. Of course it was red; nothing today had gone her way. Cars rolled past, tires spraying up water. Sleet clattered on her backpack, and she thought about her laptop and whether it was getting wet and she'd lose all the work she'd put in this afternoon. Yes, that would perfectly cap off her day. It's what she deserved for not checking the forecast. For not bringing an umbrella. For wearing these stupid shoes.

The light was still red. Was it broken? Should she ignore it and just make a dash across the street?

She was so focused on the light that she wasn't aware of the man standing behind her. Then something about him caught her attention. Perhaps it was the rustle of his nylon jacket, or the odor of alcohol drifting on his breath. All at once she knew someone was there and she turned to look at him.

He was so bundled up against the cold, with a scarf wrapped up to his chin and a wool cap pulled down to his eyebrows, that all she could really see of his face were his eyes. He didn't avoid her gaze but looked straight back at her with a stare so piercing that she felt violated, as if that stare was vacuuming out her deepest secrets. He made no move toward her but his gaze was enough to make her uneasy.

She glanced across Huntington Avenue, at the businesses across the street. The taco shop was open, its windows brightly lit, and she could see half a dozen customers inside. A safe place, with people to turn to if she needed help. She could duck in there to get warm, and maybe call an Uber to take her home.

The light turned green at last.

She stepped too quickly off the curb and the sole of

her leather flat instantly skidded across the ice-slicked road. Arms flywheeling, she fought to stay upright but the backpack threw her off-balance and down she went, her rump splashing down into slush. Soaked and shaken, she staggered back to her feet.

She never saw the headlights hurtling toward her.

TWO

ANGELA

Two Months Later

IF YOU SEE SOMETHING, SAY SOMETHING. We've all heard
that advice so many times that whenever we find a
suspicious package where it shouldn't be, or notice a
stranger lurking in the neighborhood, we automatically
pay attention. Certainly I do, especially since my daughter, Jane, is a cop, and my boyfriend, Vince, is a retired
cop. I've heard all their horror stories and if I see something, you bet I'm going to say something. So it's only
second nature for me to keep an eye on my own
neighborhood.

I live in the city of Revere, which strictly speaking
isn't in the city of Boston proper, but is more like Boston's more affordable cousin to the north. Mine is a
street of modest single-family homes tucked in side by
side. *Starter homes* was what Frank (soon to be my ex-
husband) called them when we moved here forty years
ago, except that we never moved on to anything bigger.
Neither did Agnes Kaminsky who still lives next door,
or Glen Druckmeyer who died in the house across the
street, which made it the opposite of a starter home for
him. As the years went by, I watched families move in,

then move out. The house to my right is once again vacant and for sale, waiting for the next family to cycle through. To my left lives Agnes, who used to be my best friend until I started dating Vince Korsak, which scandalized Agnes because my divorce isn't final yet, and this made me a scarlet woman in her eyes. Even though Frank was the one who walked out of our marriage to be with another woman. A blonde. What really turned Agnes against me is the fact I *enjoy* myself so much now that Frank's gone. I *enjoy* having a new man in my life and kissing him in my own backyard. What does Agnes think I'm supposed to do now that my husband's left me? Drape myself in virtuous black and keep my legs crossed until everything down there dries up? She and I hardly talk anymore, but we don't need to. I already know what she's up to next door. The same things she's always done: smoking her Virginia Slims, watching QVC, and overcooking her vegetables.

But that's not for me to judge.

Across the street, starting at the corner, is the blue house owned by Larry and Lorelei Leopold, who've lived here for the past twenty or so years. Larry teaches English at the local high school, and while I can't say we're close, we do play Scrabble together every Thursday night so I'm well acquainted with the breadth of Larry's vocabulary. Next to the Leopolds is the house where Glen Druckmeyer died, which used to be for rent. And next door to that, in the house directly across the street from me, lives Jonas, a sixty-two-year-old bachelor and former Navy SEAL who moved here six years ago. Lorelei recently invited Jonas to the Scrabble nights at my house, which should've been a group decision, but Jonas turned out to be an excellent addition.

He always brings a bottle of Ecco Domani cabernet, he has a good vocabulary, and he doesn't try to sneak in foreign words, which shouldn't be allowed. Scrabble is, after all, an American game. I have to admit, he's also a fine-looking fellow. Unfortunately he knows it, and he likes to mow his front lawn while shirtless, his chest puffed out, his biceps bulging. Naturally, I can't help but watch him and he knows it. When he sees me at my window, he makes a point of waving to me, which makes Agnes Kaminsky think something's going on between us, which isn't true. I'm just everyone's friendly neighbor, and if someone moves onto our street, I'm always the first at their door with a smile and zucchini bread. People appreciate that. They invite me into their homes, introduce their children, tell me where they're from and what they do for a living. They ask me to recommend a plumber or a dentist. We exchange phone numbers and promises to get together soon. That's how it's been with all my neighbors.

Until the Greens moved in.

They are renting number 2533, the yellow house where Glen Druckmeyer died. The house has been vacant for a year and I'm glad someone is finally occupying it. It's never good to have a house sit empty too long; it reflects on the entire street, giving it a whiff of undesirability.

On the day I see the Greens' U-Haul truck pull up, I automatically pull a loaf of my famous zucchini bread out of the freezer. As it thaws, I stand on my porch, trying to glimpse the new neighbors. I see the husband first, as he steps out of the driver's side: tall, blond, muscular. Not smiling. That's the first detail that strikes me. When you arrive at your new home, shouldn't you be smiling?

Instead, he coolly surveys the neighborhood, head swiveling, eyes hidden by mirrored sunglasses.

I wave hello, but he doesn't immediately return the greeting. He just stands looking at me for a moment. At last he raises his arm in a mechanical wave, as if the chip in his computer brain has analyzed the situation and decided the correct response is to wave back.

Well, okay, I think. Maybe the wife is friendlier.

She steps out of the passenger side of the U-Haul. Early thirties, silvery-blond hair, a slender figure in blue jeans. She too checks out the street, but with quick, darting looks, like a squirrel. I wave at her and she offers a tentative wave back.

That's all the invitation I need. I walk across the street and say, "May I be the first to welcome you to the neighborhood!"

"It's nice to meet you," she says. She glances at her husband, as if seeking permission to say more. My antennae twitch because there's something going on between this couple. They don't seem comfortable together, and my mind goes straight to all the ways a marriage can go wrong. I should know.

"I'm Angela Rizzoli," I tell them. "And you are?"

"I'm, um, Carrie. And this is Matt." The answer comes out in stutters, as if she has to think about each word before she says it.

"I've lived on this street for forty years, so if you need to know anything at all about the area, you know who to ask."

"Tell us about our neighbors," Matt says. He glances at number 2535, the blue house next door. "What are they like?"

"Oh, that's the Leopolds. Larry and Lorelei. Larry

teaches English at the public high school and Lorelei's a housewife. See how nicely they keep up their yard? Larry's good that way, never lets a weed grow in his garden. They don't have kids, so they're nice, quiet neighbors. On the other side of you is Jonas. He's retired from the Navy SEALs, and boy does he have tales to tell about it. And on my side of the street, right next door to my house, is Agnes Kaminsky. Her husband died ages ago and she never remarried. I guess she likes things just fine the way they are. We used to be best friends, until my husband—" I realize I'm rambling and pause. They don't need to hear how Agnes and I fell out. I'm sure they'll be hearing about it from her. "So do you have kids?" I ask.

It's a simple question, but once again Carrie glances at her husband, as if needing permission to answer.

"No," he says. "Not yet."

"Then you won't need babysitter referrals. It's getting harder and harder to find them anyway." I turn to Carrie. "Say, I've got a nice loaf of zucchini bread defrosting in my kitchen. I'm famous for my recipe, even if I do say so myself. I'll bring it right over."

He answers for them both. "That's kind, but no thank you. We're allergic."

"To zucchini?"

"To gluten. No wheat products." He places a hand on his wife's shoulder and nudges her toward the house. "Well, we've got to get settled. See you around, ma'am." They both walk into their house and shut the door.

I look at the U-Haul, which they haven't even opened yet. Wouldn't any other couple be anxious to move their stuff into the house? The first thing I'd do is unpack my coffeemaker and teakettle. But no, Carrie and Matt Green have left everything in the moving truck.

All afternoon their U-Haul stays parked on the street, locked up tight.

It's not until after dark when I hear the clatter of metal, and I peer across the street to see the husband's silhouette standing at the rear of the vehicle. Matt climbs inside and a moment later backs down the ramp, wheeling a dolly loaded with boxes. Why did he wait until dark to unload the U-Haul? What doesn't he want the neighbors to see? There must not be very much in the truck, as it takes him only ten minutes to finish the job. He locks the truck and retreats into the house. Inside, the lights are on, but I can't see a thing because they've closed the blinds.

During my four decades on this street I have had as neighbors alcoholics and adulterers and a wife beater. Maybe two. I've never met any couple as standoffish as Carrie and Matt Green. Maybe I was too pushy. Maybe they're having marital problems and they just can't deal with an inquisitive neighbor right now. It may be entirely my fault that we didn't hit it off.

I will have to give them some space.

But the next day, and the next, and the next, I can't help watching number 2533. I see Larry Leopold leave for his job at the high school. I see Jonas, shirtless, mowing his lawn. I see my nemesis, Agnes, puffing on a cigarette on her twice-daily march of disapproval past my house.

But the Greens? They manage to slip by me like wraiths. I catch only the briefest glimpse of him behind the wheel of a black Toyota as he pulls into the garage. I spy him hanging venetian blinds in the upstairs windows. I see FedEx deliver a box to their home, which the driver tells me was shipped from BH Photo in New York City. (It never hurts to know that your neighborhood FedEx driver is crazy about zucchini bread.) What I don't see is any sign that these people have jobs. They live irregular lives, coming and going without any apparent schedule, acting as if they're retired. I ask the Leopolds and Jonas about them, but they don't know any more than I do. The Greens are a mystery to us all.

All this I've explained over the phone to my daughter, Jane, who you'd think would be as curious about this as I am. She points out there's nothing criminal about wanting to stay away from the neighborhood snoop. She's proud of her instincts as a cop, proud of being able to sense when something's not right, but she has no regard for a mother's instincts. When I call her for the third time about the Greens, she finally loses her patience.

"Call me when something actually *happens,*" she snaps at me.

A week later, sixteen-year-old Tricia Talley disappears.

THREE

JANE

BUBBLES SPIRALED PAST A CINDERELLA-PINK CASTLE, stirring a forest of plastic kelp where a pirate's chest overflowed with gemstones. A mermaid with swirling red hair reclined on her clamshell bed, surrounded by a legion of crustacean admirers. Only one occupant of this underwater wonderland was actually alive, and at that moment it was staring through the blood-spattered glass at Detective Jane Rizzoli.

"This is a pretty fancy aquarium for one little goldfish," said Jane. "I think she's got the whole cast of *The Little Mermaid* in here. All this for a fish that's just gonna get flushed down the toilet in a year."

"Not necessarily. That's a fantail goldfish," said Dr. Maura Isles. "A fish like that can theoretically live for ten, twenty years. The oldest one on record lived for forty-three years."

Peering through the glass, Jane had a watery view of Maura, who was crouched on the other side of the aquarium, examining the body of Sofia Suarez, fifty-two years old. Even at ten forty-five on a Saturday morning, Maura managed to look coolly elegant, a trick Jane had never been able to pull off. It wasn't just Maura's tailored slacks and blazer and her geometrically clipped black hair; no, there was something about Maura herself. To most cops at Boston PD, she was an intimidating figure in bloodred lipstick, a woman who used her intellect as a shield. And that intellect was now fully engaged in reading the language of death in the wounds and the blood spatters.

"Is that true? Goldfish can really live forty-three years?" said Jane.

"Look it up."

"Why would you happen to know that completely useless piece of information?"

"No information is useless. It's just a key waiting for the right lock to open."

"Well, I am going to look it up. 'Cause every goldfish I ever owned was dead within a year."

"No comment."

Jane straightened and turned to survey once again the modest home of the woman who had lived and died here. *Sofia Suarez, who were you?* Jane read the clues in the books on the shelves, in the neatly lined-up remotes on the coffee table. A tidy woman who liked to knit, judging by the magazines on the end table. The book-case was filled with nursing textbooks and romance novels, the collection of a woman who saw death in her job, yet still wanted to believe in love. And in one corner, on a little table adorned with bright plastic flowers, was the enshrined photo of a smiling man with twinkly eyes and a handsome swoop of black hair. A man whose ghostly presence still lingered in every room of this house.

Hanging above the dead man's shrine was the wed-ding photo of a younger Sofia and her husband, Tony. On the day they'd married, joy had lit up both their faces. That day, they must have believed that many happy years lay before them, years of growing old together. But last year, death took the husband.

And last night, a killer came for the wife.

Jane circled to the front door, where a stethoscope lay coiled on the floor, spattered with blood.

Here is where the attack starts.

Was the killer already waiting for her as she walked through her door last night? Or was he surprised when he heard the key in the lock and panicked when he realized he was about to be discovered?

The first blow doesn't kill her. She's still alive. Still conscious.

Jane followed the trail of blood smeared along the floor, marking the victim's desperate attempt to escape her attacker. It led from the front door, across the living room, and past the softly burbling aquarium.

And here is where it ends, she thought, gazing down at the body.

Sofia Suarez lay on her side on the tiled floor, her legs curled up like an infant still in the womb. She was dressed in her blue nurse's scrubs and a hospital ID was still attached to her shirt: *S. Suarez, RN.* A halo of blood surrounded her crushed skull, and her face was now shattered beyond recognition. A sad remnant of the face that had beamed so joyfully in the wedding photo.

"I see an outline of footwear here, in this splatter," said Maura. "And there's a partial tread mark over there."

Jane crouched to study the footwear impression. "Looks like some kind of boot. Men's size seven or eight?" Jane turned toward the front door. "Her stethoscope's near the door. She's attacked soon after she walks into the house. Manages to crawl away until this point. Curls up into this fetal position, maybe trying to protect herself, protect her head. And he hits her again."

"Have you found the weapon?"

"No. What should we be looking for?"

Maura knelt beside the body and with her gloved hand gently parted the dead woman's hair to expose the scalp. "These wounds are well-defined. Circular. I think you're looking for a flat-head hammer."

"We haven't found any hammer. Bloody or other-wise."

Jane's partner, Barry Frost, emerged from the back bedroom. His usually pale face was an alarming shade of sunburned scarlet, a consequence of his hatless trip to the beach yesterday. It made Jane wince just to look at him. "I didn't find her purse or her cell phone," he said. "But I did find this. It was plugged into the bed-room socket." He held up a charging cord. "Looks like it's for an Apple laptop."

"Where's the laptop?" said Jane.

"Not here."

"You sure?"

"You want to look for yourself?" It was an uncharac-teristically cranky response from Frost, but maybe she'd asked for it. And that sunburn must be bothering him.

She had already walked through the house earlier, and now she walked it again, her shoe covers *whish*ing across the floor. She glanced into the spare room, where the bed was covered with folded laundry and linens. Next came the bathroom, its under-sink cabinet over-flowing with the usual face creams and ointments that promised, but never delivered, eternal youth. In the medicine cabinet were bottles of pills for hypertension and allergies as well as a prescription bottle of hydrocodone, six months expired. Nothing in the bathroom looked disturbed, which bothered Jane. The medicine cabinet was one of the first places a burglar normally raided, and hydrocodone would be a prize worth snatching.

Jane continued to the main bedroom where she saw, on the dresser, another framed photo of Sofia and her husband in happier times. Alive times. They were standing arm in arm on a beach, and the years since their wedding photo had added both wrinkles and pounds. Their waists were thicker, their laugh lines deeper. She opened the closet and saw that, along with Sofia's clothes, Tony's jackets and slacks were still hanging. How painful it must have been for her to open this closet every morning to see her dead husband's clothes. Or was it a comfort, being able to touch the fabric he'd worn, to inhale his scent?

Jane closed the closet door. Frost was right: If Sofia did own an Apple laptop, it was not in this house.

She went into the kitchen, where the countertop held sacks of masa and plastic bags filled with dried corn husks. The kitchen was otherwise uncluttered, the surfaces wiped clean. Sofia was a nurse; perhaps it was second nature for her to wipe down and sterilize surfaces. Jane opened the pantry cabinet and saw shelves filled with unfamiliar condiments and sauces. She imagined Sofia pushing her grocery cart down the aisles, planning the meals she would cook for herself. The woman lived alone and probably dined alone, and based on her extravagantly stocked spice cabinet, she must have drawn comfort from cooking. It was yet another piece of the puzzle that was Sofia Suarez, a woman who loved to cook and knit. A woman who missed her dead husband so much she kept his clothes in the closet and a shrine to him in the living room. A woman who loved romance novels and her goldfish. A woman who lived alone but certainly did not die alone. Someone had stood over her, holding the instrument of her death. Someone had watched her take her last breaths.

She looked down at the broken glass from the shattered window in the kitchen door, the point of entry. The intruder had smashed the glass in the doorframe, reached in, and slid open the bolt. She stepped out into the side yard, a stark strip of gravel with one empty trash can and a few weeds popping out. There were more shards out here, but the gravel preserved no footprints, and the gate had a simple latch, easily lifted from the outside. No security cameras, no alarm system. Sofia must have felt safe in this neighborhood.

Jane's cell phone rang with the screech of violins. It was the movie theme from *Psycho* and it set her nerves on edge—appropriately so. Without looking at the caller's name, she silenced the phone and walked back inside.

A nurse. Who the hell kills a nurse?

"Aren't you going to answer her?" asked Maura as Jane returned to the dining room.

"No."

"But it's your mother calling."

"That's why I'm not going to answer it." She saw Maura's raised eyebrow. "This is the third time she's called today. I already know what she's gonna say. *What kind of cop are you? Don't you even care about a kidnapping?*"

"Someone's been kidnapped?"

"No. It's just some girl from her neighborhood who took off. It's not the first time she's run away."

"Are you sure that's all it is?"

"I've already talked to Revere PD and the ball's in their court. They don't need me butting in." Jane looked down again at the body. "I've got enough things on my mind."

"Detective Rizzoli?" a voice called out.

Jane turned to see a patrolman standing in the front door. "Yeah?"

"The neighbor's granddaughter just arrived. She's ready to translate for you, if you want to come next door."

Jane and Frost stepped outside, where the sunlight was so bright Jane paused for a moment, blinking against the glare as she took in the audience watching them. A dozen neighbors stood on the sidewalk, drawn by the spectacle of official vehicles parked on their street. As a CSU van pulled up behind the row of patrol cars, two gray-haired women shook their heads, their hands pressed to their mouths in dismay. This was not the circus atmosphere Jane so often encountered downtown, where crime scenes were entertainment. Sofia's death had clearly shaken those who knew her, and they watched in mournful silence as Jane and Frost walked to the neighbor's house.

The front door was opened by a young Asian woman dressed in pinstripe slacks and a pressed white blouse, oddly businesslike attire for a Saturday morning. "She's still pretty upset, but she's anxious to talk to you."

"You're her granddaughter?" asked Jane.

"Yes. Lena Leong. I'm the one who called 911. Grandma called me first, in a panic, and she asked me to call the police for her because she's not comfortable speaking English. I would have gotten here sooner to translate, but I had to meet a client downtown."

"On a Saturday morning?"

"Some of my clients can't come in any other time. I'm an immigration attorney and I represent a lot of restaurant workers. Saturday morning's the only time they're free to see me. You do what you have to do." Lena waved them inside. "She's in the kitchen."

Jane and Frost walked through the living room, where the plaid sofa looked pristine under plastic slip-covers. On the coffee table was a bowl of fruit carved from stone, jade-colored apples, and rose quartz grapes. Eternally gleaming produce that would never spoil.

"How old's your grandmother?" Frost asked as they followed Lena to the kitchen.

"She's seventy-nine."

"And she doesn't speak *any* English?"

"Oh, she understands way more than she lets on, but she's too embarrassed to actually speak it." Lena paused in the hallway and pointed to the photo on the wall. "That's Grandma and my parents and me, when I was six years old. My parents live down in Plymouth and they keep asking Grandma to move in with them but she refuses. She's lived in this house for forty-five years and she's not about to give up her independence." Lena shrugged. "She's stubborn. What can you do?"

In the kitchen, they found Mrs. Leong sitting at the table with her head in her hands, her silver hair as un-kempt as dandelion fluff. A cup of tea sat in front of her, the scent of jasmine wafting up with the steam.

"Nai nai?" Lena said.

Slowly Mrs. Leong looked up at her visitors, her eyes

red from crying. She pointed to the other chairs and they all sat down, Lena taking the chair next to her grandmother.

"First, Lena, can you tell us what she said to you on the phone?" said Frost, pulling out his notebook.

"She said she and Sofia planned to get together this morning. But when Grandma went next door and rang the bell, no one answered. The door wasn't locked, so she went inside. She saw the blood. And then she saw Sofia."

"What time was this?"

Lena asked her grandmother, and Mrs. Leong responded with a long stream of Mandarin that was surely more than just the time of day.

"A little before eight A.M.," Lena said. "They were going to make tamales together. Usually they do it in January, but that was too soon after Tony died, and Sofia was still pretty shaken up."

"That would be Mr. Suarez?" asked Jane. "How did he die?"

"It was a hemorrhagic stroke. They operated on him, but he never woke up. Spent three weeks in a coma before he died." Lena shook her head. "He was such a nice man, so sweet with my grandma. With everyone, really. You'd see him and Sofia holding hands whenever they walked around the block. Like newlyweds."

Frost looked up from the notebook he'd been jotting in. "You said your grandmother and Sofia were going to make tamales this morning. How did they talk to each other?"

Lena frowned. "I'm sorry, what?"

"Your grandmother doesn't speak English. And I assume Sofia didn't speak Chinese."

"They didn't need to talk because cooking *is* a language. They watched and tasted together. They were always passing dishes back and forth. Sofia's tamales. My grandma's amazing oxtail stew."

Jane looked at the spice rack by the stove, at the collection of condiments and sauces that were so different from Sofia's. She remembered the sacks of masa in the dead woman's kitchen and imagined these two women sitting side by side, wrapping corn husks around pillows of cornmeal, laughing and jabbering in different languages, but understanding each other perfectly.

Jane watched as Mrs. Leong wiped her face, leaving wet streaks on her cheeks, and she thought of her own mother, also fiercely independent, also living alone. She thought too of all the other women in this city, alone in their homes at night. Women who would be alert to the sound of shattering glass and unfamiliar footsteps.

"Last night," said Jane, "did your grandmother hear anything unusual? Any voices, any disturbance?"

Before Lena could translate, Mrs. Leong was already shaking her head. Clearly she understood the question, and she answered in another long stream of Mandarin.

"She says she didn't hear anything, but she goes to bed at ten," said Lena. "Sofia worked the evening shift at the hospital, and she'd normally get home around eleven-thirty, midnight. By then, my grandmother would've been asleep." Lena paused as Mrs. Leong spoke again. "She's asking is that when it happened? Right after she got home?"

"We believe so," said Jane.

"Was it a robbery? Because there've been a few break-ins in the neighborhood."

"When were these break-ins?" asked Frost.

"There was one a few months ago, the next block over. The owners were at home in bed when it happened and they slept through the whole thing. After that, my dad installed new deadbolts in Grandma's doors. I don't think Sofia ever got around to doing hers." Lena looked at Jane, then at Frost. "Is that what happened? Someone tried to rob her and she walked in on them?"

"There are items missing from her house," said Jane. "Her purse, her cell phone. And possibly a laptop computer. Does your grandmother know if Sofia owned one?"

There was another rapid exchange of Mandarin. "Yes," said Lena. "Grandma says Sofia was using it in her kitchen last week."

"Can she describe it? What color, what brand?"

"Oh, I doubt she'd know anything about the brand."

"Apple," said Mrs. Leong, and she pointed to a bowl of fruit on the countertop.

Frost and Jane looked at each other in surprise. Did the woman just answer their question?

Frost pulled out his cell phone and pointed to the logo on the back. "This kind of Apple? An Apple computer?"

The woman nodded. "Apple."

Lena laughed. "I told you she understands more than she lets on."

"Can she tell us more about the computer? What color? Was it old, new?"

"Jamal," the grandmother said. "He help her buy."

"Okay," said Frost, jotting down the name in his notepad. "Which store does Jamal work at?"

Mrs. Leong shook her head. In frustration she turned and spoke to her granddaughter.

"Oh, *that* Jamal," said Lena. "That's the boy down the street, Jamal Bird. He helps a lot of the older ladies in the neighborhood. You know, the ones who can't figure out how to turn on their TVs. You need to talk to him about the computer."

"We will," said Frost, closing his notebook.

"And she says you should use cold green tea and calendula, Detective."

"What?"

"For your sunburn."

Mrs. Leong pointed to Frost's painfully red face. "Feel much better," she said, and for the first time she managed a smile. Frost *would* be the one to finally coax a smile from this sad woman. Silver-haired ladies always seemed to treat him as their long-lost grandson.

"One other thing," said Lena. "Grandma says you need to be careful when you talk to Jamal."

"Why?" asked Jane.

"Because you're police officers."

"Does he have something against cops?"

"No. But his mother does."

FOUR

"WHY DO YOU WANT TO TALK TO MY SON? You people just assuming he did something wrong?"

Beverly Bird stood guarding her front doorway, an immovable barrier against anyone who dared invade her home. Although shorter than Jane, she was as solid as a tree stump, her feet firmly planted apart in pink flip-flops.

"We're not here to accuse your son of anything, ma'am," Frost said quietly. When it came to cooling down arguments, Frost was the crisis whisperer, the voice Jane relied on to bring down the temperature. "We're just hoping that Jamal might be able to help us."

"He's only fifteen. How's he supposed to help with a murder case?"

"He knew Sofia, and—"

"So did everyone else in the neighborhood. But you folks are zeroing in on the only Black kid on the block?"

Of course that's how it must seem to her, and how could it not? To a mother, the whole world seems like a dangerous place, and when you're the mother of a Black son, those dangers are only magnified.

"Mrs. Bird," said Jane, "I'm a mom too. I under-stand why you're anxious about us talking to Jamal. But we need help identifying Mrs. Suarez's computer, and we heard your son helped her buy it."

"He helps lots of folks with their computers. Even gets paid for it sometimes. Look around the neighborhood. How many of these old folks you think can even figure out their own phones?"

"Then he's the perfect person to help us find her missing laptop. Whoever broke into her house took it and we need to know the make and model."

Mrs. Bird eyed them for a moment, a mama bear weighing whether these intruders constituted a threat to her cub. Reluctantly she stepped aside to let them into her house. "Just so you know, I've got a cell phone and I'm not afraid to film this conversation."

"If it makes you feel better," said Jane. Who didn't have a cell phone these days? This was the world the police now had to navigate, their every move recorded and second-guessed. In this mother's place, she would do the same.

Mrs. Bird led them up the hallway, her pink flip-flops thwacking her feet, and called through her son's doorway: "Honey, it's the police. They want to talk to you about Sofia."

The boy must have overheard their conversation because he did not react to the announcement, did not even turn to look at them. He sat at his computer, shoulders slumped, as if already demoralized by their visit. Scattered around his room was typical teenage boy clutter: Clothes on the bed, blue Nike shoes on the floor, plastic action figures crowding the shelves. Thor. Captain America. Black Panther.

"Mind if I sit down?" Jane asked.

The boy shrugged, an answer she took as a yes. Or

maybe just a *whatever*. As she scooted another chair beside him, she noticed a Ventolin inhaler lying on the seat. The boy had asthma. She set the inhaler on his desk and sat down.

"I'm Detective Rizzoli," she said. "This is Detective Frost. We're with Boston PD Homicide, and we need your help."

"It's about Sofia. Isn't it?"

"So you've heard what happened."

He nodded, still not looking at her. "I saw the police cars."

Mrs. Bird said from the doorway: "He stayed inside and I went out to find out what was going on. I told him not to go out, 'cause I didn't want there to be any mistakes made. You police, sometimes you assume things."

"I try not to assume anything, Mrs. Bird," said Jane.

"Then why are you here?" asked Jamal. He finally swiveled around to face Jane and she saw moist brown eyes with impossibly long lashes. He was small for fifteen, and frail looking. The asthma, she thought.

"A few items are missing from Sofia's house, including her laptop. Mrs. Leong said you helped Sofia buy that computer."

He blinked, his eyelashes glistening. "She was a nice lady. Always tried to pay me for stuff I did."

"What did you do for her?"

"Just stuff. Like helping her figure out her TV. Setting up her new computer. I felt bad for her, after her husband died."

"We all felt bad for her," said Mrs. Bird. "It's like the worst shit always happens to good people."

Frost said to Jamal: "Tell us about Sofia's laptop. When did you help her buy it?"

"It was maybe two months ago. Her old one broke, and she wanted a new one to look up some stuff online. She didn't have a lot of money, and she asked me what she should buy."

"Lot of ladies on the block ask him for help," said Mrs. Bird, with a note of pride. "He's the neighborhood tech guy."

"So where did she buy this computer?" asked Frost.

"I found her one on eBay. It was a pretty sweet deal. A 2012 MacBook Air for a hundred fifty bucks. The graphics didn't matter to her, and I figured four gigabytes of memory was all she needed. She was just gonna use it for research."

Frost jotted in his notebook. "So, a MacBook Air, 2012 . . ."

"Thirteen point three inches diagonal. One point eight gigahertz Intel Core—"

"Hold on, you're going too fast. Let me get this all down."

"How 'bout I just print up the technical specs for you?" Jamal turned to his computer and tapped on the keyboard, pulling up the information. Seconds later, his printer whirred to life and a sheet of paper rolled out. "It was silver," he added.

"And you said it was only a hundred fifty dollars?" said Jane.

"Yeah, she had the winning bid, and the seller had good ratings. When she got it, I went over there and helped set up her Wi-Fi too."

"Gee," said Jane. "I could use someone like you on speed dial."

For the first time Jamal smiled, but it was a tentative

smile. He didn't yet trust them. Maybe he never really would.

Mrs. Bird said: "Some of the ladies do pay him, you know. So his help wouldn't come free."

"But I never asked Sofia to pay me," said Jamal. "She was gonna give me some tamales instead."

"That woman, she cooked some mighty fine tamales," said Mrs. Bird.

The tamales that never got made, thought Jane. Sometimes it was small things, like tamales, that bound a neighborhood together.

"What about her cell phone, Jamal?" asked Frost. "You remember it?"

Jamal frowned. "Is that missing too?"

"Yes."

"Weird. 'Cause it's just some old Android she had forever. She was having trouble surfing on it, 'cause of her eyesight. That's why she needed the laptop for her research."

"What kind of research?"

"She was trying to track down some old newspaper articles. That's hard to do on a little phone when your eyes aren't good."

Frost flipped to a new page in his notebook and kept writing. "So it was an old Android. What color?"

"I know it had a blue case with all these tropical fish on it. She liked fish."

"Blue case with tropical fish. Okay," said Frost and he closed the notebook. "Thank you."

Jamal heaved out a sigh, clearly relieved the interrogation was over. Except it wasn't. There was one more question Jane had to ask.

"I don't want you to take this the wrong way, Jamal,"

she said. "But I need to be thorough. Can you tell us where you were last night, around midnight?"

In an instant, a cloud seemed to pass over his face. With that one question, she'd just destroyed any trust they'd built with him.

"I knew it," Mrs. Bird snapped in disgust. "Why do you want to go asking that? That's why you're really here, isn't it? To accuse him?"

"No, ma'am. This is a completely routine question."

"It's *never* routine. You're looking for a reason to blame my son and he'd never hurt Sofia. He liked her. We all did."

"I understand, but—"

"And since you want to know, I'm just gonna straight-out tell you. It was hot last night, and my boy doesn't do well in the heat. He had a bad attack of asthma. Last thing he'd want to do is go down the street and hurt someone."

While his mother raged, Jamal said nothing, just sat with his back rigid, his shoulders squared, maintaining his dignity in silence. Jane could not take back the question, a question she would have asked any teenage boy who lived in a neighborhood where there'd been burglaries. Who knew the victim and had been inside her house.

Her next question would be even more hurtful.

"Jamal," she said quietly, "because you've been inside Sofia's house, your fingerprints may be there. We need to exclude yours from any unidentified ones we find."

"You want my fingerprints," he said dully.

"It's just so we know which ones we can discount."

He gave a resigned sigh. "Okay. I understand."

"An evidence technician will be here to collect them." She looked at his mother. "Your son is not a suspect, Mrs. Bird. If anything, he's been a very big help to us, so thank you. Thank you both."

"Yeah." The woman scoffed. "Sure."

As Jane stood up to leave, Jamal asked: "What about Henry? What happens to him?"

Jane shook her head. "Henry?"

"Her fish. Sofia doesn't have any family, so who's gonna feed Henry?"

Jane glanced at Frost, who just shook his head. She turned back to Jamal. "What do you know about goldfish?"

FIVE

I N JANE'S EXPERIENCE, HOSPITALS WERE where bad things happened. The birth of her daughter, Regina, four years ago, an event that should have been joyous, had instead been both terrifying and painful, an ordeal that had ended in blood and gunfire. This is where people come to die, she thought as she and Frost walked into Pilgrim Hospital, as they rode the elevator to the sixth-floor Surgical Intensive Care Unit. During the pandemic, when COVID-19 had swept through the city, this really had been the place where people came to die, but on this Sunday evening, an eerie calmness prevailed over the ICU. A lone unit clerk staffed the desk, where six cardiac rhythms blipped across the monitors.

"Detectives Rizzoli and Frost, Boston PD," Jane said, showing her badge to the clerk. "We need to speak to Sofia Suarez's colleagues. Anyone who worked with her."

The clerk nodded. "We thought you might be coming by. I know everyone wants to talk to you." She reached for the telephone. "And I'll page Dr. Antrim too."

"Dr. Antrim?"

"Our intensive care director. He should still be in the

hospital." She looked up as a nurse emerged from one of the patient cubicles. "Mary Beth, the police are here."

At once the nurse came toward them. She was red-headed and freckled, with flecks of black mascara on her lashes. "I'm Mary Beth Neal, the charge nurse. We're all in shock about Sofia. Have you caught who did it yet?"

"It's early stages," said Jane.

One by one, more nurses joined them at the unit desk, forming a circle of somber faces. Frost quickly jotted down their names: Fran Souza, a fireplug of a woman, her dark hair cropped short as a man's. Paula Doyle, blond ponytail, lean and tanned and fit as an L.L.Bean model. Alma Aquino, huge eyeglass frames overwhelming her delicate face.

"We couldn't believe it when we heard the news last night," said Mary Beth. "We don't know anyone who'd want to hurt Sofia."

"I'm afraid someone did," said Jane.

"Then it was someone who didn't know her. God, the world has gone nuts."

The circle of nurses nodded in sad agreement. For those who pledged to save lives, the taking of a life, especially the life of one of their own, must indeed seem like an act of insanity.

The door to the unit hissed open and a doctor strode in, white coat flapping around his long legs. He made no move to shake their hands; in this postpandemic world, keeping one's distance had become the new normal, but he stood close enough for Jane to read the name on his ID badge. He was in his midfifties with tortoiseshell glasses and an earnest face. That was what stood out most for Jane, his earnestness. She saw it in his furrowed brow, the anxious gaze.

"I'm Mike Antrim," he said. "ICU director."

"Detectives Rizzoli and Frost," said Jane.

"We kept hoping they got the name wrong. That it was someone else," said Mary Beth Neal. "A different Sofia."

For a moment no one spoke, and the only sound was the *whoosh* of a ventilator in one of the patient cubicles.

"Tell us how we can help," said Dr. Antrim.

"We're trying to get a time line of what happened on Friday." Jane looked around at the staff. "When did you all last see her?"

Fran Souza said: "It was the end of evening shift. We sign over our patients to the night shift at eleven P.M. We would have finished that around eleven-fifteen."

"And then?"

"I headed home after that."

The other nurses nodded, with echoes of "Same here."

"And you, Dr. Antrim?" Jane asked.

"Friday I was here, covering the unit."

"What time did you see Sofia leave the hospital?"

"Actually, I didn't see her leave. I was busy with the patient in bed seven. He kept crashing on us. We tried for hours to stabilize him, but I'm afraid he was gone by morning." He paused, his gaze drifting toward cubicle number seven.

"Bad luck bed," said Mary Beth softly. "It's where Tony died."

Frost looked up from his notebook. "Tony?"

"Sofia's husband," said Dr. Antrim. "He was a patient in this unit for almost a month, after his operation.

Poor Sofia, working her shifts in here, while Tony was vegetating in that cubicle. He was like part of our family."

"They both were," Mary Beth said.

Another silence. Another round of sighs.

"It's true, we really are a family here," said Antrim. "When my daughter was admitted a few months ago, Sofia was her nurse and she treated Amy like her own daughter. We couldn't have asked for better care."

"Your daughter—is she all right?" Jane asked. Almost afraid to hear the answer.

"Oh, Amy's fine now. She was hit in a crosswalk by some maniac driver. It fractured her leg in three places and she needed emergency surgery for a ruptured spleen. My wife and I were terrified, but the nurses here, they all helped her pull through. Especially Sofia, who . . ." His voice faded and he looked away.

"Can you think of anyone who might have wanted to harm her? An ex-patient, maybe? A patient's family member?"

"No," the nurses said simultaneously.

"No one would want to hurt her," said Antrim.

"That's what everyone keeps telling us," said Jane.

"Well, it's true," said Mary Beth. "And she would have told us if she was being threatened by anyone."

"Was she seeing anyone romantically?" asked Frost. "Any new man in her life?"

Clearly offended by the question, Mary Beth snapped: "Tony died only six months ago. Do you really think she'd be seeing another man?"

"Did she seem worried about anything lately?" Jane asked.

"Just quiet. Of course, she would be, after losing

Tony. That's probably why she stopped coming to our monthly potlucks."

Jane noticed that Antrim was frowning. "Doctor?" she asked.

"I'm not sure if this means anything. It just struck me as odd at the time, and now I wonder."

"About what?"

"It was last Wednesday, as I was leaving the hospital. I saw Sofia in the parking lot, talking on her cell phone. This would've been just before her shift started so maybe around two-thirty in the afternoon."

"What was odd about that?"

"She seemed upset, as if she'd just heard some bad news. All I heard was, 'Are you sure? Are you sure that's right?'"

"Did you hear any more of the conversation?"

"No. When she saw me she hung up. As if she didn't want anyone to hear the call."

"Do you know who she was talking to?"

He shook his head. "You'd have access to her phone records. Couldn't you find out?"

"We're still waiting for the call log from her mobile carrier. But yes, we'll find out."

"It just struck me as odd, you know? We've all known her for ten, fifteen years, ever since she came to work at Pilgrim, and I have no idea why she'd be so secretive."

What secrets could a fifty-two-year-old widowed nurse be hiding? Jane wondered. Sofia had no criminal record, not even an outstanding parking ticket. Their search of her house had turned up no illicit drugs or stashes of cash, and her bank account was modest.

Maybe the secret wasn't about her.

"What about her husband, Tony?" Jane asked. "What did he do for a living?"

"He was a mail carrier," said Mary Beth. "Thirty years on the job and he loved it. Loved talking to people on his route. He even loved all their dogs, and they loved him."

"No, they loved his dog biscuits," said Fran Souza with a sad laugh. "Tony kept a bag of them in his mail truck."

"But he really did love dogs. They both did. After Tony died, Sofia was talking about getting one, maybe a big ol' golden retriever. Then she thought it wouldn't be fair to the dog, being left at home alone while she worked." Mary Beth paused. "It's too bad she didn't have a dog. Maybe this wouldn't have happened."

Fran asked, softly: "Was it quick? Did she suffer?"

Jane thought of the smears of dried blood across the living room floor, evidence of Sofia's desperate attempt to escape. *Yes, she did suffer.* Sofia had lived long enough to be terrified. To know she was about to die. "We're waiting for the autopsy report," was all she said.

"Is Maura Isles doing it?" asked Antrim.

Jane looked at him. "Do you know Dr. Isles?"

"Oh yes. We both play in the same orchestra."

"She's in an orchestra?"

"It's a doctors' orchestra. We rehearse once a week at Brookline High School. She's our pianist, and a very good one."

"I know she plays the piano, but I didn't know about any orchestra."

"We're just amateurs, but we have a good time. You should come to our concert in a few weeks. I'm a lowly second violinist, but Maura? She's a real musician and will be our featured soloist."

And she never told me.

What else had Maura kept from her? Jane wondered as she and Frost rode the elevator to the first floor, as they walked across the parking lot to her car. It was a small thing, yet it bothered her. She knew Maura was a private person, but they had been friends for years, had faced the worst together, and there was no more powerful bonding experience than facing death, side by side.

She slid in behind the wheel and looked at Frost. "Why didn't she tell us?"

"Who?"

"Maura. Why didn't she mention she's in an orchestra?"

Frost shrugged. "Do you tell *her* everything?"

"No, but this is different. A concert's kind of a big deal."

"Maybe she's embarrassed."

"That there's *one more thing* she can do and I can't?"

He laughed. "See? You find that annoying, don't you?"

"I'm more annoyed she didn't tell me about it." Her cell phone rang with a nerve-jarring scream of violins. "Another thing to annoy me."

"You gonna answer her? 'Cause she'll just call again."

Resignedly, Jane picked up the phone. "Hey, Ma. I'm in the middle of something right now."

"You're always in the middle of something. When can we talk?"

"Is this about Tricia Talley again?"

"You know what that Revere detective said? He told

Jackie that Tricia will come home when she runs out of money. Who says that to the mother of a missing kid? I'm telling you, the police are not taking this seriously."

"Unlike the last three times Tricia ran away from home?"

"Poor Jackie's a mess. She wants to talk to you."

"Revere PD needs to handle this, Ma. They won't like it if I interfere."

"Interfere in what, their complete dereliction of duty? Jane, you've known the Talleys most of your life. You babysat that girl. You can't ignore a missing-persons case just because you've got bigger fish to fry."

"A dead body isn't a fish, Ma."

"Well, Tricia could be a dead body. Is that what it'll take to get you interested?"

Jane rubbed her temple, trying to stave off an incipient headache. "Okay, okay. I'll come by tomorrow."

"When?"

"Sometime in the afternoon. I've got to view an autopsy. And I have a lot of things I need to follow up on."

"Oh, and you know those new people across the street? The Greens?"

"Are you still spying on them?"

"There's some kind of weird hammering going on in their house. You know what Homeland Security says. 'If you see something, say something.' Well, I'm just saying something."

Yeah, Ma. You always do.

SIX

MAURA

"**H**OW COME YOU NEVER TOLD us you played in an orchestra?" said Jane. "It seems like something you *might* have mentioned."

Maura heard the note of accusation in Jane's voice and she took her time before answering the question. Instead she remained focused on the body that was stretched out on the autopsy table. Sofia Suarez's clothes had already been removed—blue hospital scrubs, a size-46B bra, white cotton underwear—and under the bright morgue lights every flaw, every scar acquired during the woman's fifty-two years of life, was exposed. Maura did not yet focus on the shattered skull or the ruined face; instead she focused on the burn scar on the back of the left hand and the arthritic bulge of the right thumb. Souvenirs, perhaps, of hours spent in the kitchen, chopping and frying and kneading. Aging was a cruel process. Cellulite now dimpled thighs that once would have been slim and smooth. An appendectomy scar rippled the lower abdomen. On her neck and chest were freckles and skin tags and rough black seborrheic keratoses that the largest organ of the body so often acquires over the decades. Flaws that Maura was starting to find on her own skin, a depressing reminder that old age came for everyone, if you were lucky.

Sofia Suarez had not been.

Maura picked up the scalpel and began to cut.

"We also heard you have a concert coming up," said Frost. "Alice and I want to come. She's really into classical music."

At last Maura looked up at Jane and Frost, who were watching her across the autopsy table. Frost's sunburn was now in its ugly peeling phase, and above his paper mask, his forehead was flaky with dead skin. "Trust me, the concert is not going to be a big deal. Which is why I never bothered to mention it. How did you hear about it anyway?"

"Dr. Antrim told us," said Jane. "He worked with Sofia Suarez at Pilgrim Hospital."

"I didn't know that."

"We interviewed her colleagues in the intensive care unit, and he told us you were going to be the star soloist at their concert."

"It's only Mozart." Maura picked up the rib shears and snapped through bone. "Piano Concerto Twenty-one."

"Well, *that* sounds fancy enough."

"It's not a difficult piece."

"Alice loves Mozart," Frost said. "She'll definitely want to hear that."

"It's not like I'm Lang Lang." Maura cut through the last rib, freeing up the sternal shield. "We're amateurs. Just doctors, playing together for fun."

"You still should have told us," said Jane.

"I joined them only a few months ago. After their pianist fell and broke her shoulder."

"And just like that, you can step in and play some complicated piece?"

"I told you, it's not that big a deal."

Jane snorted. "You keep saying that. And I keep not believing you."

"Hey, maybe *we* should start a band or something," Frost said to Jane. "A police band. You used to play the trumpet, didn't you?"

"You do not want to hear me play the trumpet."

Maura reached into Sofia Suarez's chest and frowned. "The surface of the right lung does not feel normal. There's fibrosis here."

"Meaning?" asked Jane.

"The clue's in her chest films." Maura nodded at the computer monitor where the chest X-ray was displayed. "It was in her medical records too. That's scarring from COVID-19. She was an ICU nurse, so it's not surprising she got infected. She never needed intubation but she was hospitalized for four days on oxygen. Quite a few people are walking around right now with X-rays that look like that, and they may not even know it."

Maura picked up a scalpel and once again reached into the chest cavity. For a moment the only sounds were the wet suck of organs as she pulled them from the cavity and the splash as they landed in the basin. The sounds of a butcher's table.

She turned her attention to the abdominal cavity and out came loops of bowel, stomach and liver, pancreas and spleen. She slit open the stomach and emptied the scant contents into a basin. "Her last meal was at least four hours prior to death," she noted. "That would have been during her work shift."

"So she didn't stop somewhere to eat on the way

home," said Jane. "Four hours. She must have been hungry."

Maura sealed a sample of stomach contents for analysis. "Any matches from AFIS?"

"No hit on any of the fingerprints," said Frost. "The ones we ID'd matched her neighbor Mrs. Leong and Jamal Bird, the computer whiz kid down the street. Assuming neither of them did it, it looks like our perp wore gloves."

"And the footwear?"

"Standard garden boots, men's size eight and a half. Like you can buy in any Walmart. We're still waiting for her phone records, but that won't help us if this was someone she didn't know."

"What about those recent break-ins in the neighborhood? Do any of those details match?" Maura looked up at Jane, who shook her head.

"That burglar wore Nikes, size ten, and his fingerprints didn't turn up in Sofia's house. It would make this case *way* too easy if it's the same neighborhood burglar."

Maura moved on to the pelvis and now her scalpel laid open the uterus, revealing yet another sad secret. "Endometrial scarring. Almost the entire wall."

"She never had children," said Jane.

"This may be the reason why."

As Maura placed the resected uterus into the basin, she thought of the wedding photo hanging in the victim's house, the bride and groom both beaming with joy. When they'd married, Sofia and Tony were already in their forties, no longer young; perhaps that had made their marriage all the sweeter, because they'd found each other so late in life. But too late for children.

She turned at last to the injuries that had brought Sofia Suarez to this table. So far Maura had examined the heart and lungs, stomach and liver, but those were faceless organs, as impersonal as pig offal at the butcher shop. Now she had to look at Sofia's face, which had been cruelly transformed into a distorted version by Picasso. Maura had already examined the skull X-rays, had seen the fractures of the cranium and facial bones, and even before she peeled away the scalp and opened the skull, she knew the damage she would find inside.

"There's a depressed fracture of the parietotemporal bone," she said. "The shape of the cranial lesion is well-defined and circular, with a sharply regular edge of the wound on the outer table of the skull. On X-ray, it's clear there's bony penetration from a rupture of the outer table with comminuted fragmentation of the inner table. This is all consistent with blunt-force trauma from a hammer. The initial blow was most likely delivered from behind, with the attacker swinging at an angle to the victim."

"Right-handed?" asked Frost.

"Likely. Someone who swung it over his right shoulder. That same impact also caused a fissured fracture that ran obliquely across the temporal bone. This was all powerful enough to certainly stun her, but we know it didn't immediately kill her. The trail of blood across the living room tells us she was able to crawl away for some distance . . ."

"Seventeen feet," said Frost. "It must have seemed like miles."

As Maura reflected back the scalp, peeling the hair and skin from bone, she imagined Sofia's terrifying last moments. The crushing pain, the seeping blood. The floor slippery beneath her hands as she dragged herself away from the front door. Away from the killer.

But she cannot crawl fast enough. He follows her, past the aquarium with the mermaid in her lavish pink castle. Past the bookcase with the romance novels. By now her vision would be fading, her limbs growing numb. She knows she can't escape, cannot fend off the attack. Finally she can go no further and here is where it ends. She curls up on her side into a fetal position, embracing herself as the last blow falls.

It lands on her right temple, where the bone is thinnest. It crushes her cheekbone, collapsing the bony orbit of her eye. All this had been revealed in the X-rays and in this exposed surface of skull. Even before Maura turned on the bone saw and opened the cranium, she knew that the transmitted force of the blows had displaced bone fragments, sheared blood vessels, and lacerated gray matter. She knew the catastrophic results when blood displaced brain and axons were stretched and crushed.

What she did not know was what the victim was thinking in her final moments. Sofia was surely terrified, but did she feel surprised? Betrayed? Did she recognize the face staring down at her? This was the limit of the pathologist's knife. Maura could dissect a body, examine its tissues all the way down to the cellular level, but what the dead knew and saw and felt as the lights blinked out would remain a mystery.

A SENSE OF DISSATISFACTION HUNG over Maura as she drove home that evening. She walked in her front door and could not help thinking about Sofia, who a few days ago had walked in her own front door to find death waiting for her. In truth, it was waiting for everyone; the only question was the time and place of the rendezvous.

Maura went straight to the kitchen and poured herself a glass of cabernet. Carried it into the living room and sat down at the piano. The score of Mozart's Concerto no. 21 was already open and staring at her, a reminder of yet another commitment she'd taken on, one that carried the risk of abject humiliation if she failed.

She took a sip of wine, set the glass down on an end table, and began to play.

The andante solo was quiet and uncomplicated and did not require the skill that the more frantic sections did, and it was a soothing place to start. A way to focus on tempo and melody instead of Sofia Suarez's death. She felt her tension ease and the dark clouds lifted from her mood. Music was her safe space, where death did not intrude, a universe away from the scalpel and the bone saw. She had not told Jane about the orchestra because she'd wanted to preserve this distance between the two universes, did not want the purity of music to be polluted by her other life.

She reached the end of the andante and launched straight into the allegro, her now-warmed-up fingers racing across the keys. She kept on playing, even when she heard the front door open. Even when Father Daniel Brophy walked into the living room. He did not say a word, but listened in silence as he peeled off his priest's collar, shedding the uniform of his calling, a calling that forbade any intimate bond between them.

Yet here he was, smiling.

She came to the end of the concerto. As her hands fell away from the keys, he wrapped his arms around her shoulders and breathed a warm kiss on the back of her neck.

"It sounds wonderful," he said.

"Not as clumsy as it did last week anyway."

"Can't you ever just accept a compliment?"

"Only when I deserve it."

He sat down beside her on the piano bench and pressed a kiss to her lips. "You'll be spectacular, Maura. And don't start pointing out all your mistakes because I can't hear them anyway. And neither will the audience."

"Jane will be there. And Frost is bringing his wife, who's supposed to be some classical music expert."

"They're going to the concert? I thought you weren't going to tell them about it."

"They found out. They are detectives, after all."

"I never understood why you didn't tell them. They're your friends. It's like you're embarrassed about it."

"Embarrassed that I might screw up."

"That's the perfectionist talking again. You know, no one really cares that you aren't perfect."

"I do."

"What a heavy cross to bear." He smiled. "So far, you've managed to fool us all."

"I almost regret agreeing to this performance."

"And after it's over, you'll be so happy you did."

They smiled at each other, two unlikely lovers who should never have found each other. Who had tried to stay apart, tried to deny their need for each other, and had failed.

He noticed the empty wineglass on the table beside her. "Need a refill?"

"Definitely. I'm done practicing anyway."

She followed him into the kitchen and watched him pour wine into her glass. The cabernet was rich and meaty, one of her expensive indulgences, but when she saw he didn't pour a glass for himself, she suddenly lost her craving for that second drink and she put it down after only one sip. "You're not having any," she said.

"I wish I could, but I can't stay tonight. There's a parish finance council meeting at eight. And then I have our immigration outreach committee, which will probably go till ten." He shook his head. "There just aren't enough hours in the day."

"Oh, well. More piano practice for me tonight."

"But I'll be here tomorrow night." He leaned in for a kiss. "You're not too disappointed?"

"It is what it is."

He reached out to cup her face. "I love you, Maura."

Over the years she'd watched as more and more silver streaked Daniel's dark hair, as lines deepened around his eyes, the same changes she saw in her own face. He would always be the man she loved, but with that love came regrets as well. Regrets that they would never live as a normal couple or sleep under the same roof every night. They would never walk hand in hand in public, their love displayed to the entire world. This was the bargain they'd made with each other, and with his god. And it would have to be enough, she thought, as she heard him walk out her front door.

She returned to the piano and stared at the concerto score. There were still so many sections she needed to master, so many passages that did not flow effortlessly under her fingers. This was a challenge, yes, but also a much-needed distraction from Daniel, and from the never-ending disassembly line of bodies that passed beneath her scalpel.

She turned to the first page and once again began to play.

SEVEN

AMY

MY MOTHER IS BEAUTIFUL.

Amy often thought that about Julianne, but never more than tonight as she watched her mother knead the dough for fettucine. Back and forth Julianne rocked, massaging magic into flour and water, sending up little puffs of white from the black granite countertop. At forty-one, Julianne still had slim, toned arms from years of kneading and whisking and chopping. Her face was aglow from the effort, and her temple was streaked with flour. *Baker's war paint,* her mother called it, and tonight Julianne the baker was happily engaged in battle, her sleeves rolled up, her favorite striped apron tied around her waist. Amy's father was working the evening shift at the hospital tonight, so it was just the two of them for dinner. Girls' night, which meant they could eat whatever they wanted.

Tonight it was fettucine with fresh asparagus. Julianne fed the dough again and again through the pasta maker, rolling the sheets ever thinner. Amy grated lemon zest, releasing its sharp and bracing scent. Teamwork, her mother always said. You and me against the world.

An hour later, they savored the result: glistening

nests of fettucine, fragrant with lemon and parmesan. They bypassed the dining room and carried their plates straight to the living room. To the TV. No rules tonight, Julianne said. It's just us girls.

And a girls' movie was what they chose to watch. *Pride and Prejudice,* which would thoroughly bore Amy's dad, but tonight he wasn't there. Tonight they could sit in front of the TV in their nightclothes and swirl pasta into their mouths as they watched Keira Knightley charm the diffident Mr. Darcy. If only women still wore such beautiful dresses! If only men really *were* attracted to a woman's sharp wit and keen intelligence!

"Some men are," said Julianne. "The good ones are. Like your dad."

"Where are all those good ones?"

"You just have to be patient and not settle. Never settle. You deserve the best." Julianne reached out to tuck a lock of hair behind Amy's ear, her fingers lingering on Amy's cheek. "You deserve to be happy."

"I am happy."

Julianne smiled. "Shall I rub some lotion on your leg? We need to keep it up."

Amy lifted her nightgown to her hip, exposing the ugly scar from her operation. It had been months since the surgeons had pinned her shattered thighbone back together. Her leg still ached in cold weather and the healed wound was an angry red ridge. She could hide that scar under a skirt, but it would always be there, a flaw waiting to be exposed by a trip to the beach or a moment of intimacy. Would the cream that Julianne rubbed on every night make the scar fade? Amy didn't know, but this was their nightly ritual now, her mother stroking in the lotion, massaging it into that ridge of scar. On TV, Keira Knightley was finally kissing her Mr. Darcy, while here on the sofa, Amy's eyes drifted shut and her body went limp with contentment. Even when the telephone rang and Julianne got up to answer it, Amy didn't stir, but waited in that warm and liquid state. *Mr. Darcy. Mr. Darcy.*

"Who is this?" Julianne said.

Amy opened her eyes and languidly turned to look at her mother, who stood with the phone pressed to her ear.

"Who is this?"

The edge in Julianne's voice made Amy pay attention. She watched as her mother hung up. For a moment Julianne stood motionless, staring at the phone.

"Mom? Who called?"

"Just a wrong number."

Amy expected Julianne to come back to the sofa, to join her in watching the end credits to *Pride and Prejudice,* but Julianne went to the front window. She stood there for a moment, peering out at the street, then closed the curtains. Went to the next window and closed those curtains as well. She turned to Amy and smiled. "What do you think? Another movie?"

"No." Amy yawned. "I think I'll go to bed."

"Yes, you look tired. Do you need help getting upstairs?"

"I'm fine." Amy pushed herself off the sofa and reached for her cane. "I can't wait to get rid of this thing."

"Let's make a ceremony of it! A cane-burning party. I'll bake a cake."

Amy laughed. "Of course you will."

She hobbled up the stairs, one hand on her cane, the

other on the railing. She could feel her mother's gaze on her, watching. Always watching over her. Safely at the top of the stairs, she turned to wave goodnight, expecting to see her mother wave back, but Julianne wasn't even looking at her. Instead she was punching in the code on the foyer security keypad: 5429. System armed.

"Goodnight!" Amy called down to her.

"Goodnight, sweetheart," said Julianne, and she went to the window. She was still standing there, still staring out at the night, as Amy limped away to bed.

EIGHT

ANGELA

M Y DAUGHTER THINKS I'M WASTING HER TIME. I see it in her face as she walks into my kitchen, as she carelessly tosses her purse onto the countertop. Jane has never been a patient girl. When she was growing up, she was in a rush to learn how to walk, to wear big-girl panties, to play basketball with the boys. My smart, fierce, indomitable daughter is always ready to go up against the enemy.

Tonight what she's up against is *me,* and the battle lines are being drawn as she stands in my kitchen, pouring herself a cup of coffee.

"Bad day at work?" I ask, to make small talk. She's a homicide cop; for her it's always a bad day.

"Dead lady in Roslindale. A nurse."

"Murder?"

"Yeah. Surprise." She sips her coffee. "You heard from Vince lately?"

"He called me this morning. Says his sister's still in a lot of pain, so he'll need to stick around for another two weeks. I always thought hip replacements were a breeze. Not hers. He's been waiting on her, hand and foot."

"Tell him to make his escape and get back here. Then *he* can help you track down Tricia."

"This is your old neighborhood, Janie. Girl goes missing, you oughta take a personal interest."

"I did what you asked. I talked to Detective Saldana, found out where they are on the case."

"Jackie says he's not doing a damn thing to find her."

"What he's doing is going with the probabilities. Tricia ran away from home three times before. She came home all three times."

"This time could be different. It could be a stalker. Some creepy old guy who's lured her to his house and locked her up in his basement as a sex slave. Like that guy in Cleveland who locked up those three girls for years. Made the cops look like idiots."

At the mention of the Cleveland case, which ended up splashed all over the cover of *People,* Jane falls silent. I knew that would make her reconsider. No detective wants to screw up a case as public as that one.

"Okay," Jane sighs. "Let's go talk to Jackie."

We don't have to drive; the Talleys' house is only a block and a half away, and at this time in the evening it's a pleasant walk, the smell of cooking in the air, the glow of TV sets in windows. When we get to the Talleys', I see Rick's blue Camaro in the driveway and I wonder if he and Jackie are getting along any better these days. You'd think, after twenty years of marriage, they'd have either ironed out their differences or gone their separate ways. Jackie told me that during one of their arguments, he'd shoved her against the refrigerator and Tricia had seen the whole thing. While I have lots to complain about when it comes to Frank, mainly his running around with another woman, at least he never shoved me. Maybe because Jane would've slapped handcuffs on him.

I knock on the door and almost instantly Jackie appears, her hair in disarray, her cheek smeared with eyeliner. I have always thought she was an attractive woman—maybe *too* attractive—but today what I see is a frightened mother. "Oh Angela, you brought her! Thank you. Janie, I can't believe you're a detective now. I remember that day when you were babysitting Tricia and you put her in the playpen and told her she was in jail. Even then, you were practicing to arrest people."

Jackie keeps up the nervous chatter as she leads us into the kitchen where Rick sits reading the sports page. Although you could call him a handsome man, still with a head full of dark hair at forty-five, I never liked his looks, and I like them even less tonight. His hair is slicked back and a gold bracelet winks from beneath the cuff of his shirt. I cannot abide men who wear bracelets. When he sees Jane, he sits up straighter. Maybe it's because she has a gun on her hip. Sometimes the only way for a woman to earn a man's respect is to come packing heat.

Jackie scurries to the stove, where a pot's about to boil over, and turns down the burner. The table has been set with two plates and a careless pile of silverware. The kitchen smells like burned food and the range is filthy with grease and brown crud. The sad state shows me just how much their daughter's disappearance has disrupted this household.

"I'm sorry, Mrs. Talley. I see you're about to have dinner," says Jane.

"No, no, don't worry about it. Your visit is much more important." Jackie pulls out a chair. "Please, sit.

To think that our Janie is now hunting down criminals. If anyone can help us, you can."

"This is really Revere PD's case, strictly speaking, but I'll try to help." Jane sits down, carefully setting her sleeves on the crumb-littered table. "My mom says Tricia disappeared last Wednesday?"

"I woke up and she wasn't in her room. The chain on the front door was off, so I know she walked out that way. I figured she'd gone out to see her girlfriends, so I didn't worry about it until it got really late. Then I called the police."

"Detective Saldana said Tricia stole money from your purse. How much?"

Jackie shifted uneasily. "I don't know. Fifty dollars, maybe."

"You have any idea why she took off?"

"She hasn't been talking much to me lately. She and I, we've had a few arguments."

"About what?"

"Everything," Rick interjected with a note of weariness. "Her grades. Her smoking. Her so-called friends. Ever since she turned fourteen, it's been pretty much hell around here."

"*You're* the one who's always on her case about those things, not me," says Jackie.

"Seems to me *you're* the one she's angry at right now."

"Of course, 'cause I'm her mother. Teenage girls always take everything out on their mothers. It's normal."

"If that's normal, it's a miracle every kid isn't strangled at birth." Rick stands up and grabs his car keys from the counter.

"Where are you going?"

"I've gotta meet Ben about that project down in Quincy. I told you."

"What about dinner?"

"I'll pick up something on the way." He looks grudgingly at Jane and nods. "Thanks for dropping by, but I don't think you need to get involved. I don't know what's got into that girl lately, but she'll come home when she runs out of money. She always does."

We're all silent as he walks out of the kitchen. It's as if we don't dare say anything that will delay his exit. When we hear his car rumble out of the driveway, I can almost see Jackie's body go rubbery in relief. Jane gives me a look that says: *Why are these people still married?* It's the same thought that's crossed my mind more than once. It wasn't always this way between them. I remember them cuddling and smooching when they first moved to the neighborhood, back before Tricia was born. Kids can be rough on a marriage.

"I went on her Facebook page, but she's blocked me. Can you believe that?" says Jackie. "I checked with her friends, and they all claim they have no idea where Tricia is. But these teenagers, they're so good at keeping one another's secrets. I don't know if she's telling them to lie to me or what." Jackie drops her head into her hands. "If I just knew what set this off. Why she's so mad at me. It's like a switch suddenly got flipped. She came home from school on Tuesday, called me this filthy, filthy word, and locked herself in her room. The next morning, she was gone."

"Where did she go the last time she ran away?" Jane asks.

"She hid out at a girlfriend's house. Even the girl's parents didn't realize she was there, sleeping in their daughter's bedroom. Another time, she took the bus to New York City. I only found out after she called and asked me to send money for the ticket home."

Jane studies Jackie for a moment, as if trying to discern what's not being said. What's being left out. "Why do you think she's angry with you, Mrs. Talley?" she asks quietly.

Jackie sighs and shakes her head. "You know how she is. She's always had a temper."

"Did something happen here at home? Maybe something between her and her father?"

"Rick? No, she would've told me."

"Are you sure?"

"Absolutely," Jackie says, but then looks away, making her declaration less than convincing. I think of Rick Talley with his gold man-bracelet and his slicked-back hair. I can't see teenage girls being his type. No, I imagine him with someone showier and bustier, someone with a big, brassy laugh. A woman like Jackie used to be.

Jackie stares down at the table with its crumbs and its dried splatters and I see the beginning of jowls tugging down her face. This is not the same lively woman who moved here eighteen years ago to take a job at the high school. Back when she was the hot new addition to the neighborhood, I didn't like her much. I even avoided her, because I knew she caught the eye of every man in the neighborhood, including my Frank. But now she's just a scared mother, trapped in a clearly unhappy marriage, and she's no longer a threat to my marriage, because another bimbo's already got her claws in Frank.

Jane and I don't talk much as we walk back to my house together. The evening is warm and windows are open and I hear snippets of conversation, the clink of dishware, and the sound of TVs spilling from the houses. It may not be the nicest neighborhood in the city but it's my neighborhood, and in these modest homes live people I know, some of them friends, some of them not. We pass the Leopolds' and through the front window I see Larry and Lorelei sitting side by side on their white sofa, dining off trays in front of the TV. Something I never allowed in *my* house, because dinner should be eaten properly, at a dining table.

To each his own. Even if it's wrong.

We reach my house, and across the street, there's that silver fox Jonas, bare-chested and lifting weights in his living room. All these windows are like TV screens, where real dramas are playing out for anyone who cares to watch. *Channel 2531: Jonas, retired Navy SEAL, battling the ravages of age! Channel 2535: Leopolds on the sofa: middle-aged couple trying to keep the romance alive! Channel 2533: The Greens . . .*

I don't know what to say about the Greens.

Their blinds are shut as usual, and except for a furtive silhouette moving past the window, I can't make out any of what's happening inside.

"That's their house," I say to Jane.

"Whose?"

"Those people I told you about. The spies. Or maybe they're fugitives."

Jane sighs. "Geez, Ma. Jump to conclusions much?"

"There's something odd about those people."

"Because they won't eat your zucchini bread?"

"Because they don't socialize with anyone. They make no effort to be part of the neighborhood."

"It's not illegal to be private."

Their black SUV is parked in their driveway. The

garage is only big enough to hold one vehicle, so Mr. Green's SUV always sits outside, conveniently available for perusal by any passerby.

I head across the street.

"Ma," Jane calls out. "What are you doing?"

"Just gonna take a peek."

She follows me across the street. "You're now trespassing, you know."

"It's only the driveway. That's like an extension of the sidewalk." I put my face right up to the driver's window but it's too dark to see the interior. "Give me your flashlight. Come on, I know you always have one."

Jane sighs as she reaches into her pocket for her flashlight and hands it to me. I struggle for a few seconds to turn it on. The blue-white beam is blinding and just what I need. Aiming it into the SUV, I see spotless upholstery. No rubbish, no papers, no loose change.

"Satisfied?" Jane asks.

"It's unnatural to be so clean."

"For a Rizzoli, maybe." She takes back her flashlight and turns it off. "Enough, Ma."

The living room blinds suddenly flick open and we freeze. Matthew Green looms in the window, his broad shoulders almost blotting out the light behind him. We've been caught red-handed in his driveway, standing next to his SUV, yet he doesn't make a move, doesn't yell through the window. He just stares at us in silence, like a hunter studying his prey, and it makes the hairs stand up on the back of my neck.

Jane waves at him, a casual, neighborly gesture as if we were merely passing by, but we know he's not fooled for an instant. He knows what we were doing. Jane grabs my arm and pulls me back to the sidewalk and across the street to my house. As we mount the porch steps, I cast a backward glance.

He is still watching us.

"Well, that was a smooth operation," Jane mutters as we walk into the house.

I close the front door and lean back against it, my heart pounding. "Now he knows I've been watching him."

"Something I'm sure he already knew."

I take a deep breath. "He scares me, Jane."

She goes to the living room window and looks across the street at Mr. Green, who's still at his window, watching us. The two of them regard each other for a moment in a duel of stares. Then he flicks the blinds shut and disappears from view.

"Janie?"

She turns to me, a distracted look on her face. "Can you just stay away from those people? It would make them happier, and me too."

"But you see what I mean now, don't you? There's something strange about them. Why do they keep avoiding me?"

"Geez, I have *no* idea." She looks at her watch.

"What about Tricia? What are you gonna do about her?"

"I'll call Revere PD, see if they've got any new info. But right now, I'm still inclined to think she's a runaway. She's clearly pissed at her mom, took money from her purse, and she's done this several times before."

"I say when a teenage girl keeps running away, you should take a look at the father."

"Sounds more like Tricia's problem is with her mother."

"So how do we find her?"

Jane shakes her head. "It won't be easy. Not if that girl doesn't want to be found."

"I NEVER MUCH LIKED RICK TALLEY," says Jonas as the four of us sit in my living room, stirring Scrabble tiles on the table. "Fine-looking gal like Jackie, she could've done a lot better. He keeps moving around from job to job, never sticks it out. Jackie's probably the one who brings in most of the money in that house. High school pays pretty well, I'm guessing. Hey, Larry?"

Larry Leopold just grunts and reaches for seven new tiles. As usual, he won the last round, thanks to his triple-word score with ZYMOSIS. I had to look it up to be sure it was a real word, and yep, there it was in *Webster's Dictionary*. Anyone else would use the Z tile to spell out ZOO or ZIP. Or in a really inspired moment, OOZE. But that's Larry the high school English teacher, always showing us up. It irritates Jonas no end, because he hates it when another man defeats him at anything. Since Jonas knows he can't best Larry on the Scrabble board, he focuses his annoyance instead on Rick Talley, who isn't here to defend himself.

"When I moved to the neighborhood, Jackie came right over to introduce herself," says Jonas. "She was sweet as pie, invited me to her house for coffee. I went there and we talked for an hour. Then Rick gets home and I tell ya, if I wasn't as big as I am, he might've taken a swing at me."

"You can't be serious, Jonas," says Lorelei. "He really thought you were after Jackie?"

Jonas puffs out his chest. If he'd been wearing all his military medals, we would've heard the *clink-clank* of brass. "Some ladies prefer their men rough-and-tumble. That Rick, there's nothing rough about him. More like slick and smooth as a hairless—" Jonas pauses, gives me a wink. "Better keep it clean for the ladies in the room."

We each peruse our new sets of letter tiles. Once again, I've drawn a bad lot. Three ES, two LS, a K, and an R. All I can think of is REEK. Or LEEK.

"Definitely something uncomfortable going on in that house," says Lorelei.

"Well, of course. Their daughter ran away," her husband points out.

"No, it's something else. Yesterday I stopped by there to drop off those petitions against pesticides. I was on the front porch and heard them yelling. Jackie was screaming that he needs to move out and Rick yells that *she's* the one who needs to move out. No wonder Tricia ran away. Who can live with all that yelling?"

"When they moved here," I say, "they seemed happy enough. Like a normal couple."

"Happy is normal?" Larry mutters.

Jonas puts down his word on the Scrabble board. BOOBS.

"Last go-round, you used *breast*," says Lorelei. "Geez, Jonas, don't you ever think of anything else?"

"I meant *boobs* as in *idiots*." Jonas smirks. "*You're* the one who put the dirty spin on it, Lorelei."

"Because I know exactly how your mind works."

"Ha. You wish you did."

Larry gives a grunt of satisfaction as he plunks down seven tiles. Using one of Jonas's BS he spells out BASI-LISK, hitting a coveted double-word square. We all groan.

"Your turn, Angie."

As I ponder my wretched selection of tiles, a car's taillights glow red in my living room window. I glance up to see Matthew Green's black SUV pull into his driveway. He climbs out and stands in his driveway, looking in my direction. Scoping out my house.

"Hey, Angie, are you in there somewhere?" says Jonas, waving his hand in front of my face.

I look down at my tiles and suddenly a word screams at me, a word that hits me like a splash of ice water. I swallow hard as I spell it out on the board, using an I from Larry's last word.

KILLER.

Across the street, Mr. Green vanishes into his house.

"Such strange people," I murmur as his silhouette moves past his window. "Have any of you been inside their house?"

"You mean the Greens?" Lorelei shakes her head. "They've never invited us in, not once. And they're right next door to us."

"Well, I've never been in Jonas's house either," Larry points out. "All I've seen is his backyard."

Jonas laughs. "Don't want you to see the bodies I keep in the basement."

"Those people, they're so unfriendly. I wouldn't be surprised if *they* have bodies in their basement." Lorelei leans toward me, a conspiratorial glint in her eye. "You know what I saw the other day?"

"What?" I ask.

"I was on the upstairs balcony and happened to look over and there he was, standing on his back balcony. He was installing a video camera on the railing."

"Aimed at his backyard? Why?"

"I don't know. He saw me and went right back inside. And it's weird how you can never see inside that house. Every window's covered up tight now, even during the day. And you hardly ever see *her*. It's like she's hiding in there. Or she's not allowed to come out."

I look down at the Scrabble board, at my word, KILLER, and suddenly feel a fluttering in my stomach. I rise to my feet. "I think I'll open Jonas's wine now."

Jonas follows me as I walk into the kitchen. "Here, let me do it," he says. "I'm an old hand at opening bottles."

"Like I'm not?"

"You're not an old anything, sweetie."

I reach into the drawer for the corkscrew and suddenly feel his hand land on my ass. "Hey. *Hey.*"

"Oh, Angie. It's just a little love pat."

I spin around to face him and get a big whiff of his aftershave. The scent of pine is so overwhelming I feel like I'm about to tackle a Christmas tree. Jonas is a fine-looking man, no doubt about it, tanned with straight teeth and a thick mane of silver hair. And those muscles. But this is way over the line.

"You do know I have a boyfriend," I say.

"You mean that Korsak fella? Haven't seen him around lately."

"He's visiting his sister in California. Soon as she recovers from her hip operation, he'll be back."

"Meanwhile I'm right here. Right now." He moves in for a smooch.

I snatch up the corkscrew and wave it between us. "Okay, *you* open the wine."

He looks at the corkscrew, looks at me, and sighs in disappointment. "Oh, Angie. Such a gorgeous woman, and you live right across the street. So close and yet so far."

"So *very* far."

To my relief, he gives a good-humored laugh. "Can't blame a fella for trying," he says with a wink and opens the bottle. "C'mon, babe, let's go get clobbered again by Larry."

LONG AFTER EVERYONE LEAVES THAT NIGHT, I'm still flustered by Jonas's pass at me. I have to admit, I'm also feeling pretty darn flattered. Jonas is a few years older than Vince, but he's both trimmer and fitter and I have to admit, there's something about a navy man that can turn a gal's head. I load dirty wineglasses into the dishwasher, turn off the kitchen lights, and head to my bedroom. There I glimpse myself in the mirror, my face flushed, my hair a little out of control. That's exactly how I'm feeling: A little out of control. On the verge of . . . what? A flirtation? An affair?

The doorbell rings. I freeze in front of my mirror thinking: Jonas is back. He knows he's got me off-balance and he thinks I just might tip right over for him.

My face is tingling, nerves buzzing, as I go to the front door. But it's not Jonas standing on my porch; it's Rick Talley, and he looks exhausted. He sees me through the foyer window so I can't pretend I'm not home. Nor can I gracefully refuse to open the door. We women are too damn polite; we hate to hurt anyone's feelings, even if it means getting strangled.

"Angie," he says when I open the door. "I was on my way home and saw your lights were still on. I thought I'd stop and just tell you in person."

"Tell me what?"

"I got a text message a while ago, from Tricia. She says she's staying with a friend for a while. So you can tell Jane she doesn't need to get involved."

"Does Jackie know this?"

"Of course she does! I called her as soon as I got the text. We're both relieved, naturally."

"She texted you but not her mom?" I can't keep the skepticism out of my voice.

He pulls out his phone and holds it in front of my face, shoving it so close that I flinch. "See?"

What I see are words that anyone could have typed on Tricia's phone. *Sux at home, staying with a friend. Will tell u everything when I'm ready. Luv U.*

"So there's nothing to worry about," he says.

"With teenagers, there's always something to worry about."

"But the police don't need to. Let Jane know that." He gets back in his Camaro, which he had left idling at the curb, and roars away, toward his own house.

I stand on my porch, frowning at the receding tail-lights. Wondering if I should call Jackie to check on his story. But of course he would've told her the same thing, would've shown her the same text message from Tricia.

If it really is from Tricia.

Across the street, a slit of light shines in the window. One of the Greens is peering through the blinds, and I can almost feel a pair of eyes watching me through the slat. At once, I retreat into my house.

Looking out the window from my dark living room, I see the same row of houses that've always been here, the same street I've lived on for forty years. But tonight everything seems different, as if I've crossed into some parallel world and I'm now looking at the evil twin of my old neighborhood. A neighborhood where every house, every family, hides a secret.

I slide the deadbolt shut. Just in case.

NINE

JANE

THREE BURGLARIES IN FOUR MONTHS did not constitute a crime spree in the neighborhood, but it did establish a pattern. Jane sat at her desk comparing three police reports, looking for any similarities between those break-ins and that of Sofia Suarez's residence. One was the robbery that Lena Leong had told them about, a daring entry through an unsecured window while the occupants were asleep in bed. The burglar had netted a purse with cash and credit cards and a Lenovo laptop, but had not touched the jewelry and cell phones in the bedroom where the owners were sleeping. Perhaps that was a feat too brazen even for him. In the soil beneath the point of entry was the shoe print of a size-ten Nike. Fingerprints left on the window frame remained unidentified.

Four weeks later, those same fingerprints turned up at burglary number two, at a house around the corner. This time the owners were not home. Entry was again through an unsecured window. Cash, jewelry, and a MacBook Pro were stolen.

Another laptop. Was that significant, or was it just because they were portable items that every household now owned?

Jane moved on to the third burglary, which took place six weeks later, at the Dolan residence. Again, the homeowners were absent. This time the burglar broke a kitchen window to enter, and the police report included a photo taken by the homeowner of shattered glass littering the floor and the countertops. While cash and several watches were stolen, there was no missing laptop because the owner had been traveling with it. A size-ten Nike shoe print was found in the backyard. No fingerprints this time; perhaps the burglar had advanced to wearing gloves.

Jane studied the photo of the broken kitchen window and thought of the broken glass in Sofia Suarez's kitchen. She pulled up the Suarez crime scene photos and clicked through the images. She found photos of the shattered door pane and the kitchen floor where a few shards were lying, but she found only two photos of the side yard, its graveled walkway glittering with glass. She went back to the photo from the Dolan break-in and frowned at the amount of glass scattered across the kitchen floor.

I need to go back, she thought.

Frost had gone home for the day so she drove alone to the Suarez residence. It was just past six when she pulled up in front of the house and stepped out of the car. The crime scene had been released days ago and the biohazard cleaners had already been here to scrub and sterilize, but mops and bleach could not cleanse the images from Jane's memory. They still haunted her as she climbed the porch steps and opened the front door.

The air was sharp with the odor of chemical cleaners, and she left the front door open for ventilation. She paused in the living room, memories overlaying the now-spotless floor with images of smears and spatters from her first visit. She could still see the fallen stethoscope, and the bloody trail left by Sofia as she'd dragged herself away from her attacker. Jane followed that remembered trail through the living room, past the vacant spot where the aquarium used to be, and into the dining room. Even here, where the pool of blood had collected beneath the body, the floor was now spotless.

Good job, cleaners.

Jane walked on into the kitchen. Here was the one room where she wished the cleaners had not been so thorough, but the floor had been swept, the surfaces wiped clean of fingerprint powder. The broken windowpane in the door was boarded over, blocking out the day's last sunlight, and the room felt boxed in. Airless.

She opened the kitchen door and stepped outside, her shoes crunching onto gravel. This is how they'd assumed the killer accessed the house. Smashed open the door pane and reached through the broken window to slide open the bolt. She remembered seeing shattered glass on the ground here, as well as inside the kitchen, but it was gone now. She should have paid more attention at the time, but she'd been focused on the body and the spatters and the blood trail from the living room. She'd been trying to establish when the first blow landed. How the attack began and how it ended.

She crouched down and searched the gravel, but the cleaners had been thorough about plucking up the shards. She scanned a wider and wider radius and was all the way to the fence when she saw a reflection wink back at her. Gingerly she fished out a shard of glass that had wedged up against the board and she deposited it in an evidence bag. She turned and eyed the kitchen door, which was a good two yards away. The glass didn't just drop there against the fence; it had been propelled.

She stood listening to the hum of insects, the growl of traffic. Even here, surrounded by houses and cars and a million other people, one could be utterly alone. She felt her heart thudding, heard the *whoosh* of blood in her ears as she thought about broken windows and scattered glass and stolen laptops.

And patterns. Maybe there, maybe not.

A loud thud made her jump. The front door. Was someone inside?

She stepped back into the kitchen and paused, listening. Heard the hum of the refrigerator, the ticking of the wall clock. There is no such thing as a silent house. She walked into the dining room and paused again. Realized she was standing in the very spot where Sofia had drawn her last breath. She couldn't help glancing down at the floor and remembering the body lying where her feet were now planted.

She moved into the living room and stopped beside the spot where the aquarium used to be with its burbling water pump and bug-eyed goldfish. The front door, which she'd left wide open, was now closed. Blown shut by the wind, she thought; no reason to be alarmed.

She walked through the house anyway, to be sure. Glanced into the bedrooms, the closets, the bathroom. While no one else was here, she still felt the echoes of those who'd lived here, felt their gazes watching her from the photos on the walls. A happy house, once. Until it wasn't.

Outside, she took a deep breath. No smell of chemical cleaners out here, just the familiar scents of mown grass and car exhaust. Her visit hadn't answered any questions, but it had raised new ones. She felt the bulge of the evidence bag in her pocket, with its errant shard of glass that the cleaners had missed. Glass that might or might not have come from the window in the kitchen door. Glass that would have flown that far if the window were broken from the *inside*.

And that would change everything.

TEN

ANGELA

EVEN FROM ACROSS THE STREET, I can hear the banging of a hammer. Something is going on at the Green residence, something that takes on more and more of a sinister cast because of the perpetually closed venetian blinds in the windows. I stand in my living room, peering through binoculars and trying to catch a glimpse of either of the Greens, but they remain stubbornly out of sight, as does their black SUV, which is now parked inside the garage. They must have returned the U-Haul to the rental agency because it's no longer parked in front of the house. I never actually saw what was in that U-Haul because Matthew Green emptied it under cover of night—yet one more detail that makes me suspicious, but I'm the only one who seems to care.

I put down the binoculars and pick up the phone. Vince spent thirty-five years as a cop; he'll know what to do. It's three hours earlier in California, and by now he's probably finished his breakfast, so it's the perfect time to talk.

After five rings, he answers: "Hey, babe." A cheery greeting, but I know him well enough to hear the fatigue in his voice. It's as though he's trying to hide from me all the strain he's under. That's my Vince, always trying to keep me from worrying. It's one of the reasons I love him.

"Are you okay, honey?" I ask.

After a silence, he releases a sigh. "She's not the easiest patient to take care of, lemme tell you. I've been running up and down these stairs getting things for her, and she's never satisfied. My cooking sucks, apparently."

She's right about that, I think, but all I say is: "You're a good brother, Vince. The best."

"Yeah, well, I try. But I miss you, sweetie."

"I miss you too. I just want you home again."

"You behaving yourself?"

What an odd question. "Why are you asking that?" I say.

"I was talking to Jane and—"

"Did she call you?"

"Well, yeah. She thought I should be apprised of certain facts. Like you poking around in things that you should leave alone."

"Here's the thing, Vince. Jane isn't taking me seriously and I'd really like to know your opinion."

"Is this about that missing girl again?"

"No, I'm putting that situation on my back burner. This is about the new couple across the street, the Greens. The ones you haven't met."

"The shut-ins."

"Yeah. Something's not right about them. Why did they wait till after dark to unpack their U-Haul? Why do they keep their shades down all day? Why do they avoid me?"

"Gee, Angie, I have no idea," he says, and I think I hear sarcasm, but I'm not sure. "What does Jane say?"

"She tells me to butt out. She doesn't want to hear any of it 'cause I'm just her mother, and no one ever seems to listen to their own mother. I wish you were here to help me figure it out."

"I wish I were there too, but maybe you should listen to your daughter. She's got good instincts about these things."

"So do I."

"She's got a badge. You don't."

And that is why no one listens to me. It's the badge thing. It makes cops think they're the only ones who can sniff out trouble. I hang up feeling deeply dissatisfied with both my daughter and my boyfriend. I go back to the window and look across the street.

The shades are still down and the pounding has started up again. What is he hammering in there? My gaze suddenly shifts to the house next door to theirs. Unlike the Greens, Jonas has his curtains wide open, and he stands in full view of the neighborhood, shirtless, as he pumps iron. I watch him for a moment, not because he has a very fine body for a man his age, but because I'm thinking of the backyard barbecue he hosted for the neighborhood last August. I remember standing on his patio, sipping a frozen margarita and looking over the fence at the house of his then-neighbor, Glen, who was skin and bones because of stomach cancer and would be dead two months later. I remember Jonas and me shaking our heads at life's cruelties, that there we were grilling hamburgers while poor Glen next door was reduced to drinking Ensure.

I can't see into the Greens' backyard, but Jonas can.

I go into the kitchen and pull a zucchini bread out of the freezer. I can't just waltz over there empty-handed;

I need a golden ticket, and when it comes to men, there's no better golden ticket than baked goods.

When I knock, Jonas opens his front door wearing nothing but blue spandex shorts with red stripes down the sides. He stands grinning at me, and I'm so startled by how tightly those shorts cling to him that for a moment I can't think of anything to say.

"Have you finally surrendered to my charms?" he says.

"What? No! I had this in my freezer. I need to make more room, and I thought you might like to, um . . ."

"Help you empty your freezer?"

Well, that did take all the charm out of my offering. I stand there holding the now-defrosting zucchini bread, wondering how to salvage the conversation.

Jonas comes to my rescue with a loud laugh. "Angie, I'm only poking a little fun at you. I'm honored to get one of your treats, frozen or not. Wanna come in? I'll cut us each a slice and we can wash it down with whiskey."

"Um, no whiskey. But I'd love to come in."

As soon as I step into the house, I get the feeling this visit could turn out badly. What if he takes it the wrong way? What if he thinks I'm following up on that pass he made at me a few nights ago? The wink he gives me, that assessing gaze up and down my body, tells me I need to be very firm about what I'm really here for.

"I'll just take this into the kitchen," he says. "And then we can both enjoy a little afternoon delight, hey?"

He heads to the kitchen, leaving me alone in the living room. I go straight to the window facing his side yard, but this offers no better glimpse into the Greens' home than their front windows do, because the blinds are shut on this side as well. I back away and almost trip over one of Jonas's dumbbells. The weights are scattered all over the floor, and the air smells like sweat mingled with cologne. There are no paintings on the walls, no artwork anywhere, just a big-screen TV, a cabinet with electronics, and a bookcase filled with DVDs and military books.

"Here we go, neighbor!" Jonas says as he pads barefoot back into the room. His feet are enormous, and their size momentarily distracts me, so I don't notice at first that he's holding two tumblers with whiskey on the rocks.

"No thank you," I say.

"But this is the good stuff, straight from Scotland. I even turned your neighbor Agnes onto it."

"You and *Agnes* drink together?"

"I don't discriminate on the basis of age. I like all the ladies." He holds out a glass and winks.

"It's too early, Jonas."

"It's five o'clock somewhere."

"But not here."

He sighs and sets the tumbler meant for me down on the coffee table. "So why are you here, Angie? If not to party with yours truly?"

"Honest answer?"

"Always."

"You have a view into the Greens' backyard."

"So?"

"I need to know what they're up to."

"Why?"

"Because I've got a feeling about them and it's not a good feeling. There's been drilling and hammering going on there all morning. I just want to peek over the fence and find out what they're up to."

"Then will you have a drink with me?"

"Sure, sure," I say, but I'm not really thinking about the consequences of that drink; I'm too anxious to see what's going on next door.

Jonas leads me through the kitchen and out the back door to his patio. He hasn't done much to the yard since he bought it, and it looks pretty much the way it did when the Dalys lived here, with a weedy lawn, a cement patio, a gas grill, and a few unkempt shrubs along the perimeter. The only new addition is a toolshed. The Dalys had the yard fenced in so their golden retriever wouldn't run away, but that dog regularly managed to escape anyway. The redwood fence is still in good shape, and now it's topped with a new privacy lattice that blocks off my view into the Greens' yard.

"Did you add that lattice?" I ask Jonas.

"Naw. Neighbor put it up yesterday. I came home from the grocery store and there it was. Actually, it looks kinda classy, don't you think?"

A drill whines next door, then the hammering starts up again.

"I can't see a thing over there," I mutter.

"You wanna peek? I can fix that." Jonas ducks into his toolshed and reemerges with a stepladder. He sets it up against the fence. "My lady."

Even though he's positioned himself in just the right spot to ogle my ass, I climb up the ladder and cautiously raise my head to peer across the fence. For a moment all I notice is the open cellar hatch and a bag of concrete leaning against the wall. Then I look at the upstairs windows facing the backyard and I see the reason for all the hammering and the drilling.

Bars. Matthew Green is installing bars over the windows.

Already he's put them on the first floor, and now he's moved upstairs, where his toolbox now sits open on the balcony. I stare at those bars, wondering why he's doing this. Who is he afraid will break in? What is so valuable inside that house that he feels the need to turn the place into Fort Knox?

Then the chilling thought hits me. What if the bars aren't to keep outsiders out, but to keep someone *in*? I think of his wife. Why do we never see his wife?

Suddenly the balcony door opens and Matthew Green steps out. I duck down before he can see me.

"What? What?" whispers Jonas.

"You won't believe this."

"Let me see."

Jonas may be stocky but he's not much taller than I am so I have to get off the stepladder to let him climb on. He takes one look and instantly ducks down again.

"I think he saw me," Jonas says.

"Uh-oh."

We both huddle by the fence, listening. It's gone completely silent next door and my heartbeat thuds as I strain to listen. A few minutes go by and the drill starts whining again.

I nudge Jonas aside and climb back onto the ladder for another peek. To my relief, Matthew has his back turned as he works, so he can't see me as he installs a new set of wrought-iron bars over the balcony window. Something catches my eye, something that I see only as Matthew Green bends forward, reaching into his toolbox for something. Suddenly wobbly, I clutch the fence to steady myself and I'm not quick enough to react when he suddenly pivots and stares at me.

Straight at me.

Caught in the act, I can only stare back at him as the seconds tick by. I am still staring as he walks back into his house and shuts the door.

My legs are shaking as I climb off the stepladder.

"What's wrong?" says Jonas, frowning at my face. "What did you see?"

"I need to call my daughter."

ELEVEN

JANE

THE AVERAGE AMERICAN CELL PHONE user sends or receives 250 calls a month, and in that regard, Sofia Suarez had been utterly average, judging by the previous year's phone log. Jane sat at her desk, combing through a year's worth of calls, searching for any entry that stood out as unusual, any name that sent off a warning flare in her head, but nothing caught her attention. There were repeated calls to and from Pilgrim Hospital where she was employed, to a hairdresser and a credit card company, a plumber and an auto repair garage. And, prior to last November, numerous ones to her husband, Tony. The pattern revealed the life of an ordinary woman who had her hair done once a month, whose car needed an occasional oil change, whose sink sometimes backed up.

As Jane scanned down the list, Frost was doing likewise at his desk, another set of eyes examining the same log to and from Sofia's phone.

In November, the rhythm abruptly changed to a frantic tempo, with most of the calls going to the same number: Pilgrim Hospital, where her husband was now lying in intensive care. Here was the record of Sofia's growing desperation as she reached out again and again for updates on Tony's condition.

On December 14, her calls to the hospital abruptly stopped. That was the day her husband died.

Jane imagined the days leading up to that date, the jolt of anxiety Sofia must have felt every time her phone rang. As a nurse, Sofia would have recognized the signs that her husband's body was failing. She would have seen the end coming. Jane thought again of the couple's smiling faces in their wedding photo, a reminder that even in the happiest moments, tragedy was waiting in the wings.

She left behind that sad month and moved on to the log for January. February. March. Calls to and from Pilgrim Hospital, to a local dentist, and to Jamal Bird. No surprises. Jane turned to the month of April and stopped. Here was yet another abrupt change in pattern with a series of new phone numbers. In the last few weeks of her life, Sofia Suarez was reaching out to people and places she'd never contacted before.

She swiveled around toward Frost. "April," she said. "Have you looked at that yet?"

"Getting to it. Why?"

"Take a look at April twentieth. She called a number listed to a Gregory Bouchard in Sacramento, California."

Frost scanned down the log until he found the right date. "I see it. It was fifty-five seconds long. Not much of a conversation. Who is this Bouchard guy?"

"Let's find out." She picked up her desk phone and dialed the number. It rang three times and was answered by a man's breezy "Hello?"

Jane put it on speakerphone so Frost could listen in.

"I'm Detective Jane Rizzoli, Boston PD. Am I speaking to Gregory Bouchard?"

A beat of silence, then a cautious "Yeah, that's me. What's this about?"

"We're investigating the death of a woman named Sofia Suarez. According to her phone records, she called your number on April twentieth. Can you tell us anything about that call?"

There was a long pause. "Did you say Sofia's *dead*?"

"Yes, sir."

"What happened? Was there an accident?"

"I'm afraid not. This is a homicide investigation."

"Oh god. Katie's going to freak out."

"Katie?"

"My wife. She's the one Sofia was trying to reach."

"Did they manage to talk?"

"No, Katie was away on a work trip when Sofia left the voicemail. Katie tried calling back when she got home, but they never connected."

"May I speak to your wife?"

"She's not home. She works as a traveling nurse for Nat Geo tours. You know, keeping the rich folks alive and well. I'll check her itinerary, but I think right now they're somewhere in the South Pacific."

"What about the voicemail Sofia left on your phone? Do you still have the recording?"

"No, I'm sorry. It's been erased."

"Do you know what her message was?"

"Um, sort of. I heard it when Katie played it back and . . ." Over the phone, Jane heard him take a deep breath. "I'm sorry, I'm kind of shaken up about this. I've never known anyone who was murdered."

"Her voicemail, Mr. Bouchard?"

"Yeah. I think it was just about catching up on their old days in the ICU."

"They worked together? Your wife and Sofia?"

"It was fifteen, twenty years ago, at a hospital up in Maine. Then I got this job in California and we moved here. We went to Sofia's wedding in Boston, but that was years ago."

"Do you know why she called your wife?"

"I have no idea. Maybe for old times' sake?" A pause. "What does this have to do with her being murdered?"

"I don't know, sir. I'm just following up on every lead. Please have your wife call me if she has any information." Jane hung up and looked at Frost. "Well, that was a dead end."

"Or maybe it has something to do with these other calls," said Frost. "They're all to area code 207. Maine."

"Where Sofia and Bouchard's wife once worked together."

"She called a really weird list of places. Gas and Go in Augusta. Bangor High School. Buffalo Wings Restaurant in South Portland. Eastern Maine Medical Center. Is there a connection between all these numbers?"

Jane picked up her desk phone again. "There's only one way to find out. I'll try the first one."

As Frost swiveled around to his own phone, Jane dialed the Augusta number. After only two rings, a woman answered briskly: "Gas and Go." It was the no-nonsense voice of someone who has more immediate business to attend to.

"I'm Detective Rizzoli, Boston PD. We're investigating the death of a woman named Sofia Suarez. According to her phone records, she called Gas and Go on

Monday, April twenty-first, at ten A.M. Did you happen to speak with her?"

"Monday? Yeah, I'm probably the person who answered the phone that day. I don't remember talking to a customer by that name."

"And she would have been calling from Boston."

"I don't know why anyone would call us from Boston. Unless she was trying to sell us something, because we get a ton of those calls. Maybe she dialed the wrong number?"

"You're sure you don't remember talking to her?"

"Sorry, no. We also sell lottery and bus tickets and we get a *lot* of people calling about those. And April twenty-first, that's like a month ago. Whatever she called about, it wasn't anything that stuck with me."

So much for Gas and Go.

Next on Jane's list was the Buffalo Wings Restaurant in South Portland, a call made at two-thirty P.M. on April 24, lasting a scant thirty seconds. It was now noon, the worst possible time to be calling a restaurant, but Jane dialed the number anyway.

A man answered: "Buffalo Wings, how can I help you?"

Like the woman at Gas and Go, he could not remember a call from Sofia, nor did he even know anyone by that name.

Jane hung up, baffled by why Sofia had phoned these numbers. From the discouraged tone of Frost's voice, she figured he was having no better luck with the numbers he was calling. She scanned down to the Wednesday afternoon before Sofia's death. Dr. Antrim had witnessed her talking on the phone in the parking lot, a call that had struck him as strangely furtive, but the only call she made that afternoon was at 2:46 P.M., and it had gone to the Pilgrim Hospital central switchboard. There was no way to track which extension Sofia had ultimately connected to.

"Any luck?" said Frost.

"No. You?"

"I spoke to the secretary at Bangor High School. She didn't recognize the name Sofia Suarez and doesn't remember the phone call. But she takes calls all day from parents and students."

"And the call to Eastern Maine Medical Center?"

"It went to their medical records department. The clerk didn't remember talking to Sofia."

Jane flinched as her cell phone gave a murderous screech of violins.

"Oh no," said Frost. "I completely forgot to tell you. She called me a few hours ago."

"My mom called *you*?"

"She asked me to tell you to call back." He winced at Jane's annoying ringtone. "Why don't you answer it? She's just gonna call again."

Jane sighed and picked up her phone. "Hey, Ma."

"Why is it always so hard to reach you?"

"I'm working."

"The same case?"

"It's not like on TV. We don't wrap things up in an hour."

"'Cause this situation here in the neighborhood could use your attention."

"There is no situation in your neighborhood. You told me Tricia texted her dad and she's okay."

"I'm not convinced *that* particular situation has been

resolved. And now I'm dealing with a completely *new* matter."

Jane looked at Frost and mouthed the words *save me*.

"I just think I have a right to know if I'm in a danger-ous position here," said Angela. "They're right across the street. Who knows if this could turn into another Waco or something?"

"Is this about the new people again?"

"Yes."

"Why don't you call Revere PD? It's their jurisdic-tion."

"But I don't have a daughter in Revere PD."

"How about calling Vince? He'll know what to do." *And he'll never forgive me for suggesting it.*

"Vince can't do anything. He's still in California."

"But he was a cop. He has instincts."

"He doesn't have access to a weapons database."

Jane paused. "Weapons? What weapons?"

"To start with, that gun Matthew Green's hiding under his shirt. A handgun. It looks just like the one Vince used to carry."

"A Glock?"

"It could be. It sure wasn't some old-fashioned re-volver."

"How do you happen to know that?"

"I was looking over Jonas's fence, trying to find out what the hammering and drilling's all about. And you know what I saw? That Green fellow's installing bars over all his windows. It's like he's turning the house into some high-security prison. So I'm watching him and he bends over and there it is, on his belt. A gun. A Glock, maybe. You're always telling me how strict the state of

Massachusetts is with this kind of thing. Why would that man be carrying a concealed weapon?"

For a moment, Jane didn't say anything. There were any number of legitimate reasons why a man might carry a concealed weapon. Maybe he was in law enforcement. Maybe he was military. Maybe he was a law-abiding citizen who just liked knowing he could protect his castle.

"There might be other guns on the property," said Angela. "That house has a full basement. There's room enough down there to store bazookas."

"Okay, okay," Jane said. "I'll see if Matthew Green has a permit to carry."

"Good. We'll talk about it when you all come over for dinner. Maura's going to ask her friend Daniel, and the butcher's got a nice leg of lamb on order for me."

"Dinner?"

"Don't tell me you forgot."

"No, of course not." *Shit. I forgot.* Jane paused, her attention snagged by Frost, who was waving the call log printout. "Ma, I gotta go. Frost needs me."

"Oh, and tell that nice Barry Frost to come too." Angela paused. "Even if it means we have to put up with his wife."

Jane hung up and looked at Frost. "You and Alice are invited to dinner at my mom's house next Saturday. Leg of lamb. Is Alice still on that weird diet?"

"She can eat around the meat. But take a look at this." He pointed to an entry near the end of the phone log. "This call she made here, May nineteenth, eight A.M. Massachusetts area code. It lasted sixteen minutes."

"Sixteen minutes. That wouldn't have been a wrong number."

"And it's long enough to be a significant conversation. I've already tried calling it, but there's no answer."

"Let's try again."

Already she could feel her pulse quicken as she reached for her desk phone and dialed the number. It rang only once, then an anonymously electronic voice answered: *The person you are trying to reach is unavailable at this time . . .*

"Still no answer." Jane hung up and frowned at the call log. "There's no name attached to this number."

"That's because it's a burner phone," said Frost.

TWELVE

AMY

A BRILLIANT RED CARDINAL WAS SINGING in the dogwood tree, warning off its rivals with a loud *cheer cheer, tick tick tick tick*. During the weeks in rehab after her accident, she had spent so little time outdoors it was now a joy just to breathe in fresh air again and to listen to birdsong. While her father drove off to park the car, she savored these few moments alone in front of the cemetery gates, watching that cocky cardinal hop about from branch to branch as it loudly declared its sovereignty. In the distance, thunder rumbled and she smelled the tang of impending rain in the air. She hoped her father remembered to bring the umbrella from the car. He might be a brilliant clinician in the hospital, but in matters of everyday life, he could be as absentminded as any other man.

Did she just feel a raindrop? She looked up. In the last half hour since they'd left home, the sky had darkened to pewter. The clouds roiling overhead suddenly threw her off-balance and she had to steady herself with her cane.

She did not notice the man standing beside her.

"It's amazing how much noise one little bird can generate," he said.

She turned, startled by his sudden appearance, even if the man himself seemed perfectly harmless. He was in his mid- to late fifties, appropriately dressed for the weather in a raincoat. The coat sagged on his shoulders, as if it were a castoff from a previous owner with broader shoulders. His face was thin and colorless, his eyes an unmemorable shade of gray, yet something about him seemed familiar; she just couldn't remember how or where they might have met. The accident in March had wiped away bits and pieces of her memory, and perhaps this man was one of those lost pieces. He looked at her a little too long and then, as if sensing that made her uncomfortable, he turned his gaze back to the cardinal perched above them.

"He's defending his territory," he said. "His nest must be around here somewhere. By now, he probably has a few hatchlings to protect."

"I don't know much about birds," she admitted. "I just like watching them."

"Don't we all?" He looked at her dress, which was a modest and boring black. "Are you here for a funeral?"

"For Sofia Suarez. Are you here for hers too?"

"No. Just to visit someone I knew a long time ago."

"Oh." She didn't know if he meant someone alive or someone dead, and she was afraid to ask.

"I only wish we'd had more time together," he said quietly, and by the sadness in his voice, she knew it was someone who'd died.

"And you still come to visit? That's so sweet." She smiled at him and he smiled back. It felt like something changed between them. As if the air was suddenly charged with static.

"Do I know you?" she finally said.

"Do I seem familiar?"

"I'm not sure. I had an accident, back in March, and ever since then I've had trouble remembering things. Names. Dates."

"So that's why you need the cane."

"It's ugly, isn't it? I should've chosen something cool and fashionable. But I won't need this much longer anyway."

"How did it happen? The accident?"

"This crazy driver hit me in a crosswalk. I was just leaving campus, and . . ." She paused. "Is that where I know you from? Northeastern?"

A pause. "It's possible we ran across each other there."

"Art history department, maybe?"

"Is that what you're studying?"

"I *should* have graduated this month, but I spent two months in rehab, trying to get back on my feet. I still feel so clumsy."

"Well, you look just fine to me," he said. "Better than fine, cane and all."

His gaze was suddenly so intent it unsettled her and she turned away. She saw her father walking toward her from the parking lot, and he was carrying the umbrella. With a stork-like little hop, he jumped onto the curb.

"I'm glad you remembered it," she said. "It's going to be pouring any minute now."

"Who's that man you were talking to?"

She turned to introduce her new acquaintance but the man had vanished. Puzzled, she scanned the walkway and caught a glimpse of him as he disappeared through the cemetery gate. "That's weird."

"Is that someone you know?"

"I'm not sure. He said he's with Northeastern. Maybe he's on the faculty."

He took her arm and they started toward the gate. "Your mother called in a panic," he said. "The caterer hasn't shown up at the house yet."

"Oh, you know her. She can whip up five hundred finger sandwiches all on her own."

He glanced at his watch. "It's almost ten. We don't want to be late for Sofia."

For Sofia, who would never know that they were there. Yet somehow it mattered that they *were* there. That on this gloomy day, those who knew her would stand beside her grave and mourn her passing.

"Think you can walk the whole way?" her father asked. "The grass might be a little tricky."

"I'll be fine, Dad," she said, although the damp air made her leg ache. It probably always would. Even when a broken leg mended, the memory of that fracture remained crystallized in bone, the pain throbbing back to life with every change in the weather. But Amy didn't complain. She kept this pain to herself as she and her father walked arm in arm through the cemetery gate.

THIRTEEN

JANE

THUNDERSTORMS WERE FORECAST AND JANE could not help glancing up every few minutes as dark clouds rolled toward the cemetery. She'd read that the worst place to be standing when lightning struck was on a knoll or under a tree, and that's exactly where she and Frost were now, on a knoll beneath the spreading branches of a Japanese maple. From this vantage point they could watch the mourners gathered at Sofia Suarez's open grave. Months ago, when Sofia had buried her husband, Tony, here in this same cemetery, did she have any inkling that she'd be joining him so soon? When she visited his grave and gazed at these rolling lawns and manicured shrubs, had she pictured her own eternity in this place?

The distant rumble of thunder made Jane once again look up at the clouds. The graveside service was at an end and there was no reason for Jane and Frost to linger here much longer. They'd been watching for any guest who'd come not to mourn but to gloat or to celebrate, but Jane saw only genuine sorrow on these faces, and she recognized many of them: Dr. Antrim. The nurses from the hospital. Sofia's neighbors Mrs. Leong and Jamal Bird with his mother. Not many teenagers would bother to show up at the funeral for a middle-aged neighbor, but there was Jamal, somberly dressed in black except for his bright blue Nikes.

"It's starting to rain. Call it a day?" said Frost.

"Hold on. Dr. Antrim's coming this way."

Antrim waved as he crossed toward them, accompanied by a slender young woman who walked with a cane. "I was hoping to talk to you," he said. "We're all wondering if there's any news on the case."

"We're making progress" was all Jane could say.

"Do you have any idea who . . ."

"Not yet, I'm afraid." She looked at the young woman standing beside him, the tip of her cane sunk into the wet grass. Her jet-black hair, cut in a stylish bob, was a startling contrast to her pale skin. She had the ghostly pallor of someone who has not been outdoors in a long time. "Is this your daughter, Amy?"

"Yes." Antrim smiled. "She's finally back on her feet. Although this grass isn't the easiest place for her to walk."

"I needed to come," said Amy. "She took such good care of me in the hospital, and I never really thanked her."

"She spent two long weeks in the hospital," Antrim said, smiling at his daughter. "It was touch-and-go for a few days, but Amy's a fighter. She might not look it now, but she is." He turned to Jane. "They never caught the driver who hit her, and it's been weeks since we've had an update from the police. Maybe you could—"

"Dad," said Amy.

"Well, she can check, can't she?"

"I'll call the investigating officer and see if there's

been any progress," said Jane. "But after this much time, I wouldn't be too hopeful."

Thunder grumbled closer.

"It's raining," said Amy. "And Mom's waiting for us."

"Right. She's probably wondering where we all are." He opened an umbrella and held it over his daughter's head. "I hope you'll both come too," he said to Jane and Frost.

"Where?" asked Jane.

"Our house. We're hosting a luncheon for everyone who knew Sofia. My wife's arranged for catering, which means there'll be enough food for an army. So please come."

Something suddenly caught Jane's eye. It was a lone figure in the distance. A man standing among the gravestones, watching them.

"Dr. Antrim," she said. "Do you know that man?"

He turned to look in the direction she was pointing. "No. Should I?"

"He seems very interested in us."

Now Amy turned to look as well. "Oh, that man. We were chatting earlier, outside the gate. I thought I might know him from the university, but now I'm not so sure."

"What did he say to you?"

"He asked if I was here for a funeral."

"Did he ask specifically about Sofia's service?"

"I don't think—I mean, I don't remember."

"Excuse us," said Jane. "We're going to have a little chat with him."

She and Frost started toward the man, walking at a measured pace so they wouldn't alarm him. He turned and began walking away.

"Sir?" Jane called out. "Sir, we'd like to talk to you."

The man's pace quickened to a jog.

"Oh shit. I think we've got a runner," said Frost.

They took off after him, sprinting past gravestones and marble angels. Raindrops splattered Jane's face and trickled into her eyes, smearing the landscape into a blur of green. She blinked and her quarry came back into view. He was running full tilt now, and he rounded an ivy-smothered mausoleum and darted down a path cutting through woods.

Blood pumping, breaths coming fast, Jane followed him into the woods and her shoe suddenly skidded on wet leaves. Like an out-of-control ice-skater, she slid across the flagstones and went down, landing so hard on her rear end that the impact slammed up her spine.

Frost dashed past her, kept running.

Tailbone throbbing, the seat of her pants now muddy, Jane scrambled back to her feet and followed her partner. When she caught up with him, he had stopped and was frantically scanning the woods. The path ahead of them was deserted, the trail flanked by dense shrubbery. Their quarry had vanished.

Thunder rumbled closer and here they were, once again standing in the worst place to be when lightning strikes: under a tree.

"How the hell did we lose him?" said Jane.

"He had too much of a head start. He must've gone off the trail somewhere." He looked at her. "You okay?"

"Yeah." She brushed dirt from her pants. "Crap, and I just bought these."

A twig snapped, loud as a rifle shot.

Jane spun toward the sound and saw a thick wall of rhododendrons. She glanced at Frost, and without a word they simultaneously drew their weapons. She didn't know who this man was or why he had fled from them, but running was something you did when you were afraid. Or guilty.

She was betting on guilty.

She spied an opening in the wall of shrubbery and eased her way through, only to be trapped in a smothering thicket of green. Thunder boomed and rain splattered the leaves, rattling them like gunfire. She kept moving forward, pushing through the damp jungle and blinking away raindrops. A cloud of mosquitoes rose from the soil and swarmed her face. Waving them away, she blindly pushed forward.

From beyond the bushes came the crack of another snapping twig. The clang of metal.

Jane plunged through the last tangle of branches and burst through to the other side, her weapon raised. She came face-to-face with a man wielding a pair of hedge clippers. A man who stared at her with a look of abject terror. He dropped the hedge clippers and raised both hands in the air. In a glance, Jane took in his rain poncho and work boots and saw the mound of clipped branches in the back of the ATV.

The gardener. I almost shot the gardener.

"Sorry," she said, and holstered her weapon. "We're police. It's okay. It's—"

"Rizzoli!" yelled Frost. "He's over there!"

She turned to see a flash of gray as the man they'd been chasing vanished out the cemetery exit. He was beyond their reach now, too far for them to catch.

"Um . . . can I put them down now?" said the gardener, his arms still raised over his head.

"Yeah," said Jane. "And maybe you can help us. That

man who just ran out the gate, do you know who he is?"

"I don't think so."

"Ever seen him before?"

"I didn't get a look at his face—"

Jane sighed and turned to Frost. "Back to square one."

"—but he might be on video."

Jane's attention snapped back to the gardener. "What video?"

"IT'S A SHAME WE EVEN need cameras like this, but that's how the world is these days. No one respects private property anymore, not like when I was growing up," said cemetery director Gerald Haas, who was certainly old enough to remember the world as it once was—or as he thought it was. Gingerly he lowered himself into his chair and woke up his computer. Like the mortuary reception room, the director's office was quietly tasteful, decorated in soothing pastels and framed quotes on the walls.

It is not length of life, but depth of life.

—Ralph Waldo Emerson

For life and death are one, even as the river and the sea are one.

—Kahlil Gibran

Also hanging on the wall was a map of the sprawling 250-acre property, its pathways named after flowers and trees: Lavender Way. Hibiscus Lane. Lake Magnolia. As if these grounds were planted with gardens, not the mortal remains of people.

With arthritic hands, Haas shakily maneuvered the

computer mouse but every move, every click, took a painfully long time. Jane thought of Jamal Bird's nimble fingers typing with the dizzying speed of youth and she had to force herself to be patient as she watched Haas's gnarled hand scroll and click, scroll and click.

"Would you like me to help, sir?" Frost asked, polite as always, with not a hint of the frustration Jane was feeling.

"No, no. I know this system. It just takes me a while to remember how to do this . . ."

Scroll. Point. Click.

"Ah. Here we are."

On the computer screen, a rain-splattered image appeared. It was the passenger drop-off area at the cemetery entrance.

"This is the CCTV at our main gate, on the south end," said Haas. "It's mounted right over the archway and it should have recorded everyone who entered and exited this morning."

"What about that north entrance?" Jane asked, pointing to the map on the wall. "Is there a camera there too?"

"Yes, but that entrance is only used by our staff. That gate's kept locked at all times and it requires a key code to get in. So a visitor couldn't have come in that way."

"Then let's just look at the video from the main entrance," said Jane. "Since we know that's also how he left."

"How far back do you want to look?"

"According to our witness, the man walked onto the grounds shortly before the memorial service started. So go back to nine-thirty."

Once again the gnarled hand reached for the mouse.

In Haas's profession there was no need to be speedy. The dead are patient.

Scroll. Point. Click.

"There," he said. "This is nine-thirty."

On the video, the rain had not started and the pavement was still dry. Except for a bird flitting past, nothing moved in the frame.

"Fifty years ago, when I was growing up, we kids had respect for the dead. We'd never dream of painting graffiti on a cemetery wall or tipping over gravestones. That's why we had to install these cameras. No wonder the world's falling apart."

The lament of every generation, thought Jane. *The world's falling apart.* It's what her grandmother used to say. It's what her dad still said. And one of these days, she'd probably say it to her own daughter, Regina.

Her attention perked up when, at 9:35, a silver sedan pulled to a stop at the curb. An elderly couple climbed out and slowly walked through the gate, holding hands.

"That's just the Santoros," said Haas. "Their daughter brings them here every week to visit their son. He's buried down on Lilac Lane. Watch, the daughter's gone to park the car, but she'll show up any minute with the flowers."

Moments later, as he'd predicted, a woman walked into view carrying a vase of roses, and she followed her parents through the gate.

"Those are the saddest ones," said Haas. "I mean, every death is sad, but when you lose a child . . ."

"How did their son die?" asked Frost.

"They won't ever talk about it, but I'm told it was a drug overdose. It happened years ago, when he was only thirtysomething. And here it is, all these years later, and they still come once a week, like clockwork. We always have the golf cart ready to take them to the grave."

At 9:40 a pair of familiar figures appeared: Jamal and his mother. Then, a few minutes later, several nurses from Pilgrim Hospital all arrived together.

"We get quite a few tourists here too," said Haas.

"Is someone famous buried here?" Frost asked.

"They come to see the plantings. This cemetery is almost a hundred years old and there are some mature specimen trees you'll find nowhere else in Boston. Did you get a chance to see our gardens?"

"A little too up close," said Jane, thinking about her battle with the rhododendrons. And her dirt-stained pants.

"The garden tourists usually show up in the afternoon, but with all this rain, they won't be coming today. Garden people tend to be very respectful, so I'm happy to see them. We pride ourselves on being a welcoming place for everyone, as long as they behave."

Onscreen, a blue Mercedes pulled up to the curb and a slender woman with short black hair gingerly emerged from the passenger side, holding a cane. Amy Antrim. As her father drove away to park the car, she waited near the entrance, her head tilted upward toward a tree.

That was when the man appeared. He swooped in on Amy so suddenly, she did not seem to notice him until he was standing right beside her.

"Our man in the raincoat," said Frost.

Amy and the man were talking to each other now, and whatever he said to Amy didn't seem to alarm her. He stood with his back to the camera, so the only face they could see was Amy's, and she was smiling. It didn't seem to alarm her that he was standing so close, leaning in like a vulture about to strike. Abruptly he turned and walked away, his head drooping as he passed through the gate and into the cemetery. All they could see on camera was the top of his head, his thinning hair an anonymous shade of brown.

Now Dr. Antrim walked into the frame, carrying an umbrella. Was it his arrival that had scared off the man? If Antrim had not arrived, what might have happened next?

"What just happened between them?" said Jane. "What the hell was that all about?"

"It's like he was waiting for her. Expecting her to turn up," said Frost.

Frost's phone pinged with a text message. As he pulled it out of his pocket, Jane backed up the recording to the man's first appearance. Had he really been waiting for Amy, or were they reading too much into an innocent interaction? And why target Amy Antrim in particular?

"Now, *this* is interesting," said Frost, staring at his phone.

"What?"

"We got the data from that burner phone."

"We know who owns it yet?"

"No. But we do have the call log. The burner phone got one incoming call from Sofia Suarez—"

"Which we know about."

"And it made two outgoing calls. Both were in the last week, and both went to the same Brookline residence." He held out his phone. "Look whose name is on the account."

She stared at the name on the screen. *Michael Antrim, MD*.

FOURTEEN

AMY ANTRIM SAT IN HER FATHER'S STUDY, her cane propped against the armchair, her modest black dress a stark contrast to her pale skin. Even though months had passed since the accident, she looked as delicate as a porcelain doll. Outside, windblown rain splattered the window and the watery streaks on the glass cast her face in distorted bands of gray.

"We get spam calls all the time," she said. "Lots and lots of them, trying to sell us things. But Dad insists on keeping his phone number listed, in case a patient needs to reach him. He's good that way, even if it means we have to put up with nuisance calls."

"The first call was two minutes long, the other was about thirty seconds," said Frost. "Both were made in the evening, while your dad was at work. Your mom says she doesn't remember any unusual calls, so we're wondering if maybe you answered them."

"My mom usually picks up first, since I don't move so fast these days. Maybe they went to the answering machine?" Amy looked back and forth at Jane and Frost. "Do these calls have something to do with that man in the cemetery?"

"We're not sure," said Jane.

"Because I thought that's what you came to ask me about, that man. He seemed nice enough at the time. *Should* I have been afraid of him?"

"We don't know that either." Jane looked down at Amy's slender hands, the skin so translucent that blue veins showed through. Were those hands strong enough to fend off an attacker? Amy seemed fragile enough to be toppled by a mere gust of wind, much less a man intent on harming her. She was like the lone gazelle at the edge of the herd, the vulnerable one that a predator would pick off first.

"Let's talk about that man," said Frost. "Tell us again what he said to you."

"It was just small talk, really. About the cardinal up in the tree and how it must be defending its nest. He noticed I was wearing black and asked me if I was there for a funeral. I asked him if we'd met before, because I got the feeling that I knew him from somewhere."

"So you did recognize him?"

Amy thought about it for a moment, her brow delicately furrowed. "I'm not sure."

"Not sure?"

She gave a helpless shrug. "There was something familiar about him. I thought maybe I'd seen him at the university, but it wasn't in the art history department. Somewhere else on campus, maybe. Maybe the library. I've spent so much time in that library, working on my senior thesis. Or at least I was working on it, until *this* happened." She massaged her healing leg, something she seemed to do as a matter of habit. "I can't wait to throw that ugly cane in the trash and get on with my life."

"About the accident," said Jane. "How did it happen?"

"It was just bad luck. Wrong place, wrong time."

"What do you remember?"

"I remember walking out of the library and it was sleeting. I hadn't dressed for it. I was wearing these silly flats and they got soaked as I walked across campus. I got to the crosswalk and then . . ." She paused, frowning.

"And then?"

"I remember standing there, waiting for the light to change."

"This was on Huntington Avenue?"

"Yes. I guess I must have stepped into the street and then the car hit me. The next thing I knew, I was waking up in the ICU. Sofia was there, looking down at me. The police said the car hit me, right there in the crosswalk, and then it drove away. They never caught the driver."

Jane glanced at Frost and wondered if he was thinking the same thing she was. *Was* it an accident? Or something else?

The door opened and Amy's mother, Julianne, walked in, carrying a tray with teacups and pastries. "I'm sorry to barge in on you, but Amy barely ate any lunch. And I thought you detectives might like something to eat as well. Tea?"

Frost brightened as he saw the plate of lemon bars on the tray. "Those look great, Mrs. Antrim. Thank you."

"Everyone else has left for the hospital," said Julianne. "But there's plenty of food in the dining room if you'd like something else. I always seem to lay out more than everyone can eat."

"Old habits," said Amy with a smile. "My mom used to work in restaurants."

"And every cook's worst nightmare is running out of food," said Julianne, pouring tea. "I'll never stop obsessing about whether I've made enough for everyone." Julianne handed out teacups with the efficiency of a seasoned hostess, then settled into the chair next to Amy. They might be twenty years apart, but mother and daughter had the same slender figures, the same jet-black hair cut in identical bobs. "So what is this all about? Who was this man at the cemetery?"

"A man who seemed to take a very special interest in Amy," said Jane. "We're wondering if it's something we need to pursue."

Julianne looked at her daughter. "You didn't recognize him?"

"I thought I might know him from somewhere. Or he was just trying to be friendly. But now that everyone's asking about him—"

"What did he look like?" Julianne cut in.

Amy thought about it for a moment. "I guess he was about Dad's age."

Frost jotted this down. "So, in his late fifties. And his hair?"

"I'd call it light brown, but he didn't have a lot of it. He was going a little bald on top." She looked at Julianne and said with a smile, "Also like Dad."

"And his face?" prompted Julianne.

"It was . . . thin. Average. I know that doesn't help much, but that's all I can say about him. He seemed sad because he was visiting someone in the cemetery. Someone he said he knew a long time ago. Maybe that's why he was so hungry to talk. And I just happened to be there."

"Or was he eager to talk to you, specifically?" asked Jane.

"You think this man was targeting my daughter?" asked Julianne.

"I don't know, Mrs. Antrim."

Julianne sat up straight in her chair, a mother primed to defend her child. "Mike told me there was CCTV footage of him. Let me see this man."

Frost pulled out his cell phone and opened the video file. "The camera didn't capture a good view of his face, I'm afraid. But here's what we have."

Julianne took the phone and stared at the video of her daughter's conversation with the unnamed man. The interaction was brief, barely more than two minutes, but it was surely obvious to Julianne, just as it was obvious to Jane, that the man was intently, even ferociously, focused on Amy. This was more than a casual conversation between strangers.

"Your daughter thinks she may know him from somewhere," said Jane. "What about you, Mrs. Antrim? Do you recognize him?"

Julianne said nothing, just kept frowning at the video.

"Mrs. Antrim?"

Slowly Julianne looked up. "No. I've never seen him before. But the way he swoops in on Amy, it's almost as if he was *waiting* for her to show up."

"You could interpret it that way."

"And then, just as my husband approaches, this man takes off. As if he doesn't want to get caught. As if he knows he shouldn't be there." She looked at her daughter. "He didn't tell you his name?"

"No, and I didn't tell him mine. Really, Mom, this was just a random event. We were both at the cemetery at the same time."

A random event, thought Jane. *Like her accident.*

"But looking at this video," said Julianne. "It seems like he was *waiting* for you."

"How would he know I'd be there today?" said Amy.

"Sofia's funeral announcement was in the newspaper," said Jane. "It was public information."

There was a long silence as Julianne considered what that might mean. "You think this has something to do with the *murder*?"

"Every homicide case attracts attention," said Jane. "Sometimes it's the attention of odd people. People who attend the victim's funeral because they're curious or they're drawn to tragedy. But every so often, the killer himself shows up. To gloat or to play games or to see firsthand the damage he's done."

"Oh god. And now he has his eye on Amy?"

"We don't know that. It's too soon to be alarmed."

"Too *soon*?" Julianne's voice rose in agitation. "I don't think it's ever too soon to imagine the worst when it comes to your own children."

Amy reached out to take Julianne's hand, the child comforting the mother, and she gave Jane an apologetic smile. "My mom worries about the littlest things."

"I can't help it," said Julianne. "Ever since the day she was born—"

"Oh no. You're going to tell that story again?"

"What story?" asked Frost.

"How I almost died as a baby."

"Well, it's true," said Julianne. "She was born almost a month early." Julianne pointed to the bookshelf, to the photograph of Amy as a black-haired infant, so impossibly tiny she looked like a doll nestled in her mother's arms. "It was a small hospital in Vermont, and they weren't sure she would make it. But my daughter pulled through. By the skin of her teeth, maybe, but Amy pulled through." She looked at Jane. "I know what it's like to almost lose my baby. So no, it's not too soon to be alarmed."

This Jane understood. When you have a child, you also grow new nerve endings that sense the slightest vibration of danger, of anything that's not quite right. Julianne was feeling that now, and so was Jane, even though she had no evidence of a real threat. Just a man in a raincoat who'd been too friendly. Who'd been waiting at precisely the right time and place where a murdered woman's friends would be gathering.

It wasn't enough to make a cop say *this is important, this means something.* But a mother doesn't need evidence to know when something is wrong.

"If you see this man again, Amy, call me. Anytime, day or night." Jane took out a business card with her cell phone number. Amy stared at the card as if it were coated in poison, as if accepting it meant accepting the danger was real.

Her mother took the card instead. "We will," she said.

It was Julianne who walked with them out of the study and ushered them out the front door. On the porch, Julianne closed the door behind them, so her daughter wouldn't hear what she said to them next.

"I know you don't want to scare Amy, but you scared *me.*"

"There may be nothing at all to worry about," said

Jane. "We just want you and Dr. Antrim to keep your eyes open. And if you get any more calls from that phone number, get a name."

"I will."

Jane and Frost started down the porch steps and suddenly Jane stopped and looked back at Julianne. "Dr. Antrim isn't Amy's biological father, is he?"

Julianne paused, clearly taken aback by the question. "No. I married Mike when Amy was ten years old."

"May I ask who her father is?"

"Why on earth do you want to know?"

"She said the man at the cemetery seemed familiar, and I wondered if—"

"I left him when Amy was eight years old. Trust me, that man in the video wasn't him."

"Just out of curiosity, where is her father now?"

"I don't know." Julianne's mouth tightened in disgust and she looked away. "And I don't care."

FIFTEEN

JANE SIPPED A GLASS OF BEER as she sat at her kitchen table, reading the Boston PD report of Amy Antrim's hit-and-run accident. The accident report was a far shorter document than the pages and pages of documents that a homicide case usually generated, and Jane quickly absorbed the essentials. Two months ago, at approximately 8:38 P.M. on a Friday, a male witness saw Amy Antrim step into a crosswalk on Huntington Avenue, right in front of Northeastern University. She had taken only a step or two when she was struck by a black sedan moving west. The witness said the vehicle was moving at high speed, perhaps fifty miles per hour. After hitting Amy, the driver did not even slow down but sped away in the direction of the Massachusetts Turnpike on-ramp.

A day later a black Mazda, matching the witness's description and caught on video by four separate CCTVs in the area, was found abandoned just outside the city of Worcester, forty-five miles away. Damage to the front bumper, along with blood that matched the victim's, confirmed it was the vehicle that hit Amy. The registered owner of the Mazda had reported the vehicle stolen two days before the accident. The thief was never identified.

And probably never would be, thought Jane. She took another sip of beer and leaned back in her chair, stretching the stiffness from her shoulders. Tonight it was Gabriel's turn to give Regina her bath, and judging by the happy squeals from the bathroom, they were having such a splashy good time that Jane was tempted to close the laptop and join them. Or at least bring a few extra towels to sop up the water before it seeped into the floorboards. Was she wasting her time, reviewing an accident that was probably not relevant to the Sofia Suarez murder? Maybe it was just bad luck that had placed Amy in that crosswalk at that particular moment. Maybe the man in the gray raincoat who'd struck up a conversation with Amy at the cemetery was just another unconnected incident that had nothing to do with Sofia Suarez's murder.

So many distracting details. So many ways to lose sight of the killer.

Bath time was over; she could hear the tub draining and suddenly four-year-old Regina scampered into the kitchen stark naked, her skin slick and rosy from the bath. Gabriel was right behind her, and judging by his soaked shirt, he'd caught the brunt of Regina's splashing.

"Whoa, baby." He laughed, trying to corral their daughter with a towel. "Let's get ready for bed. Mommy's working."

"Mommy's *always* working."

"Because she has an important job."

"But not as important as you are!" said Jane, and scooped her wet daughter onto her lap, where Regina sat wriggling, as slippery as a seal. Gabriel handed her a towel and Jane wrapped her daughter into a snug little Regina enchilada.

"Any breakthroughs?" asked Gabriel as he uncapped a beer for himself.

"More like alleys. Lots and lots of blind alleys."

He leaned against the kitchen counter and took a swig from the bottle. "So. A normal day, then."

"All these things feel like they *should* connect to the case, but I don't see how they can."

"Maybe they don't connect. It's normal for humans to see patterns in random events. Just like when we look at the surface of Mars and see random hills and valleys, we think we see a face."

"I've just got this *feeling*."

He gave her his maddeningly impassive smile. As usual he was Mr. Calm and Logical Special Agent who did not believe in gut feelings, only in facts. Who once told her that when a cop relies on his instincts, it too often leaves him blind to the truth.

After Gabriel coaxed Regina off to bed, Jane turned back to the accident report, which was still nagging at her. What was it about Amy and the accident and the man at the cemetery? She looked up the responding officer's contact information and reached for her cell phone.

"Officer Packard," he answered. Jane could hear the buzz of conversation in the background and a woman's voice calling out: *Number eighty-two! Order eight-two!* He was on his dinner break, and for a hungry cop, mealtime was holy. She'd make this short.

"I'm Detective Rizzoli, following up on a hit-and-run that you responded to back in March. It happened on Huntington Ave. Victim's name is Amy Antrim."

"Oh yeah." Mouth full, chewing. "I remember that one."

"You ever ID the driver?"

"Nope. Asshole hit her and just left the poor girl bleeding in the street. She was in pretty bad shape. I wasn't sure she'd make it."

"Well, I just saw Amy yesterday and she's doing fine. She's still using a cane, but not for much longer."

"Glad to hear she pulled through. I heard she had a ruptured spleen and her mother was really freaking out 'cause the girl needed a lot of transfusions and she's got some kind of rare blood type."

"I don't see a lot of details here in your interview notes."

"That's because I couldn't talk to her until a few days after her surgery, and she had no memory of the accident. Didn't even remember stepping into the crosswalk. Retrograde amnesia, the doctor said."

"She didn't remember anything about the driver?"

"Nope. But there was a witness who saw it all. Homeless guy, standing right behind her on the sidewalk. He said the light turned green, she entered the crosswalk and slipped on the ice. He was about to help her when that car came roaring down the street."

"You trust the word of a homeless guy?"

"It was caught on surveillance camera. Everything he said checked out." There was the sound of more chewing and in the background, a voice called out: *Number ninety-five! Junior Whopper and fries!*

"Did you ever go back to interview her again?"

"Didn't really need to. And by then, we'd found the

vehicle abandoned out in Worcester. Unfortunately, it had been stolen a few days earlier and we never identified the thief."

"Fingerprints?"

"Lots of unidentifieds, but none of 'em had a match on AFIS."

"And this vehicle, where was it stolen?"

"It was parked on the street outside the owner's residence, in Roxbury. By the time the vehicle was recovered, it was pretty beat up, not just from the accident. Undercarriage looked like someone took it joyriding in the woods. Hey, what's this got to do with Homicide?"

"Did I mention a homicide?"

"No, but you're Detective Rizzoli. Everyone knows who you are."

Is that a good thing? Jane's cell phone beeped and she glanced at the screen to see she had a call waiting, from Sacramento, California.

". . . that Chinatown case you cracked, that was, like, *legendary*," said Packard. "How many cops get to chase down a ninja?"

"I've got another call coming in," she said. "You remember anything else, call me."

"You bet. Nice talking to you, Detective."

Jane switched to the other caller. "Detective Rizzoli."

"This is Katie Bouchard," a woman said.

It took Jane a few seconds to remember the name. *Sofia's phone calls. The number in Sacramento.* "You're Sofia's friend. In California."

"My husband told me you called a few days ago. I'm sorry I couldn't return your call earlier, but I just got home from Australia yesterday."

"Did he tell you why I called?"

"Yes, and I couldn't believe it. So it's true, then. Sofia was murdered?"

"I'm afraid so."

"Have you caught him yet? The person who did it?"

"No. Which is why I need to talk to you."

"I wish I could help you, but it's been years since I saw her."

"When was the last time?"

"It was at a nursing conference in Dallas, maybe five years ago. We hadn't seen each other since her wedding to Tony, so we had a lot of catching up to do. We met for dinner, just the two of us, and she seemed so happy. She talked about the cruise she and Tony went on to Alaska. How they planned to buy an RV someday and see the country. Then last December I got a card from her that Tony died. Oh, that was awful. And now this." She sighed. "It's so unfair, how anyone can be that unlucky, especially Sofia. She was such a *good* person."

On that point, everyone agreed: Sofia Suarez did not deserve such a terrible fate. That could not be said for every victim; more than once in her career, Jane had caught herself thinking: This one had it coming.

"Do you have any idea why she reached out to you?" Jane asked.

"No. I work as a traveling nurse for a tour company and that month, I was with a group in Peru."

"Sounds like a pretty cool job."

"It is. Until you have to deal with octogenarians with high-altitude sickness puking on the bus."

Oh. Never mind.

"When I got home a few weeks later, my husband

told me Sofia had left a voicemail. I tried calling her back, but she didn't answer. By then, I guess, she was already . . ." No need to finish the sentence. They both knew why Sofia never answered.

"Do you remember what was on the voicemail?"

"Unfortunately, I've already deleted it. She said she wanted to talk to me about some patient we had in Maine."

"Which patient?"

"I have no idea. We worked for years together and we took care of maybe a thousand post-op patients. I have no idea why she'd be calling me about one after all these years." Katie paused. "Do you think this has anything to do with what happened?"

"I don't know," said Jane. Three words she'd been saying a lot lately.

She hung up, frustrated by yet another loose thread. This case had so many of them and as much as she wanted to, she could not see how to weave them together into a bigger picture. Maybe this was the face on Mars that Gabriel had talked about, just random hills and shadows that she'd transformed, with wishful thinking, into a pattern that did not exist.

She powered down the laptop and snapped it shut. Common things were common, and burglary was one of the most common crimes of all. It was easy to envision the most likely sequence of events: The burglar breaking in. The sudden return of the homeowner. The panicked thief attacking her with the same hammer he'd used to shatter the window. Yes, it was all perfectly logical except for that shard of glass she'd found against the fence, glass that the crime lab confirmed was from the broken pane in the kitchen door. Was it kicked there when the killer fled in panic? Or was it propelled there because the window was broken from the inside?

Two different possibilities. Two very different conclusions.

SIXTEEN

AMY

NO MATTER HOW HARD SHE tried to remember his face, the image kept slipping away from her, like a reflection that disintegrates when you plunge your hand into water. There and gone. There and gone. She knew that face lurked somewhere deep in her memory, but she could not reach it. Instead, when she closed her eyes and thought about him, she saw cornflowers. Faded blue cornflowers on wallpaper that was streaked with mold and stained an ugly yellow from years of cigarette smoke.

Even all these years later she could still picture that bedroom, scarcely larger than a closet, with one small window. A window that might as well not even have been there, because the house was tucked up against a hillside, which blocked all the sunlight. Her room was a grim little cave that her mother had tried to dress up and make cheerful. Julianne had hung curtains she'd made herself from remnant lace bought at a yard sale. From that same yard sale, she'd also bought a painting of roses that she'd hung over Amy's little bed. It was an amateurish painting—even at eight years old, Amy could tell the difference between the work of a real artist and that splotchy attempt, signed on the bottom by someone named Eugene. But Julianne was always thinking up ways to brighten their lives in that cramped house, where the walls themselves reeked with the accumulated odors left by countless previous tenants. Her mother always tried her best.

But it was never good enough for *him*.

For too long she'd suppressed the memories of those days and now she could not conjure up an image of his face, but she could still remember his voice, raw and angry, yelling in the kitchen. Whenever he was in one of his moods, her mother would send Amy to her room and tell her to lock the door, leaving Julianne to deal with his rage the way she always dealt with it. Which usually meant quiet pleading and an occasional black eye.

"If I lose, you lose" was what he always screamed at her. Amy did not understand why it had such power over her mother, but those words inevitably defeated Julianne and made her go silent.

If I lose, you lose.

But it was her mother who bore the bruises, who got in the way of his fists. The one who trudged off to work at the local diner every morning at five A.M., where she'd heat up the griddle and brew the coffee before the farmers and the long-haul truckers showed up for breakfast. She was the one who dragged herself home every afternoon to cook dinner and help Amy with her homework before he got home. Then they'd both watch him get drunk. *Family values,* that's what he called it, what he threw in Julianne's face whenever she tried to leave him. *Family values* was a threat, the cudgel he used to keep them forever locked with him in battle.

Most of the time that battle played out in other

rooms, where Amy couldn't watch it. But she could hear it through the wall as she lay curled up in bed, staring at the wallpaper with the blue cornflowers.

Even now, and hundreds of miles from that house under the hill, she could still hear those voices in her head, his growing louder and louder, and Julianne's fading to silence. Family values meant keeping your head down and your voice soft. It meant having dinner on the table by six and your paycheck in his hand every other Friday.

It meant keeping secrets that at any time might explode in your face.

Was that miserable shack still standing? Was some girl now sleeping in her old bedroom, or had it all been torn down, its ghosts bulldozed into the earth where they belonged? The ghosts of those cornflowers would never vanish; they were here in her head, still so vivid she could see their nicotine-stained petals, but why couldn't she remember his face? Where had that memory gone?

All she remembered was the voice screaming in the kitchen, vowing that he would never let them go, would never give them up. No matter how far and fast they ran, he said, he would find them.

Is it possible? Is he coming for us now?

SEVENTEEN

ANGELA

I'VE ALWAYS LIKED SHOPPING FOR DINNER PARTIES. As I wheel my cart through the supermarket, I imagine the guests seated around my table, feasting on the meal I've so lovingly prepared. Not that this is a particularly large dinner party, just Jane's family and nice Barry Frost with his annoying wife, Alice, plus Maura and—I hope—Maura's friend Father Brophy. Once it would have bothered me, seeing the two of them together, because I was raised a good Catholic girl. But perspectives change. At my age, none of the old rules seem set in stone anymore, certainly not when it comes to love. Just in case he does come, I'll plan on dinner for seven. Seven and a half, counting little Regina. That's not much bigger than the dinners for five I used to cook every night when my kids were young, when cooking was a duty, more about just getting something edible on the table.

This meal will be more than edible. I want it to feel like a feast.

At the meat counter, I pick up the beautiful leg of lamb, which my butcher lovingly wraps in paper. I'm going to stud it with garlic cloves and roast it a juicy medium rare. What a shame Alice Frost is on some sort of diet and probably won't even touch it. Her loss. I cruise through the produce section, plucking up tender lettuces and yellow onions, potatoes and green beans. And asparagus. That's for me. It's the season for fresh asparagus and it makes me happy to see it because it means summer's on the way.

I push my cart up and down the aisles, searching for olive oil and pasta, coffee beans and wine. Six bottles, at least. Again, some of it just for me. With my cart almost full, I head to the frozen desserts section. It never hurts to have an extra carton or two of ice cream on hand. I round the corner into the freezer aisle and come to a halt when I see who is standing there, staring at the offerings.

Tricia Talley. So she's not kidnapped and murdered after all, but alive and apparently shopping for ice cream.

"Tricia!"

She looks at me with a blank teenage stare. Either she's too zoned out to recognize me or she just doesn't care.

"It's me. Angela Rizzoli."

"Oh, yeah. Hi."

"I haven't seen you around in a while."

On this warm day she's wearing blue-jean cut-offs and an oversize T-shirt that's sagged off one shoulder, leaving it bare. That skinny shoulder shrugs at me, a halfhearted greeting as I wheel my cart closer.

"What's going on, Tricia? I talked to your mom and she's been worried sick about you."

Her face stiffens. She looks at the freezer, glaring at the shelves.

"At least give her a call, why don't you?" I suggest. "Tell her you're okay. Don't you think she deserves at least that much?"

"You don't know a thing about her."

"She's your mom. That's enough reason to call her."

"Not after what she did."

"What? What'd Jackie do?"

Tricia turns away from the freezer. "Guess I don't want anything after all," she mutters and walks away.

I stare after her, baffled by what just happened. I've known this girl all her life. I remember bringing over a pink onesie and a bag of Pampers when she was born. When she was a Girl Scout, I bought Thin Mints from her every year, and I donated to her class trip to D.C. But this isn't the same sweet girl. This Tricia is angry and resentful, every mother's nightmare teenager.

Poor Jackie.

THAT AFTERNOON, AFTER I PUT AWAY THE GROCERIES, I walk down the street to Jackie's house. She'll be relieved to hear I've seen her daughter alive and kicking. When she answers the door, I can see the strain in her face, the saggy eye bags, the unkempt hair. She's been crying and that only makes me angrier at Tricia. Thank god my Janie never put me through anything like this.

"Oh honey," I say as I walk into the house. "You look like you need some good news."

"I'm really not in the mood for a visit right now."

"But this'll make you feel better. I guarantee."

We head straight to the kitchen. For women, it's an automatic destination, the first place you go for tea and comfort. I'm not sure Jackie even uses her living room these days, because everything there seems frozen in place, never moved, as if someone has coated it all in wax to keep it presentable just in case an important guest turns up. I'm not that guest. I'm just a friend—or so I thought, but she doesn't look happy to see me and clearly wants me to go away. Something has changed.

Yes, I think as I step into the kitchen. Something has definitely changed. The place is even more of a mess than the last time I visited. There are dirty dishes piled up in the sink, and judging by the food crusted on the plates, they've been there for at least a day. A few shards of glass sparkle on the floor by the refrigerator. Who leaves broken glass on the floor? Jackie doesn't offer me tea or coffee—again, that's unlike her. We sit down at the table but she doesn't look at me, as if she's afraid to. Or embarrassed by her haggard appearance.

"Tell me what's going on," I say.

She shrugs. "Marriage. It's complicated."

"You two had a fight, huh?"

"Yeah."

"So who broke the glass, you or Rick?" I point to the shards on the floor.

"Oh, Rick. He threw it and . . ." She's sniffling now, trying to hold back tears.

"He didn't hit you, did he? Because if he did, I'm gonna—"

"No, he didn't hit me."

"But he's throwing dishes around."

"Angie, don't make it more than it is."

"It looks pretty bad as it is."

"We had a fight. He left to cool down. That's it. That's all I'm gonna say."

"Is he coming back?"

"I don't know." Her sniffles grow more desperate. "He might not. I'm just afraid he'll do something."

"To you?"

"No! Stop thinking that!" Abruptly she gets up. "I need to lie down. So if you don't mind."

"I never told you what happened today."

"Angie, I really don't feel like talking right now." She starts to walk out of the kitchen.

"It's Tricia. I saw her at the supermarket just a few hours ago. She was alive and well and looking at ice cream."

Jackie halts in the doorway and turns to look at me. What I see in her face puzzles me. Despite the fact I just gave her some very good news, she looks frightened. "Did you—did you talk to her?"

"I tried to, but you know. Teenagers."

"What did she say?"

"She seems really mad at you."

"I know."

"What happened between you two? She said it was something you did."

"She didn't tell you, did she?"

"No."

Jackie sighs, a sound of relief. "I can't talk about this. Please, will you just give me some privacy? It's something we have to work out by ourselves."

I exit her house feeling bewildered. As I walk away, I'm aware she's watching me, her haggard face framed in the window. I don't know what blew that family apart, and clearly not one of them is going to tell me. At least now I know this isn't a case of a kidnapped teenager. Instead it's a case of a pissed-off teenager and a marriage in the process of disintegrating.

Just another day in the neighborhood.

EIGHTEEN

MAURA

As Maura looked down at the keyboard, she felt her heartbeat quicken, keeping pace with the allegro tempo the orchestra was now playing, every note, every measure, counting down toward her solo. She knew her part so well she could play it with her eyes closed, yet her hands trembled, her nerves drawing tighter and tighter as the strings and woodwinds called to one another. Now the bassoons joined in and the flutes trilled, and it was time.

She launched into her solo. The notes were seared into her muscle memory, as familiar to her now as the act of breathing, and her fingers moved effortlessly through the cadenza, slowing into the dolce, and then launched into the final trill. It was the cue for the string section to raise their bows for the tutti section. Only then, as the rest of the orchestra took over, could she lift her hands from the keys. She took a deep breath and felt her shoulders relax. *I did it. Made it through without a single flubbed note.*

Then the rehearsal fell apart. Somewhere among the strings, notes collided in a sour jumble, throwing off the woodwinds. In the midst of that dissonant scrimmage, the conductor's baton rapped sharply on the music stand.

"Stop. Stop!" the conductor called out. The bassoon gave one final honk and the orchestra fell silent. "Second violins? What happened there?" He frowned at the offending string section.

Mike Antrim reluctantly raised his bow in the air. "My fault, Claude. I lost my place. Forgot which measure we were on."

"Mike, we've got only two weeks till the concert."

"I know, I know. I promise, it won't happen again."

The conductor gestured toward Maura. "Our pianist here is doing a bang-up job, so let's try to match her performance, shall we? Now let's go back to five measures before the tutti. Piano, lead us in with the trill, please?"

As Maura raised her hands to the keyboard, she glimpsed a red-faced Mike Antrim looking her way as he mouthed the word *sorry*.

He still looked abashed when the rehearsal ended half an hour later. While the other musicians packed up their stands and instruments, he approached the piano, where Maura was gathering up her sheet music. "Well, that was pretty humiliating. For me anyway," he said. "But you made it seem effortless."

"Hardly." She laughed. "I've done nothing but practice for the last two months."

"And it certainly shows. Obviously, I should've been doing more of it myself, but I've been distracted." He paused and looked down at the violin case he was holding, as if trying to come up with a way to broach the subject on his mind. "Are you in a rush to leave? Because I wondered if we could talk about the investigation."

"The Suarez case?"

"Yes. It really shook me up, not just because I knew her. But now Detective Rizzoli's raised the possibility that the killer has his eye on my daughter."

"I hadn't heard that."

"It happened at Sofia's funeral. There was this man at the cemetery who seemed far too interested in Amy. And that worries us."

The other musicians were already heading out of the auditorium, but Antrim made no move to leave. The door banged shut, sending an echo through the deserted building. Only Maura and Antrim were left in the performance hall, standing alone among the empty chairs.

"Detective Rizzoli hasn't told us anything since then," said Antrim. "Julianne's so anxious she can't sleep. Neither can Amy. I need to know if there's something we should be doing. If it's something we even need to be worried about."

"I'm sure Jane would tell you if there is."

"I get the feeling she likes to keep her cards close to her vest. You know her pretty well, don't you?"

"Well enough to know you can trust her."

"To tell us the truth?"

Maura slipped the sheet music into her portfolio and looked at Antrim. "She's the most honest person I know," she said, and it was true. Too often people avoided speaking candidly because there were consequences to honesty, but that had never stopped Jane from delivering the truth, however painful.

"Do you think you could talk to her? Let her know how worried we are?"

"I'm having dinner with her tomorrow night. I'll find out if there's anything she's willing to share with you."

They walked out of the building, into a night so thick with humidity it felt like wading into a warm bathtub. She took a breath of syrupy air and looked up at a cloud of moths, swarming and battering themselves against the streetlamp. Theirs were the only cars still left in the lot, Maura's Lexus parked half a dozen stalls away from Antrim's Mercedes. She unlocked her vehicle and was about to slide in when he called out with a question.

"What else can you tell me about Detective Rizzoli?"

She turned back to him. "In what respect?"

"Professionally. Can we count on her to follow through with every detail?"

Maura eyed him over her car, its roof glistening with a wet film of humidity. "I work with a lot of detectives, Mike. I've never met a better investigator. Jane's smart and she's thorough. You could even call her relentless."

"Relentless is good."

"In her job, it definitely is." Maura paused, trying to read his face under the glow of the parking lot lights. "Why are you asking about her? Are you wondering if she's up to the job?"

"Not me. It's my wife. Julianne has this old-fashioned image of what a homicide detective *should* look like and—"

"Let me guess. It's not a woman."

Antrim gave an embarrassed laugh. "Yeah, crazy, isn't it, in this day and age? But Julianne's scared. She won't admit it, but on some level she really believes it takes a man to protect a family. Last night I woke up to find her out of bed and watching the street, to see if someone was lurking outside."

"Well, you can tell Julianne that you and your family couldn't be in better hands. I mean it."

He smiled. "Thank you. I will."

She climbed into her Lexus and had just started the engine when Antrim tapped on her window. She rolled it down.

"You know about the party we're having after the concert?" he asked.

"There's a party?"

"Yeah, I was worried you missed my announcement because you got here late tonight. Julianne and I are throwing a party for all the musicians and their guests. A proper cocktail party with enough food to feed the Philharmonic. So bring a guest."

"That sounds like fun. After this concert, I'm definitely going to need a few cocktails to unwind."

"Great. See you at rehearsal next week. Assuming I don't get booted out of the violin section. Oh, and Maura?"

"Yes?"

"You were brilliant tonight. It's a shame you chose cadavers instead of Chopin."

She laughed. "That's for my next lifetime."

MAURA WAS THE FIRST TO ARRIVE, and now she stood in Angela Rizzoli's kitchen, sipping a glass of wine and feeling useless as her hostess swooped around the room with the efficiency of a seasoned cook, zipping from refrigerator to sink to the chopping board to the stove, where all four burners were covered with simmering pots. This was the downside of being obsessively punctual; it meant standing in your hostess's kitchen making small talk, something Maura had never been good at. Luckily, Angela talked enough for both of them.

"Since Frankie moved to D.C. and Vince is stuck out in California, I've got no one to cook for anymore," said Angela. "All those years, all those meals. Christmas and Easter and Thanksgiving, and now it's just dinner for one. I'm feeling deprived, you know?"

Judging by all the pots simmering on the stove, no one else was going to feel deprived this evening.

"Are you sure I can't help you?" said Maura. "Maybe wash the lettuce?"

"Oh no, Maura, you don't need to do a thing. I've got it all under control."

"But you've got so much going on here. Give me a job."

"The sauce. You can stir the marinara sauce. Aprons are in that bottom drawer. I wouldn't want you to stain your pretty blouse."

Relieved to finally have a task, however mindless, Maura tied on an apron embroidered with *Cucina Angela* and gave the marinara a stir.

"You know, I really was hoping he'd come tonight," said Angela. "Your friend."

Friend. A euphemism for the man who shared Maura's bed.

"Daniel wanted to," said Maura. "But there was a death and he needed to be with their family tonight."

"I guess it comes with his job, doesn't it? You never know when people will need you."

His job. Another euphemism, another way of talking

around the uncomfortable reality of Daniel's calling. Maura said nothing as she stirred the marinara.

"Life is complicated, isn't it?" Angela said. "All the twists and turns. You never know who you're going to fall in love with."

Maura kept stirring the sauce, the steam bathing her face.

"I was raised a good Catholic girl. Look at me now," said Angela. "I'm about to get a divorce. I'm shacked up with my boyfriend." She sighed. "I just want to say I understand, Maura. I understand completely."

At last Maura turned to face her. They had never spoken about her and Daniel, and this conversation among all the simmering pots took her by surprise. Angela's face was flushed from the hot kitchen and the steam had frizzed her hair, but her gaze was direct and steady. And kind.

"We love who we love," said Maura.

"Ain't that the truth? Now let me refill your glass of wine."

"Ma?" a voice yelled from the front door. "We're all here!"

Footsteps pattered into the house and four-year-old Regina came charging into the kitchen. "Nonna!" she shrieked and threw herself into Angela's arms.

"Hey, hey, hey!" called out Barry Frost as he walked into the kitchen, carrying a six-pack of beer. "Looks like this is where the action is!"

Everyone invaded the tiny kitchen. Gabriel walked in carrying two bottles of wine. Frost's wife, Alice, brought in a bouquet of roses and wasted no time rummaging under the sink for a vase. That was classic Alice, getting straight to business. The kitchen was now so crowded there was scarcely room for Angela to work, but she looked delighted by the chaos. She had raised three children in this house, cooked thousands of meals in this kitchen, and she beamed as wine corks popped and steam curled up from the pots on the stove.

"Wow, Mrs. R," said Frost. "You've cooked up a feast!"

And a feast it certainly was: salads and pasta, roast lamb and garlicky green beans. When all the dishes were on the table and they'd settled into chairs, Angela regarded her guests with a weary but happy smile.

"Oh my, but I've missed doing this," she said.

"What, Ma?" said Jane. "Slaving all day in the kitchen?"

"Having my family here."

Though they were not really family, thought Maura, tonight it felt like they were. She looked around the table at people she'd known for years, people who knew about her imperfections and her sometimes unfortunate choices, yet accepted her anyway. In all the ways that mattered, they *were* her family.

Well, all but one of them.

"I hear you're a featured soloist," said Alice Frost as she passed the salad to Maura. "Barry and I are looking forward to the concert."

"You're coming?"

"Oh yes. Didn't he tell you how much I love classical music?"

"I hope he also told you we're a strictly amateur orchestra, so I hope you're not expecting Carnegie Hall. We're just doctors who love playing music together."

"Don't you find those two skills reinforce each other? Higher education and musical ability? I believe it's all about enhancing brain development. When I was in law school, we had our own orchestra. I played the flute. We were amateurs, but we were pretty darn good."

The bowl of pasta, cloaked in marinara sauce, moved around the table. As the bowl reached Alice, she frowned and slid it straight to Maura. The snub wasn't missed by Angela, whose lip twitched in irritation. Maura deliberately served herself a generous swirl of pasta.

"This meal is *perfect,* Mrs. Rizzoli," said Frost.

"I *do* appreciate a guest with a hearty appetite, Barry," Angela said, casting a not-so-subtle side-eye at Alice, who was fussily picking out the croutons, as if they were bugs infesting her salad.

Frost sliced into a medium-rare slice of meat. "Amazing as always! It's been a long time since I've had your leg of lamb."

"No, I imagine you don't get it at home very often," said Angela, aiming another look at Alice.

"How is Vince doing in California?" Maura asked, quickly changing the subject. "Is he coming home soon?"

Angela sighed. "Oh, it's all up in the air. His sister had some complications after her hip surgery and at her age, bones don't heal so fast."

"She's lucky she has a brother like him."

"But I don't think she appreciates it. Complains about everything. His cooking, his driving, his snoring. They've always had a complicated relationship."

Which relationship isn't? thought Maura, looking around the table. Angela, raised Catholic, was now on the verge of divorce. Barry and Alice had only recently pulled their marriage out of the fire after Alice's affair with a law school classmate. *And then there's Daniel and me.* Perhaps the most complicated relationship of all.

"So Mrs. R," said Frost. "Whatever happened to that girl who went missing from the neighborhood?"

Angela brightened. "I'm so glad you asked."

"I'm not," said Jane.

"To answer your question, Barry, that particular mystery has been solved. I saw Tricia at the supermarket. She's alive and well."

"As I knew she would be," said Jane. "She just ran away from home. Again."

"Doesn't that deserve further investigation?" said Alice, offering her unasked-for opinion. "Is something going on in that house? Is it the father? You know that twenty-five percent of sexual abusers are fathers." Alice looked around the table, ready to argue with anyone who challenged her.

No one did. No one ever wanted to argue with Alice Frost about anything.

"But now we've got another mystery that needs to be addressed," said Angela. "The Greens."

"Who are the Greens?" asked Alice.

"Those odd people across the street."

"Why are they odd?"

"They're hiding something," said Angela. She dropped her voice, as if the secret mustn't go beyond this room. "And he has a *gun*."

Gabriel, who'd been wiping Regina's greasy hands, glanced up. "You actually saw his weapon?"

"Didn't Jane tell you? I saw it strapped to his hip when he bent over. It was tucked under his shirt, which makes it a concealed weapon, right? And he looks like the kind of man who knows exactly how to use it."

"Where did you see him when he had the gun?"

"He was up on the balcony. In his backyard."

There was a silence as everyone around the table processed that detail.

"Ma, you were *spying* on him," said Jane.

"No, I happened to be in Jonas's backyard when I heard all this hammering next door. I just had a little peek over the fence to see what was going on."

"One has the expectation of privacy in one's own backyard," said Alice. It was true, of course, but no one wanted to hear it when it came from Alice the lawyer.

"What were you doing in Jonas's backyard?" said Jane.

"I've lived on this street for forty years and I try to keep an eye on it, that's all. You can't prevent bad things from happening if no one even notices those things."

"She does have a point," said Frost.

Angela looked at Jane. "Did you ever find out if he has a concealed weapons permit?"

"I haven't gotten around to it, Ma."

"Because the whole thing's very suspicious."

"*Appearing* suspicious isn't a crime, thank god," said Alice, unable to stop herself from sharing her lawyerly perspective.

"Come on, all of you. Let me show you their house," said Angela. She tossed her napkin onto the table and heaved herself to her feet. "Then maybe you'll understand what I'm talking about."

Frost dutifully stood up to follow her, and a second

later, so did Alice. And that was it, the migration was off and running. Maura set down her wineglass and she followed the others, if only to be polite.

They all gathered at the living room window and looked across the street. This was a solidly middle-class neighborhood of modest houses set on modest lots, a neighborhood where a man once could raise three kids on his salary alone. Jane had grown up here, and Maura imagined her riding her bike on this street and shooting hoops with her brothers in the driveway. She glanced at Jane and saw the pugnacious scowl and square jaw that Jane must have had as a little girl. Angela had that same stubborn jaw. In the Rizzoli family, determination clearly ran down the female line.

Jane muttered to Maura: "I'll apologize later."

"For what?"

"For being drafted into the Angela Rizzoli Detective Agency."

"I meant to tell you, I saw Mike Antrim last night at rehearsal. He's worried, Jane. Their whole family is."

"Yeah, I imagine they would be."

"He wants to know if there's anything on that guy at the cemetery."

Jane sighed. "I wish I had something to report, but I don't."

"What about that burner phone? Have there been any other calls made from it lately?"

"None. That phone's gone silent."

"Okay, tell me what you all see," said Angela, still focused on the house across the street. She handed Frost a pair of binoculars.

"What am I supposed to see?" he asked.

"Tell us if anything about that house bothers you."

Frost peered through the binoculars. "I can't see anything. All the blinds are down."

"Exactly," said Angela. "Because they're hiding something."

"Which is their right," pointed out Alice, the annoying voice of authority. "No one's obligated to expose themselves to the world. Although Mr. America over there seems happy to be doing it."

"Oh, that's just Jonas," said Angela. "Ignore him."

But it was hard to ignore the silver-haired man lifting weights next door to the Greens. He stood in front of his living room window, bare-chested and pumping iron in full view of the neighborhood.

"That man doesn't *want* to be ignored," said Jane.

"Well, he is in awfully good shape for a man his age," Alice noted.

"Sixty-two," said Angela. "He was a Navy SEAL."

"And it, um, shows."

"Forget Jonas! It's the Greens I want you to look at."

Except there was nothing to look at. All Maura saw were lowered blinds and a closed garage door. Weeds grew through the cracks in the driveway, and if she did not already know that someone lived there, she would assume the place was vacant.

"And look, it's back again," Angela said as a white van slowly drove past. "Second time this week I've seen that van come by. That's something else I need to keep my eye on."

"So now you're doing neighborhood vehicle surveillance?" said Jane.

"I know it doesn't belong to anyone on this block." Angela's head slowly swiveled as she watched the van make its way down the street and out of sight. Maura wondered how many hours a day Angela stood at this window, taking in this view. After four decades here, she must know every car, every tree, every shrub. Now that her children had grown up and her husband had walked out, was this what her world had shrunken down to?

A few houses away, a lawn mower roared to life as a skinny man in Bermuda shorts trimmed his grass. Unlike Jonas, this man seemed completely disinterested in his appearance, flaunting knee-high socks and sandals as he pushed his mower.

"That's Larry Leopold. He's so good about keeping up his yard," said Angela. "He and Lorelei are the kind of neighbors everyone wants. Friendly people who take pride in their property. But the Greens, they're different. They won't even talk to me."

Maura saw the twitch of a window blind in the Greens' house. Someone inside that house was watching them right back. Yes, it did indeed seem strange.

A cell phone rang.

"That's mine," said Frost and he headed back to the dining room, where he'd left his phone.

"So now you see the situation," said Angela.

"Yeah. Too much time on your hands," said Jane. "Vince really needs to come home."

"*He'd* pay attention to me, at least."

"I have been paying attention, Ma. I just don't see any reason for law enforcement to get involved with people whose only suspicious behavior is avoiding *you*. How about we leave those poor people alone and go back to the dining room for dessert?"

"Sorry to say we'll have to skip dessert, Mrs. R," said Frost, returning to the living room. "Just got a call. Jane and I need to leave."

"Where are we going?" asked Jane.

"Jamaica Pond. They found Sofia Suarez's laptop."

NINETEEN

JANE

THEY PARKED ON PERKINS STREET, right behind a police cruiser, and walked down the shallow bank to the water's edge, where Patrolman Libby was waiting for them. Jamaica Pond was the largest body of fresh water in Boston, and the mile-and-a-half path that encircled it was a popular route for joggers. With daylight quickly fading toward dusk, there was now only one runner on the path and he was so focused on keeping up his pace that he didn't glance at them as he pounded past.

"A couple of nine-year-old boys spotted it this afternoon, right about here," said Officer Libby. "They were playing around skipping stones, and one of 'em noticed something shiny in the water. Waded out up to his knees and got it."

"How far out was it?"

"The pond's fifty feet deep at the center, but it stays shallow for quite a ways from the edge. It was maybe ten, fifteen feet in from this bank."

"Close enough that it could've been thrown from here."

"Yeah."

"Did the boys see anyone do it? Notice anyone nearby?"

"No, but we don't know how long it was in the water. Could've been tossed in days ago. The kids gave it to their mom, and she brought it to the Jamaica Plain substation. Our IT guy matched the serial number to the laptop you reported stolen. He says the hard drive's been pulled out, which is weird for a burglar, you know? Who steals a laptop and then goes to the trouble of destroying it?"

"Any fingerprints?"

Libby shook his head. "The water took care of that."

Jane turned to look at the cars moving past on Perkins Street. "Drive-by disposal. Too bad we don't have the hard drive to look at."

"Whoever removed it didn't care about preserving any data. The laptop looked like someone took a hammer to it."

Jane turned back to the pond, where ripples gleamed with the last light of day. "Why go to all that trouble? I wonder what was on it?"

"Well, we're not going to find out now," said Frost. "That data's destroyed."

Jane looked down at shoe prints tracking across the mud, prints left by boys who'd just happened to choose this particular spot, on this particular pond, to skip stones. Until now, Jane had assumed the thief would put the laptop on the market, hoping for a quick buck. Instead, this was where it ended up, ruined and discarded, no longer of use to anyone. This was definitely not what a garden-variety thief would do. *What was on that laptop, Sofia? What did you know that was worth killing you for?*

The boys' footprints were fading into the gloom of twilight. Once again the jogger came around, his breaths now quick and labored, his shoes thudding along the path behind them.

"If you want to talk to the boys who found it, I have their contact info," said Officer Libby. "But I don't think they can tell you anything useful."

Jane shook her head. "I don't think some nine-year-old's going to crack this case for us."

"Although they'd probably get a big kick out of talking to a detective. You know how boys are."

Boys.

Jane stared down at the almost invisible shoe prints and suddenly remembered a pair of blue Nikes lying in a boy's cluttered bedroom. A boy who just might be able to dig up some answers.

She turned to Frost. "You know the data on that hard drive?"

"Yeah?"

"Maybe there's a way to retrieve it."

ARIEL THE MERMAID WAS STILL reclining on her clamshell bed, surrounded by her usual crustacean admirers, but the watery wonderland was now in Jamal Bird's bedroom. Jane leaned in close to look at Henry the goldfish, who stared back at her with a gaze so intent she almost believed there was a brain behind those googly eyes.

"The fish looks happy," Frost said to Jamal. "You must be taking really good care of him."

"I had to look up a lot of stuff, to make sure I was doing everything right," said Jamal. "Did you know goldfish can recognize faces? And you can teach them tricks?"

"Did you know they can live up to forty years?" said

Jane. "I learned that just the other day." *From a certain know-it-all medical examiner.*

Jamal shrugged, unimpressed. "Yeah, I already knew that." Everyone, it seemed, knew about a goldfish's lifespan. Everyone except Jane. "I can't have a dog, 'cause of my asthma," said Jamal. "But a fish is okay. He'll live longer too, as long as I take good care of him."

"Come on, you folks didn't come here to talk about the fish," said Jamal's mother. Mrs. Bird stood watching them from the doorway, her face stony with skepticism. The moment they'd stepped into her house she had pulled out her cell phone and it was in her hand now, ready to record any threat to her son.

"We're here because we need Jamal's help," said Jane.

"Again?"

"Sofia's laptop was found yesterday afternoon in Jamaica Pond. The hard drive is missing and whatever data she had on it is probably destroyed."

Mrs. Bird's eyebrow lifted. "You don't think my son had anything to do with that?"

"No. Not at all."

"So how's he supposed to help you?"

"Mom," said Jamal.

"Honey, you gotta be careful. Ask yourself why the police would come around asking for help from a fifteen-year-old boy."

"'Cause maybe I know stuff they don't?"

"They're the police."

"But they probably don't know shit about computers."

"Actually, he's right," admitted Jane. "We don't."

Jamal swiveled around in his chair to face Jane. "Tell me what you want to know."

He might be only fifteen, but at that moment, looking into his eyes, Jane saw a confident young man looking back. "You said that Sofia bought the laptop to do online research," said Jane.

"That's what she told me."

"Do you know what sort of research?"

"No. She just asked me to set up the laptop for her. I installed some software, got her a new Gmail account." He laughed. "I mean, she was still using AOL for her email."

"So you're the one who signed her up for Gmail?" said Frost.

"Yeah."

"Do you happen to know her log-in information?"

Jamal regarded him for a moment, as if trying to discern some unspoken reason for the question. A question that could get him into trouble. "I didn't hack her account, if that's what you're asking."

"That's not at all what we're saying," said Jane. "But we *are* hoping you can do it for us now."

"Hack her account?"

"You seem like you'd remember details. Like user names and passwords."

"Maybe I do. So?"

"If we can read her emails, find out who she's been corresponding with, we might be able to catch her killer."

Jamal thought this over, weighing the risks of trusting them. Helping them. At last, he took a breath and swiveled around to his keyboard. "Her password is Henry plus her address. I told her that wasn't secure enough, but she said it's the only way she'd remember it."

"Her password has her fish's name?"

"Why not?" He typed, his fingers moving so fast they were a blur. "There. You're in."

Just like that. Jane and Frost glanced at each other, both of them stunned by how quickly their problem had been solved by a fifteen-year-old.

"And here's her inbox," said Jamal. "There's not a lot in here 'cause she only had the account for a few weeks."

But those weeks were the all-important ones just before she died.

Jamal scooted out of the way to let Jane and Frost see the screen. Jane grabbed the mouse and began to click through the messages.

In the three weeks before her death, Sofia Suarez had received emails from Pilgrim Hospital regarding her work schedule, a message from the hair salon confirming her appointment, a nursing journal renewal reminder, two alerts from Amazon about new romance releases, and messages that were clearly spam. Lots and lots of spam. There were no threatening messages, nothing that seemed out of the ordinary.

Then Jane clicked on an email that was sent from a Hotmail address. It was only two lines long.

Your letter was forwarded to me from my old apartment. I want to know more. Call me.

Jane stared at the phone number in the message, a number she'd seen before. "Frost," she said.

"That's the number on her call log," said Frost. "The call she made to that burner phone."

Jane looked at Jamal. "Did Sofia say anything about this email to you?"

He shook his head. "I was just her computer guy. I don't know anything about any phone call. Why don't you just call the number and find out who it is?"

"We've tried. No one answers."

"Well, you've got the email address. Lemme see what's in the header." He tapped a few keys, made a few clicks of the mouse.

Frost frowned at what was now on the screen. "IP address."

Jamal nodded. "Maybe it'll point us to the sender's location." He navigated to a new website, pasted the data into the search box, and sighed. "Sorry. It goes to Hotmail in Virginia. Why don't you just send him an email?"

"And if he doesn't answer?" said Frost.

Jane stared at the computer, thinking for a moment. "He says he got a letter from her, forwarded from his old address. Which means she was the one reaching out to find *him*. She probably searched for him online."

"So let's check out her search history," said Jamal.

"We don't have her laptop."

"You don't need it. You're already signed into her Gmail account." He reached for the mouse, then stopped and looked at Jane. "Just because I can do this doesn't mean I'm a hacker or anything, okay? I just know a few tricks. And I swear this is the only time I've accessed her account."

"Okay, we believe you," said Jane.

His mother said: "And just so you folks know, I'm recording this on my phone. To make it clear you're *asking* him to do this. So don't go putting words in his mouth later."

"We wouldn't dream of it," said Frost.

"Since we're already logged in, all we need to do is go into her Google account." *Click.* "Go to Activity and Timeline." *Click.* "And open My Activity." *Click.* "And there's a list of her online searches, by date." He swiveled around and smiled at Jane and Frost. "You're welcome."

Jane stared at the screen. "Shit. Boston PD needs to hire you."

Mrs. Bird called out from the doorway: "I got that on video too!"

Jane and Frost crowded in close as Jamal scrolled down the screen, revealing the websites that Sofia had visited in the last weeks of her life. Weather.com. *USA Today.* An online nursing journal. An article about the genetics of blood types.

"Stop," said Jane, pointing to the screen. "There. April tenth. She did a Google search for someone named James Creighton. What's that about?"

"Seems like a pretty common name," said Jamal. "You're gonna get a lot of hits."

"Do it. Let's see what turns up."

Jamal clicked on the search term and snorted. "Seventeen million hits. There's a famous hockey player. A psychologist. An actor. Plus a thousand other guys on Facebook with that name. Which one you want?"

"The one she was searching for."

"How many years you want to spend on it?"

"Keep scrolling through her search activity. What other websites did she visit?"

Jamal's hand was back on the mouse, scrolling backward through early April, past links to the *Portland Press Herald* and the *Bangor Daily News*.

"And we're back to Maine again," said Jane.

"She did use to live there," said Frost.

"But that was fifteen years ago. Why is she suddenly searching their newspapers?" Jane pointed to the *Bangor Daily* link. "Click on that one. Let's see where it goes."

Jamal clicked on the link and the screen filled with an old newspaper article: EX-HUSBAND SOUGHT IN MURDER OF COLBY COLLEGE PROFESSOR.

"What the hell is this all about?" Frost said. "This story's nineteen years old. How does it connect with anything else?"

"*That's* how it does," said Jane, and she pointed to the screen. To a sentence buried midway through the article.

. . . *a warrant has been issued for the arrest of the victim's ex-husband, James T. Creighton.*

"That's the man she was searching for," said Frost. "Maybe she found him."

Jane looked at Frost. "Or he found her."

TWENTY

THUNDERSTORMS HAD ROLLED IN OVERNIGHT and rain lashed the car as they drove north. Jane had insisted on driving because when the weather turned nasty and roads were slick, the driver she most trusted behind the wheel was herself. She and Frost had come this way on earlier investigations, following leads north across the Kittery bridge and into Maine. They had been partners for so long, they were now like an old married couple, both of them comfortable with long silences, and for an hour they scarcely spoke as the windshield wipers swiped back and forth and wind buffeted the car.

They were fifty miles past the border when he finally said: "I'm sorry about Saturday night."

"What?"

"Dinner at your mom's house. Alice is on this weird diet, see. I was worried your mom might be upset about her not eating very much."

"What is this weird diet of hers anyway?"

"It's from a book by this health guru and it changes from week to week. One week she loads up on protein. The next week she only eats salads. This happens to be her salad week. I was hoping your mom wouldn't notice."

"Trust me, she notices every forkful that goes into everyone's mouth. She's got this mental calculator so she has it down to the calorie." Jane glanced at him. "How's it going by the way? You and Alice?"

He shrugged. "Good days and bad. Mostly good."

"Does she ever talk about, you know. Him."

"We're past that. In any relationship you have to learn to move on, you know? The important thing is, she came back to me." He stared at the rain sheeting down the windshield. "I was no good being single. Hated being on my own, signing up for those stupid dating sites. You remember."

Yes, Jane did remember because he'd shared his woes after every rejection, every disastrous date. She'd heard about them all, and even if she didn't particularly care for Alice, Frost clearly loved her and was miserable without her.

"Anyway, when you talk to your mom, tell her it had nothing to do with her cooking. It was just Alice's diet."

"I'll tell her," Jane said, but she knew that unless you were in a coma, you had no excuse for refusing to eat Angela's lovingly cooked meals.

"I think the storm's letting up," he said.

The rain had lessened to a drizzle, but when she peered up at the sky, she saw black clouds looming to the north. The direction they were headed. "It'll be back."

TWO HOURS LATER, THEY TURNED onto a dirt road. The storm had scattered an obstacle course of branches and Jane had to slalom around them as she drove toward what had once been the home of Colby associate profes-

sor Eloise Creighton. A vehicle with State of Maine official plates was already parked in the driveway, and as
they pulled up beside it, the driver's door opened and a
bear of a man stepped out. He was in his forties, dressed
for the weather in an oilskin slicker, but his buzz-cut
hair was uncovered and he stood bareheaded in the
drizzle, patiently waiting for them to climb out of their
car.

"Detective Rizzoli? I'm Joe Thibodeau."

"And this is my partner, Detective Frost," she said,
and turned toward the residence. It was a handsome log
house with expansive windows and a soaring roofline,
perfectly suited for this heavily wooded setting. "Wow.
Nice place."

"Yeah, it's like a dream house, except for the history
that comes with it." He squinted up at the sky. "Let's
get inside before it starts pouring again."

"You said someone's living here now?" Jane asked as
they climbed the stairs to the front porch.

"Noah and Annie Lutz. Annie's expecting us. Not
particularly happy about the reason for our visit. It's got
to be disturbing, being reminded of what happened
here."

Before they could knock, the front door swung open
and a young woman appeared, holding a blond toddler
on her hip.

"Hey, Annie," Thibodeau said to her. "Thanks for
letting us take a look around."

"I have to admit, this is kind of freaking me out a
little. Having this come up again." Annie looked at Jane
and Frost. "So you're from Boston PD?"

"Yes, ma'am," said Jane.

"I hope this visit means you're finally going to arrest

him. Because I hate thinking he's still out there. The truth is, if I'd known about what happened here, I never would have let my husband sign the lease."

They stepped into the house and Jane looked up to see open beams arching twenty feet overhead. The floor-to-ceiling windows faced a backyard that was surrounded by forest. Although the house itself was spacious, those encroaching trees and the black clouds gathering overhead made the view uncomfortably claustrophobic.

"How long have you lived here, Mrs. Lutz?" Jane asked.

"Eight months now. My husband teaches at Colby College. Chemistry Department. We moved here from L.A. and when we saw this house, we couldn't believe how reasonable the rent was. Then my babysitter told me about . . ." Annie set down her squirming toddler and he ran off to pick up a stuffed koala lying on the floor. "I was shocked when I heard there'd been a murder here."

"You had no idea when you moved in?" said Frost.

"No, and I think the agent should have told my husband, don't you? It doesn't bother Noah so much, but he's not the one who's home alone all day with a kid. I know it happened a long time ago, but still." She hugged herself, as if a cold wind had suddenly swept in. "That kind of history never really leaves a place."

"I'm going to walk them through the house, Annie," Thibodeau said. "Okay to show them the bedrooms?"

"Yes, go ahead." She looked at her son, who was sitting on the floor, babbling happily to his zoo of stuffed animals. "I'll just stay down here with Nolan. Feel free to poke around wherever you want."

"Thank you, ma'am," said Frost, but Annie had already sat down on the floor beside her son and she wasn't looking at them. Perhaps she didn't want to be reminded of why they were here in her house.

Thibodeau led the way upstairs to a second-floor loft. Jane looked down over the railing, at Annie huddled with her son in the great room below. From this high perch, she could see over the trees to mist-cloaked mountains beyond the panoramic windows. The sky had grown even darker now, the clouds moving in like a black curtain. In the distance, thunder boomed.

"The victim's bedroom is this way," said Thibodeau.

They followed him along the open gallery and into the main bedroom where the encroaching woods and thickening storm clouds cast an ominous gloom. As soon as they stepped inside he closed the door, and Jane understood why. Annie was already unnerved by the visit, and what he was about to tell them would only disturb her more.

"Nineteen years ago, the lead detective on this case was Dan Tremblay," said Thibodeau. "Smart guy, very thorough. Unfortunately, he died last year of lung cancer. I've made copies of the relevant files for you— they're out in the car—but I can sum up everything you need to know about the case. I was just a lowly patrol officer when it happened, but I was the first one on the scene. And I remember every awful detail." He looked around the bedroom, his gaze distant, as if he were looking backward in time to the day he first visited this house, although the room had surely changed since then. The Lutzes had furnished it in Scandinavian modern and it now had a sleek maple bed and a crisply geometric area rug. On the blond wood dresser was a photo of the smiling Lutz family: Annie, her husband, Noah, and their pink-cheeked son. With his trim beard and glasses, Noah Lutz looked every bit the part of a college chemistry professor, a man of science who probably didn't believe in haunted places. While standing in this room, did he ever feel just the slightest chill, knowing what happened here? Did he look out the bedroom windows at the ever-advancing woods and wonder what else might be closing in on their house? Jane did not believe in ghosts, but even she sensed darkness hovering over this space, echoes that would never completely fade.

Or maybe it was just the thunderstorm moving in.

"It was a Tuesday morning," said Thibodeau. "The victim hadn't shown up for two classes she was supposed to teach the day before, and she wasn't answering her phone. I got tasked with coming to her house to do a welfare check."

"What did she teach at Colby?" asked Frost.

"English lit. She was an associate professor, thirty-six years old, recently divorced. She'd been living in this house for about a year. That day I came to check on her, I figured she was just ill and forgot to inform the college that she wasn't coming in. Murder isn't the first thing that crosses your mind around here. This is a safe area. Families, college kids. None of the crime you folks probably see down in Boston. You just don't expect . . ." He let out a breath. "Anyway, I wasn't prepared for what I found.

"I got here about eleven A.M. It was mid-October, beautiful day, fall leaves at their peak. At first I didn't notice anything wrong. The front door was locked. I rang the bell but no one answered. Her vehicle was in the carport, so I figured she must be home. I started to get that feeling you get, in the pit of your stomach, when you know something's not right. Maybe she was *really* sick, or she'd fallen down the stairs. Or there was a problem with the furnace and she was dead from carbon monoxide poisoning. I walked around to the backyard, where those big windows face the woods, and that's when I saw the door to the deck was open. It didn't look like it'd been forced, so either she forgot to lock it, or someone used a key."

"Who else had a key?" asked Jane.

"We know the ex-husband did, but folks up here don't always lock their doors at night. It's that kind of place. And she always kept a spare key under a rock on the back deck. We found it there, still under the rock."

"Who knew about that key?"

"Lots of folks. Babysitter. House cleaner. The work crew who renovated her kitchen."

"In other words, half the town."

"Just about." He went to the window and looked out at the darkening sky. "It was clean and crisp that day. No rain in weeks, no mud to track into the house. Just lots of leaves blown in through the open back door. I came inside and started to climb the stairs. That's when I noticed the flies. And I got my first whiff of—well, you folks know the smell. It's something you never forget. I came up the stairs, reached the landing, and that's where I found her, lying in the hallway right outside this bedroom. She was wearing a nightgown, and her bedroom door was wide open. It looked like she'd climbed out of bed, walked out into the hallway, and came face-to-face with the intruder." He looked at Jane and Frost. "There were strangulation marks on her neck, bruises clearly left by fingers. Whoever did it was strong enough to choke a woman with his bare hands. And based on the smell, and the flies, it happened at least a few days earlier. I didn't touch anything, move anything. I left her just the way I found her and was about to call it in when I noticed the rabbit."

"What rabbit?" said Jane.

"This stuffed pink rabbit. It was lying on the floor, in the hallway. And I started to get a really sick feeling. No one had told me there was a child in the house. I went down the hall, looked in the next bedroom, and it was clearly a kid's. Pink curtains, princess comforter on the bed. I looked everywhere. The bedrooms, the cellar, the area outside the house, but I didn't find her. Neither did the search team, who combed all those woods." He shook his head. "That little girl was gone."

TWENTY-ONE

THEY SAT IN A CAFÉ IN DOWNTOWN WATERVILLE, a twenty-minute drive from the late Eloise Creighton's residence. The torrential rains had kept most people at home, and only one other table was occupied, by a couple too engrossed in their smartphones to pay attention to each other, much less to anyone else. As thunder boomed and rain pounded the street outside, inside there was only the sound of quiet conversation and the hiss of the cappuccino machine.

"I never stopped thinking about the case, even all these years later," said Thibodeau. "I wasn't the investigating officer, but at that particular time in my life, it hit me hard, because of that missing little girl, Lily. She was only three years old when she vanished, and I couldn't stop thinking about what she might have gone through that night. Did she see what happened to her mother? Was the killer someone she knew, maybe even trusted? My daughter was a year old then, and I thought about what it'd be like to have her taken. To not know if she was even still alive. Four years ago, when I joined the Major Crime Unit, Dan Tremblay had just retired, so I pulled out his cold case files and took another look at the Eloise Creighton murder. That folder I gave you contains copies of his notes and interviews, and I'll email you the autopsy report. I've gone over the case again and again and I keep coming to the same conclusion Tremblay did. It was her ex-husband who did it. It *had* to be him."

Jane paged through the sheaf of interviews. "There were no other viable suspects?"

"Tremblay considered just about everyone who came into contact with the victim. In the end, he still believed it was the ex-husband, James. Their divorce was pretty much a knock-down, drag-out fight. Truth is, their marriage seemed doomed from the start. She was an academic, he was a musician—and not a very successful one. He played guitar in bars at night and taught music part-time at the high school in Bangor. It must've been a case of opposites attracting. Women always seem to have a thing for scruffy musicians."

"Do they?" said Jane.

"You tell me."

"I never got the musician bug myself."

"Well, a lot of ladies seem to catch it. Maybe it's the bad-boy mystique. Whatever, it didn't last long for the Creightons. They were married for four years and then she filed for divorce. They fought over everything—the furniture, the bank account, the kid. They finally agreed to share custody of their three-year-old daughter, but even then they were barely speaking to each other. So you can see why he was Tremblay's number one suspect. Especially since whoever killed the mother also made off with the kid."

"What other suspects did Tremblay look at?"

"The victim taught four classes a semester at Colby, so her students came under consideration. Maybe she'd

pissed off a student with a bad grade. Maybe she became the object of a student's obsession. She was a
nice-looking woman, with no current man in her life as
far as anyone knew. And a week before the murder,
she'd hosted a wine-and-cheese reception in her house
for a few dozen of her senior students, so they knew
where she lived and the layout of the house." He paused.
"And they would have seen her little girl that night too."

"You said her name was Lily?" asked Frost.

"Yeah."

"You ever consider the possibility that the mother
wasn't the target? That maybe the child was the real
prize?"

Thibodeau nodded. "Yeah, and that girl was cute as
a button. Long blond hair, just like her mother's. Tremblay wondered if maybe someone saw Lily around town
and decided he wanted her for himself. That maybe the
mother's murder was just incidental, a kidnapping that
went wrong."

"Who took care of Lily while her mother was teaching at the college?" asked Jane.

"She attended a private daycare. It was run by a local
woman, and she checked out totally clean. Forty-five
years old, lived in Waterville all her life."

"You make that sound like a badge of purity," said
Jane. "Being local."

"In a way, it is. You grow up in a small town, you're
always under a magnifying glass. Everyone knows who
you are—and what you are. So no, it wasn't the daycare
lady. Tremblay also considered the possibility it was
someone from out of town who was passing through the
area. Saw the girl, decided to snatch her, and killed the
mom in the process."

"Wouldn't an outsider be noticed around here?" asked Frost.

"Right now the town's quiet, but wait till September, when classes start up at Colby and the other local college. That's two thousand students arriving, plus all the tourists who come through here to ogle the fall colors. In a crowd like that, you never know what kind of weirdo might turn up. So yeah, it's possible it was an outsider. Someone who came for the girl, who must've kicked up a fuss. Mom hears the kid screaming, tries to stop it. So he had to kill her."

"Did forensics turn up anything useful?" asked Jane.

"Fingerprints galore, but then she'd hosted that reception for her students a few days before she was killed. And there'd been a crew working in her house weeks earlier, renovating her kitchen. A carpenter, a plumber, and an electrician. Plus the ex-husband's prints were everywhere."

"So we're back to James Creighton again."

"He still had a key to the house, so he had access. He had a motive. And he had absolutely no alibi for the night his ex-wife was killed."

"Where did he say he was that night?"

"Out on Penobscot Bay. He owned this crappy little sailboat and he claimed he was sleeping aboard it all weekend. No witnesses, of course."

"Of course."

"And then there was the blood."

Jane perked up. "What blood?"

"Trace blood on the floorboards in the upstairs hallway. Just a few feet from where the victim was found."

"The ex-husband's?"

"Type A negative, a match for James Creighton. He

claimed the blood was from a year before, when he'd cut himself while shaving."

"Did he have any fresh injuries?"

"He had a healing cut on his finger, claimed it happened on his sailboat. There *was* blood on the boat too, so that didn't really help us. They held him for forty-eight hours while they searched his rental house and his crappy sailboat, looking for the kid. Her hair and fingerprints were all over the place, of course, but there was no Lily. Since the girl visited him regularly, all that trace evidence added up to nothing. They had to let him go, but he's still my number one suspect." Thibodeau looked straight at Jane. "Now explain to me what Creighton has to do with *your* homicide case."

"We were hoping you could tell us," said Jane.

Thibodeau shook his head. "I have no idea. I don't even know where he is at the moment."

"You weren't keeping tabs on him?"

"It's been nineteen years. Tremblay kept hoping that one day he'd be able to prove Creighton did it. Maybe a witness would start talking, or the man would confess. Or, god forbid, they'd find the little girl's body. A few years ago, we thought we *did* find her when a skeleton turned up at the state park twenty miles away."

"A kid's?" asked Jane.

"Yeah. Based on their condition, the bones had been there for a while, maybe a decade or more, and they belonged to a little girl around three years old."

"Just like Lily."

"Right after they found those bones, I pulled James Creighton in for questioning. Ran him through the wringer. I wanted so badly to nail him for the kid's murder, but then we got back the DNA on those bones, and they didn't match either him or Eloise."

"Then whose bones are they?"

"They're still unidentified. She's just Little Girl Doe, left out in the woods." He shook his head. "I thought I fucking *had* him."

"What happened to Creighton?"

"The high school didn't want him teaching music classes, so he lost that gig. From there he moved around, looking for other jobs. Worked at a Gas and Go in Augusta. A restaurant down in South Portland."

That explained all the Maine phone numbers on Sofia Suarez's cell phone records. She'd been trying to track down James Creighton, tracing his work history job by job. The gas station. The Buffalo Wings restaurant. Had she ever contacted him? Did the burner phone she called belong to Creighton?

"We want to show you a video," said Frost, handing Thibodeau his cell phone. "It's surveillance footage recorded at a cemetery in Boston. This isn't the best way to view it, but I'll send the file to you later, so you can watch it on your desktop."

"What am I supposed to look for?"

"We're hoping you recognize the man."

Thibodeau studied the video once, then replayed it as the cappuccino machine once again hissed in the background.

"Is that man James Creighton?" Frost asked.

Thibodeau huffed out a sigh. "I don't know."

"*Could* it be him?"

"I suppose. The height seems right, and the hair color. But if it is him, he's changed a lot since I last saw him. He's lost weight, a lot of weight. And some hair too." Thibodeau handed Frost's phone back. "I wish I could be more certain, but it's not a very clear video."

"Do you have any idea where he is now?" Jane asked.

"No. After I took on the cold case, he dropped out of sight. Probably because he knew I was watching him, waiting for any reason I could find to yank him behind bars. Okay, maybe I *did* harass him a little, so he had a reason to avoid me. For all I know, he's still up here in Maine. Or he could be anywhere in the country."

"And killing again."

"Maybe. But I'm not sure I see the connection between Eloise Creighton's murder and your case down in Boston."

"Sofia Suarez *is* the connection."

"Just because she did a Google search for Creighton?"

"*Why* did she search for him, and did she find him? Is that why she ended up dead?"

Thibodeau gave a grim laugh. "Death by Google. That's a new one."

They sat in silence for a moment, all three of them mulling the question. Across the dining room, the couple kept staring at their smartphones, oblivious to the detectives' conversation and to each other. The café door swung open and two women ducked in from the storm, shaking off raindrops from their jackets. The barista cheerily greeted them both by name. In this town where all the locals seemed to know one another, murder must seem like the work of outsiders.

Until it isn't.

"What about other suspects?" Jane said.

"There was a student who'd threatened Professor Creighton when she flunked him. There was a drunk guy who lived up the road from her. Neither one panned out."

"You have the list of those students who attended Professor Creighton's reception the week before?"

"It's in those files I gave you. Some of the students had alibis for the night of the murder. Some of them didn't."

"And the work crew who renovated her kitchen?" asked Frost.

"Three guys. Their names are in that folder too. They knew how to access the house and their fingerprints were on the outside door and all over the kitchen. They would've seen the little girl while they were doing the renovations, so naturally Tremblay talked to them."

Jane flipped through the file to the interviews with the work crew. *Scott Constantine. Bruce Flagler. Byron Barber.* Yet more names to add to their ever-growing list of possible suspects. "Any of these guys have criminal records?"

"Just minor stuff. Drunk driving, domestic abuse. But all three men claimed to be at home on the night of the murder, and their wives or girlfriends vouched for them. Two of them have moved out of state and I have no idea where they are. Byron Barber's still in town, still building kitchens."

Jane turned to a photo of Eloise and Lily Creighton, mother and daughter beaming at the camera from beneath a spreading oak tree. Both of them were pale and flaxen-haired and they wore matching summer dresses with pink sashes. It hurt to see how happy they looked together. Jane thought of her own daughter, Regina, and the Easter photo they'd taken together. They had not been wearing pretty spring dresses, because Regina was an overalls kind of four-year-old, but like the Creightons, they had also posed under a tree and worn the same happy smiles. Jane flipped over the picture and saw it was taken June fifteenth.

Four months later, Eloise Creighton would be dead.

"You can see why this case haunted me," said Thibodeau. "Those faces. Those smiles. I kept thinking about my own daughter."

"So would I," said Jane softly.

Thibodeau looked at his watch. "Sorry to take off, but I've got a meeting. Most of what you need should be right there in those files, and I'll email you whatever else I have. If you crack your case, call me. I'm curious as hell what connects these murders." He stood up. "If there's any connection at all."

TWENTY-TWO

"BASED ON WHAT I READ in Eloise Creighton's autopsy report," said Maura, "I'm having trouble seeing many similarities between these two murders. Which makes me think you're not dealing with the same killer."

Jane watched as Maura washed her hands in the morgue sink, seemingly oblivious to the stench from the postmortem she'd just completed. Jane stood near the door, her elbow lifted to her nose to shield it, but the smell had already seeped into her nostrils, her lungs. Even if she stripped off her clothes and took a shower, she wouldn't be able to erase the memory of that odor.

"What the hell did you just slice up in there anyway? It smells like a sewer."

"Eighty-eight-year-old female, lived alone. She was dead for eight days in a warm house before anyone found her." Maura shut off the water and reached for a paper towel to dry her hands. "A very sad but ultimately natural death."

"Can we get out of here? I need some fresh air."

"Gladly." Maura tossed the paper towel into the trash can. "Let's go outside."

Another storm system had rolled in overnight, and dark clouds hung low over the city. The air was cloying and damp and Jane could taste more rain in the air. They sat outside on the bench behind the building, facing the underpass, where concrete magnified the roar of traffic. It was a decidedly unscenic view, and auto exhaust tinged the air, but at least it did not smell like death. Something they had both had their fill of today.

"I *want* this to be the same killer," said Jane. "It would make things so much simpler. All I'd have to do is find James Creighton."

"The Maine police never proved beyond a doubt that he killed his ex-wife."

"Detective Thibodeau's pretty sure he did. And if Creighton killed one woman—"

"It doesn't mean he killed a second one."

"But there are similarities. Both were home invasions. And it looks like both victims were caught by surprise."

"If it is the same killer, he's changed his MO. Sofia was clubbed with a hammer, an efficient and matter-of-fact killing. Eloise Creighton was strangled in her upstairs hallway. That's a very personal, very intimate way of killing someone. It requires strength and skin-to-skin contact, close enough for the killer to feel her struggles, the last twitches of her body."

"You're saying it's someone who knew her."

"It doesn't rule out a stranger. Maybe it was someone forced to use his own hands because that's all he had at the time."

"James had a motive. He and his ex-wife were battling over child custody."

"If he did it, then where's the child? Why would he kill her?"

"You know the way some of these exes think. *If I*

can't have her, nobody can. They just haven't found Lily's body yet. And that was his blood in the upstairs hallway."

Maura nodded. "I saw that detail on the report: A negative."

"*His* blood type. And he had a fresh cut on his finger."

"Which he had an explanation for. Plus they found blood on his sailboat, where he said he hurt himself."

"Conveniently enough."

"You're still reaching, Jane. Think about the ways these cases are dissimilar. One victim was in her thirties, the other in her fifties. They lived in different cities, different states. And the first murder was nineteen years ago."

"Nineteen years ago, Sofia was working as a nurse in Maine. The murder of Eloise Creighton was splashed all over the local newspapers, so Sofia would have heard about it at the time."

"Why was she looking it up now? Nearly two decades later?" asked Maura.

"That's what I have to figure out." Jane looked at a slice of gray sky above. Took a deep breath to wash the fetid air from her lungs. They sat silent for a moment, listening to the clang of a manhole cover as cars rattled across it.

"Maybe she just came across something. Heard a conversation, read a news item," Maura said. "It reminded her of the murder and curiosity sent her to the web."

"There's that sequence of dates, Maura. Early April, she starts her online search for Creighton. She tracks down his old address and sends him a letter. A month later, she gets an email from someone who tells her to call his burner phone. That's got to be *his* phone. James Creighton's."

"It's also possible the burner's not his and Sofia's death had nothing to do with the Creighton murder."

"So why was she searching for him online?" asked Jane.

"People search the web for all sorts of crazy things. If I were to show you my recent search history, you'd be surprised."

"Let me guess. Something to do with dead bodies."

"Do you really think that's all I have on my mind?"

"It's the only thing you and I ever seem to talk about."

"Penguins."

"What?"

"My last Google search was about penguins."

Jane laughed. "Yeah, okay. That is a surprise. If I may ask, why penguins?"

"I'm planning a trip to Antarctica."

"While everyone else in the world heads to a warm beach, you choose icebergs. Typical."

"Penguins are fascinating, Jane."

"Yeah. Like goldfish."

A raindrop fell on Jane's nose. She looked down at the splatters now hitting the ground and inhaled the scent of wet pavement, the smell of a city rainstorm.

"Time for me to get back to work," said Maura.

"You think I'm wasting my time, don't you? Trying to connect these two murders."

"I don't know, Jane. One thing I've learned, after all these years of working with you, is to never doubt your instincts."

But back at her desk that afternoon, as she reread the documents in the Eloise Creighton folder, Jane wondered if this might be the one time when her instincts had sent her in the wrong direction. Maura was right. The two victims, as well as the way they'd been killed, were very different. Eloise Creighton had been an attractive young academic who lived in a rural neighborhood with a young daughter. Sofia Suarez was a middle-aged widow who lived alone with her goldfish in the city of Boston. Other than their gender and their ultimate fates, they had little in common.

She opened the autopsy document and studied the morgue photos of Eloise Creighton. Except for the bruising around her neck, her skin was flawless, her hair almost silvery under the morgue lights. There'd been no evidence of sexual assault. She was wearing a nightgown and her bed had been slept in, so something had awakened her during the night. Was it the creak of footsteps? Her daughter, calling to her? Something made her climb out of bed, open her door, and step out into the hallway. And there she had encountered the intruder. Had he been surprised by her sudden appearance, and killed her in a panic?

Jane flipped back to the photo of mother and daughter, both so blond, both so happy. She thought of Regina, imagined her own little girl vanishing into the night. *What would I do to find her? Anything.*

Everything.

At five p.m. Jane was still at her desk, still reviewing the Eloise Creighton file. Det. Tremblay, the original in-

vestigator on the case, had generated hundreds of documents, which were now nearly two decades old. They
may not have any connection to the Suarez murder, but
all those phone calls Sofia made to Maine, plus Sofia's
search for information about James Creighton, made
Jane think there had to be a link here. Frost had left half
an hour ago, and she'd soon have to pick up Regina
from daycare, but Jane kept sifting through Tremblay's
notes and interviews, looking for some all-important
detail she'd missed the first time. A detail that would tie
Creighton to both murders.

She flipped to the next document in the stack. It was
an interview with Tim Hillier, one of the students who'd
attended Eloise Creighton's wine-and-cheese evening
the week before the murder. He was twenty-one years
old, a senior from Madison, Wisconsin, who hoped to
attend medical school after graduation. There was no
photo, but the State Police had collected his fingerprints
for exclusionary purposes. He had no criminal record,
he claimed he was with his girlfriend on the night of the
murder, and Tremblay did not consider him a suspect.
Attached to the interview was an addendum, written
soon after Det. Thibodeau had taken on the cold case.

Tim Hillier, MD, is currently a dermatologist
practicing in Madison, WI. Per telephone
conversation, he has no additional recollection
or further info about Prof. Creighton's death.
He is now married to former Colby classmate
Rebecca née Ackley, who also attended
Prof. Creighton's reception. (cross-reference
to Ackley interview)

Det. Thibodeau had certainly made Jane's task a great deal easier. He'd tracked down most of the students' current addresses, occupations, and phone numbers. A quick search online told Jane that Dr. Tim Hillier was indeed still in active practice in Wisconsin. His and his wife, Rebecca's, fingerprints, collected for exclusionary purposes during the investigation nineteen years earlier, showed no hits on the AFIS database. A squeaky-clean couple.

Jane set Tim Hillier's and Rebecca Ackley's files off to the side and moved on to the next interview.

Nineteen students attended the cocktail party and Thibodeau had followed up on every interview. Good detectives suffer from at least a touch of OCD, and he clearly had a serious case of it, doggedly tracing the current whereabouts of everyone who'd been inside Prof. Creighton's residence the week before her murder. He'd discovered that two students were now deceased, one from a brain hemorrhage, the other from a climbing accident in Switzerland. After graduation, most had left the state of Maine and scattered to cities around the world. Only one currently lived in the Boston area: Anthony Yilmaz, a financial adviser at Tang and Viceroy Investments, someone who would probably be worth talking to. Most of the students had gone on to impressive careers: doctor, attorney, financial consultant. None had been in trouble with the law and none of their fingerprints had turned up at any other crime scenes.

Finally, Jane turned to the file on James Creighton. Other than an OUI at age nineteen and a charge of vandalism as a juvenile, the man had no criminal record and no history of violence, but he and his ex-wife had

been locked in a bitter custody battle for three-year-old
Lily. Eloise had recently been offered a position at a
university in Oregon, which meant moving the child
three thousand miles away from her father. Communi-
cations between the opposing lawyers had grown more
and more rancorous.

He told me I'd be sorry if I took her away from him,
Eloise said in her affidavit. *I considered that a threat.
Which is why I don't think his visitation rights should
continue.*

And this was why Tremblay zeroed in on James as the
killer. The man had a motive, he had access, and he had
no alibi. Traces of his blood were found in the hallway
near his ex-wife's body. He was clearly the number one
suspect but he never tried to flee the state of Maine.
Even though the murder poisoned his reputation, even
though his neighbors shunned him and police continu-
ally tramped through his backyard, searching for Lily's
remains, he did not flee his home—not at first. Then
parents at the high school complained that their children's music teacher could be a murderer; he lost his
position and was forced to cycle through a string of
dead-end jobs, none of which lasted long. When the police keep dredging up your past, keep pursuing and ha-
rassing you, who would hire you?

Her cell phone rang. She looked at the caller's name
on her phone. *Revere Police Dept.*

"Detective Rizzoli," she answered.

"This is Detective Saldana, Revere PD."

"Hey. What can I do for you?"

"You can start by talking to your mother, Angela."

Jane sighed. "Now what's she done?"

"Look, I understand it all started off as well-intentioned, all her calls about Tricia Talley. Who, by the way, turns out to be alive and well. It was just a typical teenage blowup with her parents."

"I'm sorry about those calls. When my mom gets an idea in her head, she runs with it. And runs." *And runs.*

"That was fine. That was just neighborhood watch sort of stuff, and we appreciate her keeping us informed. But this is going too far. She's gotta stop calling us about her neighbors."

"Is this the couple across the street?"

"Yes."

"She told me the man carries a concealed weapon. I haven't had a chance to check on his CCW permit, but—"

"Don't bother. Just tell her to stop calling about them."

"Have they complained?"

"They're well aware of her interest in them."

"Is this, like, an impending restraining order?"

"She has to stop drawing attention to them. It's important, so have that talk with her. I'd appreciate it."

Jane paused, puzzled by what was being left out. She said, quietly: "You want to tell me what's going on with those neighbors?"

"Not at this time."

"When, then?"

"I'll let you know," Det. Saldana said and hung up.

TWENTY-THREE

ANGELA

M Y DAUGHTER HAS LAID DOWN THE LAW: *Stay away from the Greens.* It's not as if I've trespassed or in any way harassed those people, but apparently they've complained to Det. Saldana at Revere PD and he told Jane, and she warns me that a restraining order is not out of the question, although I think she's exaggerating. Somehow I have turned into the bad guy, all because I'm trying to keep my neighborhood safe. Because I saw something and I said something.

But nobody cares what a mature woman has to say, so my opinion gets ignored, the way women my age are always ignored. Even when we're right.

I tell this to the Thursday night Scrabble group as we sit in my living room, and Lorelei nods vigorously when I talk about the trouble we women face, trying to be heard. At that moment her husband is certainly not listening to us because he's too busy studying his Scrabble tiles. Larry has never been a great listener anyway. Maybe it's because he thinks I have so little of importance to say. I watch him stare at his tiles, his eyes narrowed, his miserly lips pursed as though to deliver the sourest of kisses. He knows he's clever, but just because he beats me all the time at Scrabble doesn't mean I'm not worth listening to. He may have a master's degree in English, but I have a life degree in motherhood, which comes with eyes in the back of my head. Something that a dictionary snob like Larry Leopold will never appreciate.

At least Jonas is listening to Lorelei and me. He's just taken his turn and he put down his tiles to spell out RIVER, which is a pretty clever way to dispose of a v, so now he can fully focus on me. Maybe he's too focused; he's leaning so close I can smell the Ecco Domani wine on his breath.

"I think we men miss out if we ignore women," Jonas says. "I *always* listen to what the ladies say."

Larry snorts. "I wonder why."

"Think of how much wisdom goes unheard when we don't listen."

"Sexual."

I frown at Larry. "What?"

"Six letters. Got rid of my x."

I look down at the Scrabble board, where Larry has just set down his tiles. So it's going to be that kind of night.

"As for words of wisdom," says Larry, picking up a fresh set of tiles, "I prefer to hear opinions from informed sources."

"Are you saying I'm not informed?" I ask him.

"I'm saying that people place too much emphasis on instinct. On gut feelings. That's how we get into trouble, relying on the most primitive parts of our brains."

"I disagree with that and let me tell you why," says Jonas. "It goes back to when I was on active duty as a Navy SEAL."

"Of course."

"And keen instincts saved my life. It was during Operation Desert Shield, and my SEAL team was right off the Kuwaiti coast, planting explosives. I could sense this little fishing boat coming toward us wasn't what it seemed."

"Jonas," said Larry, "we've all heard that story."

"Well, I never get tired of hearing it," says Lorelei. "Just because you never served, Larry, doesn't mean you should be disrespectful of another man's service."

"*Thank* you," says Jonas, gallantly tipping his head. There's a moment there, a look between them, that rattles me. Jonas and Lorelei? No, not possible. He has eyes only for me, or so I thought, and even though I'm not interested in him, it's still a thrill to think I've got what it takes. What does Lorelei have that could possibly be alluring to a man like Jonas? She may be thinner than I am, a skin-and-bones type of thinness which might be fashionable, but it makes me think of a naked baby bird.

"Are you going to take your turn or aren't you, Angela?" says Larry.

I tear my gaze from Jonas and Lorelei and look at my seven tiles. I've drawn a variety of letters, but my brain can't seem to rearrange them in any usable order. All it sees is CAT and RAT and HAD. Words that will only reinforce Larry's poor opinion of my intelligence. But I can't come up with anything better, so CAT it is. I glare at Larry, expecting him to say something denigrating, but he just shakes his head and sighs.

Lorelei puts down ROCK, which isn't bad, even if it's not Larry-worthy, and she says to me: "So what *are* the Greens up to? Did Jane tell you anything?"

"All she says is I'm not allowed to go near those people or Revere PD will come after me."

"That sounds like an exaggeration," says Larry.

"It's not. It's exactly what my daughter said. The Greens are off-limits to me, even though that man has a gun. Even though there's clearly something not right about them." I look at Jonas. "Don't you think? You live right next door to them."

Jonas shrugs. "I hardly see 'em. They always keep their blinds down."

"Exactly. Which tells me they're hiding something. Obviously Revere PD knows more about them than they're letting on. I have a feeling they're connected to the white van that keeps coming around."

"What white van?" Lorelei asks.

"You haven't noticed it? It drives by really slowly, like it's casing houses or something. I've seen it four times now. It always slows down as it gets near your house."

Larry looks up from his Scrabble tiles. "What's this about a white van?"

"See, Larry?" says his wife. "When you don't listen to us women, you miss important things."

"Maybe it's just a plumber or something," says Jonas. "Seems like they all drive white vans."

"It has no logo on it," I tell them. "I haven't gotten a good look at the license plate, but next time it comes around—"

"Call me," says Lorelei. "So I can take a look."

"Better yet," says Larry, "why don't you two ladies grab your broomsticks and chase him off? Because good god, we can't have plumbers coming around the neighborhood."

Lorelei gives him a sour look. "Really, Larry?"

But Larry is no longer listening because he's back to perusing his tiles, plotting another way to humiliate the rest of us.

"What about Tricia Talley?" Lorelei asks. "You ever find out what's going on with that girl?"

"Yeah, what happened to Tricia?" asks Jonas.

I sigh. "Nothing. I was wrong about that."

"Stop the presses!" says Larry. "Angela Rizzoli is wrong about something!"

"I'm admitting it, aren't I? But only because I saw Tricia at the supermarket, and then I spoke to Jackie, and she told me they had some sort of blowup. Tricia's alive and well but she still hasn't returned home. She's very troubled, that girl."

"Is there a boyfriend?" Lorelei leans closer and murmurs, "When girls act out, it's always about a boy."

"I don't know. Jackie wouldn't tell me. She's been so closemouthed lately, which is odd, because *she's* the one who asked me to get Jane involved. Now it's like she wants me to butt out."

"Can we just get on with Scrabble?" says Larry. "I didn't come here to gossip about the neighbors."

His wife ignores him. "I saw Jackie last week at the gas station and I asked her about Tricia. I could tell she didn't want to talk about it. We've known that family since Jackie got hired at Larry's school, and I have to say, she never really warmed up to me. It's like she wears this ice shield whenever I'm around her. Don't you think so, Larry?"

"No."

"I haven't noticed that at all," says Jonas.

Lorelei looks at me. "I swear, men never notice anything."

"I notice no one's interested in playing Scrabble," says Larry, and he picks up his rack of tiles and unceremoniously dumps them into the box. "So I'm going home."

The rest of us are so startled we don't know what to say. Lorelei jumps up and follows her husband to the front door.

"Larry? Larry!" She looks back at us and shakes her head. "Sorry, I don't know what's gotten into him! I'll call you later, Angela."

Jonas and I hear the front door thud shut and we look at each other, stunned. Then he picks up the bottle of wine. "It'd be a shame to waste this," he says, and fills my glass to the brim.

"What just happened?"

"Larry's turning into a grumpy old man, that's what."

"No, tonight was different. He's grumpier than usual." The Scrabble game has been ruined now, and I'm about to toss my tiles into the box when I suddenly realize what I could have spelled with them: HAZARD, and it would have earned a triple-word score. *That* would have been a slap in Larry's snooty face, and I'm annoyed he's not here to see me claim those points. But whenever he is here, I'm so intimidated by him that my brain shuts down. "I don't know why Lorelei puts up with that man."

"She doesn't know why either."

"What?"

"That's what she told me."

"When did she tell you this?"

Jonas shrugs, takes a sip of wine. "Might've been a few years ago, when we were meeting for coffee."

"You two met for coffee?"

"I would have preferred meeting *you,* but you were still married then."

"*She* was married too. She still is."

"What can I say? Ladies tell me their problems and I listen. I listen very well."

"What else went on between you two?"

He smiles, an I-ate-the-canary smile. "Are you jealous?"

"No! I'm just—"

"Relax, Angie. Nothing happened between us. She's not my type. Way too skinny, with nothing to grab on to. I like a woman with generous handles, you know?"

What he's saying is that I have handles, and I'm not sure I like hearing that, but I let it pass. I'm more interested in what he has to say about Lorelei and Larry.

"Does he abuse her?" I ask.

"What, *Larry*?" Jonas laughs. "With his skinny chicken legs? No, that's not the problem."

"Then what is?"

"It's not something I can talk about. I promised her."

"You've told me this much. You can't stop now."

He puts his hand over his heart. "There are some things a gentleman never does. And one of those is spilling a lady's secrets. In that way, you can trust me, Angie. Because I'd never spill any of yours." He gazes into my eyes and I can almost feel him crawling around inside my head, probing the folds of my brain.

"I don't have any secrets."

"Everyone does." He gives me a sly smile. "Maybe it's time for you to come up with a few more."

"Do you ever stop, Jonas?"

"Can you blame me for trying? You're an attractive woman and you live right across the street. It's like staring into a candy-store window and never getting a chance to buy anything." He drains his wineglass and sets it down. "Look, I know you've got your heart set on Vince. But if you ever change your mind, you know where I live."

I walk him to the door because it's the polite thing for a hostess to do. And because he really does look disappointed, which I should find flattering, but instead it just makes me sad for him. I watch him cross the street to his own house and think about him climbing into bed alone, waking up alone, eating breakfast alone. I, at least, can look forward to Vince coming home to me once his sister can fend for herself again, but Jonas has no such prospects. Not now, at least. The lights come on in his house and now he appears in his living room window. Once again, he's lifting weights, keeping those muscles toned and ready for his next conquest.

Another movement catches my eye. This time it's not one of the Greens who draws my attention; it's Larry Leopold, backing out of his driveway. I don't think he notices me as he drives past my house, which is good; I don't want him to think that all I do is spy on my neighbors. But it's after ten P.M., and I wonder where he's driving at this hour. These past few weeks, I've been so focused on Tricia and then on the Greens that I haven't been paying attention to what else is going on in the neighborhood. It's true what Jonas said: Everyone has secrets.

Now I'm wondering about Larry's.

I'm about to close the door when I notice something

white lying at my feet—a slip of paper. It must have been stuck in the door and fluttered free when my guests left. I pick it up and carry it inside to read by the light of the foyer.

The message is only three words long, and judging by the looping handwriting, a woman wrote it.

Leave us alone.

I go to the window and stare at the Greens' house. Carrie Green wrote it; it had to be her. What I don't know is whether the note is a plea or a threat.

Leave us alone.

In the house across the street, there is the flick of a blind, and I glimpse a silhouette. It's her, afraid to be seen.

Or is she not *allowed* to be seen?

I think of the bars on their windows and the gun on her husband's hip. I think of the day I met them, and how he laid his hand so possessively on her shoulder, and I realize she's not afraid of me; she's afraid of *him*.

Just ask me, Carrie, I think. Give me a signal and I'll help you get away from that man.

But she walks away from the window and turns off the lights.

TWENTY-FOUR

JANE

THE AFTERNOON HEAT HUNG HEAVY over the garden, where the luscious scent of lilacs perfumed the air. Anthony Yilmaz, dandelion fork in hand, bent down to pry up a weed and he shook the soil from its roots.

"I know this looks like work, but for me it isn't," he said. "After a day at the office, where all we talk about is investments and taxes, this is how I relax. Pulling weeds. Deadheading old blossoms. I come home, strip off the suit and tie, and head right into my garden. It keeps me sane." He smiled at Jane and Frost, and even with his silvered hair and deeply creased laugh lines, he still had a boy's smile, bright and mischievous. "And out of my wife's hair too."

Jane drew in a breath, inhaling the glorious scents, and wondered if she would ever have a garden of her own. A garden with plants that she would manage not to kill, like almost every houseplant that was unfortunate enough to come into her possession. Here, rhododendrons and poppies were in full bloom and peony bushes lined the stone path where an enormous orange cat lounged in the sun. Clematis and climbing roses had scrambled up the stump of a dead tree and over the fence, as if trying to escape into the wild. Nothing in this garden was orderly, yet all of it was perfect.

The sound of the patio door sliding open made Anthony turn toward the house. "Ah, thank you, dear," he said as his wife, Elif, walked into the garden, carrying a pitcher filled with a brilliant red liquid, rattling with ice cubes. She placed it on the patio table and gave her husband an inquiring look.

"They're here to ask about that murder I told you about. The lady professor at Colby College."

"But that happened years ago." She looked at Jane. "My husband was just a student."

"The case was never solved," said Jane. "We're just following up on it."

"Why ask Anthony about it? You don't think—"

"It's nothing to worry about," Anthony said, patting his wife's hand. "But I might be able to help them. I hope I can anyway." He reached for the pitcher and filled the glasses. "Please, Detectives, sit down. This is hibiscus tea, all the way from Turkey. Refreshing and full of vitamins."

On this hot and humid afternoon, chilled tea was a welcome beverage and Jane drank down half of hers in just a few gulps. When she set down the glass, she saw that Elif was watching her, clearly disturbed by this visit from the police. But Anthony seemed not at all concerned as he sipped his tea, ice cubes clinking.

"Even after all these years," he said, "I remember it very well because it was such a shock at the time. Terrible things stick with you, like scar tissue on your brain that never goes away. I even remember exactly where I was when I heard the news. In the cafeteria on campus, sitting with a classmate I was interested in at the time."

He looked at his wife and gave an apologetic shrug. "It took only two dates for me to realize I wasn't interested in her after all. But the news about the murder—it's a very vivid memory." He looked down at his glass. "Because Professor Creighton was so special to me."

"What do you mean by special?" asked Frost.

"I only came to appreciate it in later years, how much she went out of her way to help me, a foreign student. I was just a skinny boy from Istanbul, not sure if I would fit in there. And those terrible winters! We have snow in Istanbul too, but I was not prepared for how cold it is in Maine. I was in Professor Creighton's freshman English class one morning, shivering, my lips blue. And she handed me her wool scarf, just like that." He smiled, his gaze drifting up to a vine of wisteria blossoms overhead. "One remembers gestures like that. Simple acts of kindness. She became my faculty adviser. Invited me to Christmas dinners when I couldn't afford to fly home for the holidays. Encouraged me to apply to graduate school. My own mother was so far away, and Professor Creighton was almost like a substitute mother for me. That's why her murder was . . ." He shook his head. "It was hard, especially for me."

"When was the last time you saw her alive?" asked Jane.

"It was at that cocktail party, at her house. I was in my senior year then, and she'd invited maybe two dozen other seniors she'd been advising. It was sometime just before Halloween, I think. I remember it got dark very early and the leaves had already changed color. It seemed so festive, all of us sipping wine, chatting about what we planned to do after graduation. Grad school, jobs. Travel. We all *assumed* we had a future, but you never know, do you? Which one of us might be dead in a few days."

"That evening, how did Professor Creighton seem to you?" asked Jane. "Did she look worried? Upset?"

Anthony considered the question. "No. I don't believe so."

"Were you aware of the child custody battle she was having with her ex-husband?"

"I know she'd been offered a faculty position on the West Coast, and he didn't want her to take their daughter. Which, to be honest, I completely understand. I'd fight tooth and nail if someone tried to take our daughters away." He reached out for his wife's hand. "Something I've never had to face, thank god."

"Did you meet Professor Creighton's daughter?"

"Oh yes. She was there that night at the party. I can't recall her name."

"Lily."

"That was it, Lily. A beautiful girl with long blond hair, like a little princess. But very quiet. She was still recovering from some sort of heart surgery, and I think she was a little wary of people. We all fawned over her, of course. Who can resist a little girl?"

Jane and Frost glanced at each other. *Maybe someone couldn't.*

Jane said, "I read your interview with Detective Tremblay. I know a lot of time has passed since then, but maybe you've had a chance to think more about that evening. Remember other details."

Anthony frowned. "I told him everything I could think of. Maybe my classmates can be of more help?"

"Yes, about your classmates. Did you ever wonder

about any of them? Whether they could have been involved?"

"In the murder? Absolutely not. It's not a very big college and after spending three and a half years in the same school, you get to know people. I can't picture any one of them attacking Professor Creighton. Besides, wasn't her ex-husband arrested for it?"

"He was later released."

"Still, I assume they had a reason to arrest him in the first place. And who had a better motive to take that little girl than her own father?"

"What about the other students who were at the reception?" asked Elif. "Have you spoken to them?"

"No."

Elif looked back and forth at Jane and Frost. "Why do you focus only on my husband? What is it you think he did?"

"Elif, please," said Anthony. "I'm sure this is just routine."

"I don't think so." Elif looked at Jane. "There's something you haven't told us yet."

"The reason we're talking to your husband," said Jane, "is because he's the only one from that reception who now lives in the Boston area."

"Why does that matter? Professor Creighton was killed in Maine."

"Two weeks ago, a woman was murdered in Boston. Her death may be linked to Professor Creighton's case."

For a moment, the only sound was the chirp of sparrows and the distant growl of a motorcycle as both husband and wife registered the significance of what Jane had said.

"*Another* murder," said Elif. "And just because my

husband's the only student who lives in Boston, you assume—"

"We don't assume anything. We're just trying to find out if there *is* a connection."

"Who was this other woman?" asked Anthony.

"Her name was Sofia Suarez. She worked as a critical care nurse at Pilgrim Hospital."

"Suarez?" He shook his head. "I don't know anyone by that name. And I don't believe I've *ever* set foot in Pilgrim Hospital."

"Neither of us has," said Elif. "Both our daughters were born at Brigham and Women's Hospital."

"The victim's name isn't familiar to either one of you?"

Both Elif and Anthony shook their heads.

"Why do you think these murders are connected?" Anthony asked. "Was this nurse killed in a break-in, like Professor Creighton?"

"It happened in the victim's home, yes." Now for the question that would surely rattle them both: "Where were you on the night of May twentieth, Mr. Yilmaz?"

His wife opened her mouth to speak, but he quickly held up his hand to stop her. Calmly he reached into a pocket for his cell phone and looked at the calendar. "May twentieth. That was a Friday night," he noted.

"Yes."

"Friday?" said Elif, and she looked at Jane with a confident glint of satisfaction in her eyes. "That's the night Rabia came home."

"Rabia is our daughter," said Anthony. "She flew home from London, where she attends boarding school. Elif and I picked her up at Logan Airport and we took her out to dinner. Then we all came home for the night."

"And you stayed home all night, sir?"

He looked straight at her. "That night, my precious daughter was home for the first time in months. Why would I suddenly leave my house to go kill a woman I didn't even know?"

"WELL THAT WAS A DEAD END," said Frost as they climbed into the car.

Jane buckled her seatbelt but did not immediately start the engine. Instead she sat for a moment looking out at the quiet street where the Yilmazes lived. It was a leafy neighborhood where people had room to grow roses in their backyards, where the sound of traffic was little more than a distant hiss. A place where an immigrant from Turkey could mingle comfortably with other professionals and raise his family and feel he belonged.

Anthony Yilmaz was not their man. Yes, they would check with British Airways to see if his daughter, Rabia, really had arrived that night at Logan Airport, but Jane already knew it would only confirm what the Yilmazes had told them. This man did not kill Sofia Suarez. But he had revealed a piece of information that might be relevant, something she hadn't heard before.

She took out her cell phone and called Det. Thibodeau in Maine. "I have a question," she said.

"Yes?"

"Lily Creighton. Did she have some kind of heart surgery?"

"Why's this coming up?"

"I just spoke to one of Professor Creighton's students, and he remembered the little girl had had surgery. I'm wondering if it was at Eastern Maine Medical Center."

"Well, I'm not sure how that's relevant, but yeah. Hold on, let me check Tremblay's notes." She heard the click of his keyboard as he typed. "Yeah, here it is. She had a diagnosis of atrioventricular defect, whatever that is. Had open-heart surgery at EMMC two months before she was taken. Why?"

"Sofia Suarez worked as a critical care nurse at EMMC. It could be a connection."

"Maybe. But I'm not seeing how it all fits together."

"I'm not sure I see it either," Jane admitted. "But it's another link between these cases. There's got to be something here."

Thibodeau grunted. "Call me when you figure it out."

TWENTY-FIVE

AMY

S HE HAD ALWAYS LOVED SHOPPING for new shoes. She loved their curves, the way they gleamed like works of art on their little Plexiglas pedestals, and when she stepped into the shop on Newbury Street she inhaled deeply, smiling at the scent of polished leather. It had been months since she last visited a shoe store—or any store, for that matter. This was the first week she'd finally set aside her cane and even though she wasn't ready to wear high heels again, what was the harm in simply admiring the new arrivals?

Slowly she circled the displays, pausing every so often to pick up a spike-heeled masterpiece, admire its silhouette, and fondle the curves. Because this was Newbury Street, of course the prices were ridiculous, extravagant enough to make her mother whisper *put it back,* if she were here. But this evening Amy was on her own, no longer the invalid and happy to be out of the house. She held one jewel-toned shoe up to the light and imagined how nice it would be to slip her foot into that narrow cradle. How it would accentuate her calf and lengthen her leg and add a fetching curve to her lower back, as high heels did. Both of the saleswomen were helping other customers, which left Amy free to wander the shop without anyone hovering over her. She was just looking anyway, with no plans to buy. Not at these prices.

She wandered over to the display in the window, where her eye went straight to a silver evening shoe with a four-inch heel. It was a shoe fit for a ballroom or the opera and she certainly didn't need it, but she picked it up anyway and considered the narrow toe box. Such a pretty shoe, but would the pain of wearing it be worth it? Maybe. But not today.

She was about to put the shoe back on the pedestal when she noticed through the window a man in a raincoat standing across the street. He was looking straight at her. She froze, still clutching the shoe, her gaze fixed on his face, a face she'd seen before. She remembered a stormy morning, the air charged with the static of an impending thunderstorm. A cardinal singing in a tree. And a man smiling at her, a man with drooping shoulders and gray eyes in a gray face.

"Would you like to try that shoe on?"

Amy flinched and turned to the saleswoman, who had chosen just that moment to finally offer her assistance.

"I'm—I'm just looking . . ." She turned back to the window and looked across the street. She saw people strolling past, a couple holding hands. The man. Where was he?

"A different evening shoe, maybe? Some new Manolos have just come in, and they're *really* cute."

"No. Thank you." Amy was so rattled that when she tried to set the shoe down, it missed the pedestal and clattered to the floor. "Oh. Sorry."

"No problem," the saleswoman said, picking up the

shoe. "If there's anything I can help you find, just let me know."

But Amy was already heading out the door.

Standing outside on the busy sidewalk, she looked up and down the street but she didn't spot the man in the evening crowd. Had he rounded the corner? Stepped into one of the shops?

Maybe he was never there at all and she'd imagined him. Or he was someone else, someone who merely *looked* like the man at the cemetery. Yes, that had to be it, because how could he know that on *this* particular evening she would step into *that* particular shoe store? No, it had to be a mistake. She'd been under so much stress these past two months. The accident. Her time in the hospital. The weeks of pain and rehab as her pinned femur healed and she learned to walk again. Plus all the worry about how she'd catch up at school after missing the final weeks of class. She still hadn't finished her senior thesis on Artemisia Gentileschi, something she'd been putting off because it seemed unimportant in light of everything else that had happened to her. Instead of shoe shopping, she should be at home right now, working on those revisions.

She took a deep breath. Calmer now, she started walking along Newbury Street, toward the garage where she'd parked her car. Today was the first time she'd driven in months, the first time she'd felt comfortable walking without the cane, but her pace was still slow and her leg ached from this unaccustomed exertion. Everyone else walked at a far brisker pace, streaming past her like swifter fish in a river, no doubt wondering why someone so young and apparently healthy had the pace of an old woman.

A few more blocks to go.

Then she saw him. A block ahead, almost lost among the crowd. Even on this warm night, he was wearing the raincoat he'd worn at the cemetery. She halted, not sure how to avoid him. Hoping he hadn't seen her.

Too late. He turned and their gazes met. Held. That's when all her doubts vanished. This was no random encounter; he had followed her here.

And now he was heading straight toward her.

TWENTY-SIX

JANE

Jane and Frost found Amy sitting alone at a table at the back of the bar, huddled into such a small silhouette that she was almost invisible in the gloom. It was eight P.M. on a Friday and the crowd was wall-to-wall, young people liberated from their workweek, ready to drink and dance and maybe find that special someone. In a room of thumping music and loud voices, Amy Antrim was a silent wraith, hiding in the shadows.

"Thank you for coming so quickly," Amy said. "My dad's at work and I can't reach my mom. I didn't know what else to do, and you did tell me to call you."

"You did just the right thing," Jane said.

"I was afraid to walk to my car." Amy looked around at the crowd. "I thought I'd be safer if I stayed right here, with all these people around."

Jane and Frost sat down at her table. "Tell us exactly what happened," said Jane.

Amy took a deep breath to steady herself. "I came downtown to do some shopping. Well, window-shopping, actually. I went into a shoe shop just up the street and I was browsing inside when I saw him, through the window. He was standing across the street, looking at me. Not just looking, but staring with this expression of . . . of *hunger*."

"Are you sure it was the same man?"

"I wasn't, not at first. I caught only a glimpse before he walked away. And I thought, okay, it might be someone else. It *had* to be someone else, because how would he know where to find me?"

"You said you parked your car here," said Frost.

"Yes. In the garage down the street."

"Did you drive here alone?"

She nodded. "It's the first time I've driven since the accident. I've avoided coming downtown because my leg hurts if I walk too long."

"You came here straight from your parents' home?"

"Yes."

"Did you tell anyone you were coming downtown?"

"No. My mom was at her yoga class, and I needed to get out of the house. After all these weeks, it's time for me to get back on my feet. To do something fun for once. My mom was worried about that man, but I wasn't. I never really thought . . ." Amy glanced around the crowded bar, searching the faces. Even with two detectives sitting at her table, she acted like prey, scanning for predators.

"What happened next?" said Jane. "After the shoe store?"

"I stepped outside, to see if the man was still around. When I didn't spot him right away I thought, okay, maybe I was wrong. Maybe it was someone else." Again she scanned the bar, still wary, still on high alert. "Then I saw him, on the street. It *was* him, I know it. He started coming toward me, and that's when I freaked out. I ducked into the first crowded place I could find and hid out as long as I could in the ladies' room. I thought he'd never attack me in here. Not with all these people around."

But would anyone in this room pay attention? Jane wondered. They were all too busy tossing back drinks to register the scared young woman in the shadows. In this crowd, with this loud music, who would notice a gun, a knife, until it was too late?

"Amy," said Frost, "why do you think this man is following you?"

"I wish I knew. I've tried and tried to remember where we met before, but I can't come up with an answer. I just know there's something *familiar* about his face."

The music thumped and a waitress glided past with a tray of martinis as Jane studied Amy's face in the gloom. She let a moment pass before asking, "Do you know the name James Creighton?"

"No. Should I?"

"Think hard, Amy. Does that name ring *any* bells at all?"

"I'm sorry, ever since the accident, my memory . . ." She shook her head.

"What about your father? What do you remember about him?" Jane asked.

"You know my father."

"I don't mean Dr. Antrim. I mean your biological father."

Even in the gloom, Jane could see the young woman suddenly stiffen. "Why are you asking about him?"

"How well do you remember him?"

"I try not to."

"Your mother said you were eight years old when

you last saw him. Is it possible this man following you is—"

"*Don't* call that man my father."

Taken aback by her vehemence, Jane regarded Amy in silence. The young woman stared straight back at her, as if daring Jane to cross some invisible line.

"Was he that awful, Amy?" Jane finally asked.

"You should ask my mother that question. She's the one who put up with his abuse. Who got all the bruises and the black eyes."

"Do you know where he is now?"

"I have no idea. And I really don't care." Abruptly Amy stood up, a clear signal the conversation was over. "I'd like to go home now."

"We'll escort you to your car," said Jane, also rising from her chair. "But let me have a look around first. To make sure he's not still in the area."

Jane threaded through the tightly packed bodies crowded at the bar, inhaling their clashing scents of perfumes and aftershave and stale booze, and stepped outside. It was a relief to breathe fresh air again as she scanned the busy street. On this Friday night, the dinner crowd was out in force strolling the sidewalks, women in short skirts and high heels, businessmen in ties, roving wolf packs of young men.

And then she spotted him, off in the distance: a man in a gray raincoat, walking away from her toward the Boston Common.

She started after him.

He was too far away for her to be certain it was the man from the cemetery, but he had the same lanky build. Jane tried to keep him in sight as he bobbed and weaved through the sea of pedestrians, but he was moving at a brisk pace, straight toward the gloom of the Common. If he crossed into the park, she would lose him in those shadows.

She began to run, pushing past pedestrians who were too oblivious to move aside. She tried to slip through a tight knot of people and slammed into a man's shoulder.

"Hey, lady!" he snapped. "Watch where you're going!"

That encounter was just enough to distract her. When she refocused on her quarry, he'd vanished.

She ran to the corner of Newbury and Arlington, dashed across the street to the Common. Where was he, where was he? A couple ambled past, arm in arm. A circle of teenagers sat on the lawn, trading songs on their guitars. She scanned the area and suddenly saw him, standing on the opposite corner. As she crossed the street toward him, he looked up and smiled, but his smile wasn't directed at Jane. It was meant for a different woman, a woman who walked straight to him and gave him a peck on the cheek. Then he and the woman linked hands and walked together, right past Jane.

The wrong man.

Swiftly Jane surveyed the street, but Cemetery Man was nowhere in sight. If indeed he was ever there at all.

"AMY COULD BE WRONG," SAID Frost. "Maybe she saw the same guy you did, and she thought it was the man from the cemetery."

"She insists she's absolutely certain." Jane sighed. "And if she's right, it means we've got ourselves a problem."

She and Frost sat in her car outside the Antrim residence, where they had just escorted Amy to the care of her mother and father. This was a neighborhood of handsome houses and mature trees, with neatly tended gardens and shrubs, a neighborhood where violence seemed a million miles away. In truth, there were no such neighborhoods. Even here, on this quiet street, Jane could feel the threat of it closing in on that house. On Amy Antrim.

"If that really was him on Newbury Street, that's no coincidence," she said. "He didn't just *happen* to find her in that shoe shop."

"She said she drove there straight from home. If he followed her there—"

"It means he knows where she lives."

They fell silent. Both of them stared at the Antrim residence, where Amy and her parents were still sitting in the living room. They were shaken, of course, but perhaps not fully aware of just how dangerous Amy's situation might be.

"It's got to be *his* burner phone. He made those calls to the Antrim residence," said Jane. "And when Julianne answered, he hung up. Because the person he really wanted to talk to was Amy."

"Their house has an alarm system," said Frost. "The residence should be secure."

"What about when Amy leaves the house, like she did today? They can't watch her every second."

A silhouette moved across the living room and stood framed at the window. It was Amy's mother, looking out at the street. Mama tiger, watching for danger. In Julianne's place, Jane would be just as vigilant.

"I'll give Brookline PD a call," said Frost. "See if they can send a cruiser by the house every so often."

They tensed as car headlights approached, the vehicle moving slowly enough to make Jane's pulse kick into a gallop. A dark sedan rolled past the Antrim house and turned in to a driveway two doors down as a garage door rumbled open.

They both relaxed.

Jane turned her attention back to the house, where Amy was now standing beside her mother at the window. "Did it strike you as odd, what Amy said tonight?"

"Which part?"

"How she refused to talk about her biological father. How upset she was when I brought up the subject."

"Sounds like it was a pretty traumatic childhood. Watching her mother get beat up."

"I wonder where he is now. If it's possible he's the one who—"

"I know where you're going with this, but come on. She'd be able to recognize her own father, even after thirteen years."

"You're right." Jane leaned back in the seat and let out a weary sigh. She wanted to go home. She wanted to eat dinner with her family and read a story to Regina and climb into bed with Gabriel, but she could not stop mulling over what happened tonight. And what else they should be doing to keep Amy safe.

"What if this man's been stalking her for a while? Not just weeks, but months?" Frost said. "We assumed he first saw her at the cemetery, but he could have latched on to her earlier. And where's the most likely place she would have picked up a stalker?"

"The university."

Frost nodded. "Pretty girl spends four years walking around campus. Some guy notices her, starts to follow her. Gets obsessed with her. Maybe even tries to kill her."

"Okay. But what does *any* of this have to do with Sofia Suarez?"

"Maybe nothing."

She looked at the house again. Mother and daughter were gone and the window was now empty. She thought of other stalking victims, lifeless women she had not laid eyes on until the moment she stood over their bodies. That was the burden of working in homicide; you are always too late to change the victim's fate.

This time is different, she thought. This time the victim is still alive and breathing, and we are going to keep her that way.

TWENTY-SEVEN

"**Y**OU EVER WISH YOU COULD GO BACK TO COLLEGE?" Frost asked as he and Jane descended the stairwell of the campus parking garage. The concrete echoed with their footsteps, multiplying the sound into the boots of an invading army.

"Not me. I couldn't *wait* to get out of college," said Jane, "and get on with the rest of my life."

"Well, I miss it," said Frost. "I miss sitting in class, soaking up all that knowledge. Imagining all the possibilities lying in front of me."

"Yet here you are."

"Yeah." Frost sighed. "Here I am."

They pushed out through the ground-floor exit door and stepped onto the Northeastern campus. The summer session had started three weeks ago and this warm spring day had brought out shockingly skimpy outfits. Since when did halter tops and short shorts become suitable campus wear? Jane thought of her daughter, Regina, fifteen years from now, strolling this campus half naked like some of these girls. No, not if Jane had anything to say about it.

Oh god. I really have turned into my mother.

"If I could do it over again," said Frost, watching students stream past, "if I could go back to college . . ."

"You'd still become a cop," said Jane.

"Maybe. Or maybe I would've gone in a completely different direction. I could have gone to law school like Alice."

"You'd hate it."

"How do you know?"

"Sitting in some courtroom all day when you could be out on the hunt with me?"

"I'd wear nicer suits."

"This sounds like Alice talking."

"She thinks I'm not living up to my potential."

"How many lawyers do you think are practicing in this country?"

"I don't know. A million? Two million?"

"And how many homicide detectives?"

"Not so many."

"*Way* fewer. Because not many people can do what we do. You tell *that* to Alice." She stopped, stared at the map on her phone, and pointed. "It's that way."

"What?"

"Harthoorn's office. And we're late."

Twenty minutes late, in fact, but Prof. Aaron Harthoorn did not seem to notice their tardiness when they walked into his office. He was so preoccupied by the papers on his desk that he merely glanced up and waved them toward two empty chairs.

"I'm Detective Rizzoli," said Jane. "And this is—"

"Yes, yes, I saw you on my schedule. I'll be with you in a minute. First let me finish grading this atrocity." He flipped to the next page. In his late seventies, he was old enough to have retired a decade ago, yet here he was, a seemingly permanent denizen of an office crammed with books. Twin towers of stacked volumes loomed on either side of him, like chess rooks guarding his desk.

He gave a snort of derision, scrawled an *F* on the page, and tossed the paper into his out basket.

"Was it that bad?" said Frost.

"I *should* report that student for plagiarism. Did he really think I wouldn't recognize a paragraph from a book that I myself edited? The first time they do it, I give them an F. But the second time?" He cackled. "There's never *been* a second time. Not after I'm through with them."

And that's why he hasn't retired, thought Jane. Without his students, who would he have to terrorize?

"Now," he said, giving them his full attention. "You said you have questions about Amy Antrim?"

"She told us you're her senior adviser," said Jane.

"Yes. A shame about the accident. She couldn't graduate with the rest of her class, but she can finish her coursework in the fall, if she chooses to return. Have you caught the driver who hit her?"

"I don't believe there's been any progress."

"But isn't that what *you're* investigating?" He looked at Frost and then Jane, head swiveling on his skinny neck like an ostrich searching for prey.

"No, we're here on a different matter. It seems someone is stalking Amy, and it's possible it started on this campus."

"She never mentioned it to me."

"She only became aware of it in the last few weeks, when he approached her at a local cemetery. Then he popped up again, on Newbury Street. He's an older man, in his late fifties, maybe early sixties."

Harthoorn scowled. "Hardly what I consider *older*."

"Take a look at this footage," said Frost, pulling up the CCTV video on his tablet. He slid the device to Harthoorn. "It's from the cemetery surveillance camera. Maybe you can recognize him."

"How? I can hardly see the man's face on this video."

"But maybe there's something about him you recognize. His clothes, his gait. Does he look like anyone you know on campus?"

Harthoorn replayed the video. "I'm sorry, I don't know him. Certainly he's not anyone in my department." He handed the tablet back to Frost. "When you said someone was stalking her, I assumed you were talking about someone younger, like one of her classmates. I can see how Amy might attract attention. Unwanted or otherwise."

"And has she? Attracted unwanted attention?" asked Jane.

"I have no idea."

"You're her faculty adviser. Did she ever mention anything about—"

"Her adviser in *academics*. It's not as if students come in here and spill their guts about their personal lives."

No, I can't imagine they do, thought Jane. Who would confide in a cranky old fart like you?

"Amy's bound to have an admirer or two. An attractive young woman like her." His gaze drifted toward a ceramic figure perched on the bookcase, the bust of a voluptuous woman in a toga with one breast spilling out. "Not that I ever pay much attention to such things. My meetings with Amy were purely about academic matters. Her prospects for grad school. Employment possibilities, given her field of study."

"How is the job market?" asked Frost.

"In art history?" He shook his head. "Dismal. Which was discouraging because financial security is important to her. She said her mother struggled to make ends meet as a single parent. Even though it was only for a few years, poverty and abuse leave a mark on a child."

"Did she mention abuse?"

"She didn't go into detail, but she said there was violence in her mother's earlier relationship. It's probably why Amy chose the topic she did for her thesis." He shuffled through the stack of papers on his desk. "I have it here somewhere. When you called to say this meeting was about Amy, I thought you might want to see it." He pulled out a folio and slid it to Jane.

"Amy wrote this?" said Jane.

"It's the first draft of her thesis about the artist Artemisia Gentileschi. She was a female painter of the baroque era. The paper still needs work because Amy failed to address an important issue in Artemisia's life, probably because she found it too uncomfortable to write about. But what she has written so far is very good."

"What could be uncomfortable about art history?"

"Let me pull up an image, to help illustrate the point." He typed on his laptop, then turned the screen toward them. "This is a painting by Artemisia. It hangs in the Uffizi Gallery in Florence. Many people find it disturbing."

With good reason. Jane frowned at the grotesque image of two grim-faced women pinning a terrified man to a bed as one of them brutally sliced his throat with a sword. Every detail, from the blood spurting from his neck to the folds of the dying man's sumptuous robe, had been rendered with shockingly exquisite accuracy.

"This is *Judith Beheading Holofernes*," said Harthoorn.

"That's not something I'd want on my wall," said Jane.

"And yet, look at the detail, the power. The cold rage on Judith's face! This is a portrait of female vengeance. It was a personal theme in Artemisia's life."

"Why?"

"As a young woman, Artemisia was raped by her teacher. In this painting you can see her fury, feel her satisfaction in delivering her own brand of justice. It glorifies violence, but it's violence in the name of justice. That's why so many of my female students are fascinated by Artemisia. She gives life to female fantasies of punishing the men who abused them. It's power to the powerless." He closed the laptop and looked at Jane, as if she in particular understood what he was talking about. "You can see why the subject appealed to Amy."

"Power to the powerless."

"A universal theme. Victims fighting back and winning."

"You think Amy saw herself as a victim?"

"She told me one of the reasons Artemisia's work fascinated her was because of the abuse her mother suffered from that previous partner. I gather this happened years ago, but these sorts of traumas echo through the rest of your life. And now, if she's being stalked—" He paused, a thought suddenly occurring to him. "That hit-and-run accident in March. Does it have something to do with her stalker?"

"We don't know."

"Because if it wasn't an accident . . ." He looked at Jane. "Then this man is trying to kill her."

TWENTY-EIGHT

ANGELA

SOMETHING IS HAPPENING ACROSS THE STREET.

As much as I try not to be nosy, despite the warnings from my daughter and the Revere Police Department, I simply can't ignore what's in plain view from my living room window: That white van is back again. The van that's been hanging around my neighborhood for no apparent reason. This time it's parked a little way down the street, almost directly in front of the Leopolds'. Yesterday afternoon I saw it cruise down the street, moving slowly enough that I caught a glimpse of the driver, a man with short hair, his head turned toward the Greens' house.

Now here it is parked at the curb, facing in my direction.

I don't know when it arrived. I didn't see it at five P.M., when I glanced out the window, but now at eight-fifteen it's sitting at the curb, the engine and lights turned off. A parked vehicle isn't necessarily alarming, but when the driver's just sitting there, something is not right. It's too dark to see the driver's face; from this distance he's just a silhouette in the windshield.

I call the Leopolds. Lorelei picks up.

"The van's parked outside your house," I tell her.

"The van?"

"You know, the white one that keeps showing up in the neighborhood. Don't draw his attention! Turn off your lights before you look out the window."

"What am I supposed to look for?"

"Check out his profile and maybe you'll recognize him. I want to know why he keeps coming back."

I wait on the line as Lorelei turns off lights and goes to the window.

"I have no idea who that is," she says. "Let me ask Larry. Hey, Larry!" she yells.

Over the phone I hear her husband grumbling as he comes into the room. "Why are the lights off in here? What are you doing?"

"Angela called to say the white van's parked outside. Do you know who that is?"

A moment's silence. Then he says, "No. Why should I care?"

"Because it's been here three times this week," I tell Lorelei.

"Angela says it's been here three times this week. That seems strange, doesn't it? Do you think he's spying on someone in the neighborhood? Maybe he's a private detective or something."

There's another silence. Larry is thinking about this, and I fully expect him to make some denigrating remark about silly women and their silly imaginations. I'm sure that's what he thinks about me, because he truly believes he's far more intelligent than I am. When it comes to Scrabble, he's right. But that's only Scrabble.

It doesn't make me wrong about this particular matter.

To my surprise, I hear him say simply: "I'm going to find out who the hell that is spying on me."

"What? Larry!" his wife calls out. "What if he's dangerous?"

"I want this to stop here and now" is the last thing I hear him say.

Through my window I see the porch lights come on and Larry comes charging out his front door.

"Hey!" he shouts. "Who the hell hired you?"

The engine lights suddenly come on and the van lurches away from the curb and shoots off into the night.

"Leave me the hell alone!" Larry yells after it.

Well, this is unexpected. I'd assumed the van was here to watch the Greens. After all, they're the ones who've been acting suspiciously, who seem to be hiding something. Now I wonder if I've been completely wrong. Maybe it's not about the Greens.

Maybe it's all about Larry Leopold.

I don't dare talk to Lorelei about this. After Larry goes back into his house, I head across the street and knock on Jonas's door. I know he's home because I saw him in the window, lifting weights. After dinner, he always lifts weights. He answers my knock dressed in his usual skimpy workout gear, his shirt steamed to his skin with sweat.

"Angie baby! You finally ready for that martini?"

I ignore the offer and charge straight into his house. "I need to ask you something."

"Shoot."

"It's about Larry Leopold. What do you know about him?"

"You've lived on this street longer than I have. You should know more than I do."

"Yeah, but you're a man."

"How nice that you noticed."

"Men share things with one another that they don't share with women."

"This is true."

"So why would someone in a white van be spying on Larry? What's he been up to?"

Jonas lets out a deep sigh. "Oh boy."

"You know something."

"I know nothing. Nothing that I can confirm."

"Oh, for Pete's sake."

He gestures to the sofa. "Have a seat, Angie. Make yourself comfortable while I get us some rehydration."

He heads into the kitchen and I sit down on his sofa. Through the window facing my house, I notice movement in my neighbor's house. It's my nemesis, Agnes Kaminsky, and she's standing at her living room window, smoking a cigarette and looking right at me. While people may think I'm the neighborhood snoop, Agnes is the real deal, and now she probably assumes Jonas and I have a thing going on. I can't blame her for assuming the worst. I've been guilty of the same. I simply wave at her, to let her know that I see her and I don't care what she thinks. It's less suspicious to be blatant rather than sneaky.

She glowers at me and walks away from the window, no doubt with one of her usual harrumphs of disgust.

From the kitchen comes the merry sound of ice jingling in the cocktail shaker. Oh no, he's going to rehydrate with booze, and I suppose I'll have to sip some too if I hope to get any information out of him. Jonas comes back into the living room deftly carrying two very full martini glasses, each with an olive bobbing inside, and he hands me a drink.

"Bottoms up, Angie!"

One drink. Only one drink. I take a sip and oh my, it's good. He does know how to make a martini.

"So you want to know about Larry," he says.

"You're going to tell me, right?"

"I have no proof. Only suspicions. Not exactly *actionable,* as we used to say when I was a Navy SEAL."

"Yes, yes, I know."

"The thing is, all men are alike. We red-blooded ones are, anyway. We're always perusing the, er, merchandise. And sometimes we do more than just look."

"Larry's got a girlfriend?"

Jonas pops the olive into his mouth and smiles. "You see? I didn't even have to tell you."

"But—but what about Lorelei?"

He sighs. "Sad, isn't it? What some wives will put up with?"

I sink back against the sofa cushions, momentarily breathless from the revelation.

"Why do you seem so surprised, Angie?"

"I just never . . . I mean, Larry *Leopold*?"

He shrugs. "As I said, it's in a man's nature."

Something I, of all people, ought to know. After all, that's why my own marriage broke up, because Frank left me for another woman. In the long run, his leaving me turned out to be the best thing that could've happened, because that's how I ended up with my sweet Vince.

Vince. He wouldn't do that to me, would he? Men aren't *all* alike, are they?

For a moment I get the panicky urge to get Vince on the phone, to have him reassure me that he really is in California taking care of his sister. Then I think of all the good men I know, like my son-in-law, Gabriel, and Barry Frost—kind and steadfast men who are nothing like Frank or Larry Leopold.

Assuming Larry really is the sleazebag that Jonas implies he is.

I study Jonas, who's already gulped down half of his martini and is looking very relaxed and happy with himself. "How do you know Larry's got another woman?" I ask him.

"Lorelei herself suspected it."

"She told you that?"

"It may have slipped out during one of our afternoon coffees."

"How could I have missed seeing *those*?"

"Because we meet at Starbucks, down by the beach. Just neighborly chats, you know?"

For which they leave the neighborhood, probably so no one sees them. Specifically, so I don't see them. No wonder it escaped my attention. I wonder how many other things have escaped my attention over the years, how many affairs and crimes I'm completely ignorant of because I'm blind to what's really going on around me. As blind as I was to Frank's affair.

It turns out I'm a lousy detective. It's a depressing thing to admit, but I see that now and I sit slumped on the sofa, demoralized.

"Don't you want your martini, sweetie?" Jonas asks.

"No." I slide it to him across the coffee table. "You drink it."

"If you say so." He pops my olive into his mouth. "I

don't know why this Larry-and-Lorelei thing has gotten you down so much. It's what happens."

"Who's the girlfriend? Who's Larry seeing?"

"No idea."

"Does Lorelei know?"

"Nope. I'm guessing that's why the van was out there, watching their house. I bet she's hired someone to follow him. Collect a little ammunition against him, for the divorce."

I think about this for a moment and realize it doesn't make sense. When I called Lorelei about the van parked outside, she sounded genuinely baffled. She didn't try to brush me off or tell me to ignore it. Then she called Larry over to the window to show him. She wasn't the one who'd ordered the surveillance.

Then who did?

I get up from his sofa. Even though I'd had only a few sips of the drink, I can feel the effects of the gin. Jonas makes a powerful martini and not only has he finished his, now he's gulping down the rest of mine.

"Aw. Leaving so soon, Angie?"

"You're drunk."

"I'm just getting started."

"That's what I'm worried about. I'm going home."

For a Navy SEAL, Jonas doesn't hold his liquor as well as I'd expect. His eyes are already glassy and when I leave, he's too tipsy to get up off the sofa and see me to the door. I cross the street back to my house, and from my living room, I look out at my neighborhood. Each lit window is a diorama into the lives of people I'd thought I knew, but now I realize how little I actually saw. I'd never imagined that Larry with the chicken legs was a Lothario. That Lorelei and Jonas shared secrets at

Starbucks. It turns out I'm just a clueless housewife, so clueless I didn't even know my own husband was cheating on me.

I go into the kitchen and pour myself a glass of merlot. I'm not dumb enough to get drunk at Jonas's house; no, the place to get plastered is in the privacy of my own home, where no one's around to see it. It's only nine-thirty, too early to go to bed, but I'm ready for this day to be over.

I finish my glass of wine and pour another.

What else is going on in my neighborhood that I don't know about? The Greens are still a mystery to me, their blinds perpetually closed, their secrets forbidden to me by my daughter and Revere PD. Then there's Tricia Talley, who still hasn't returned home, and her parents, Jackie and Rick, who now avoid me. Only a few weeks ago, Jackie asked for my help finding her daughter. Now she wants nothing to do with me. Something's going on in that house too, something that's blown that family apart, and I have no idea what it is.

Maybe I should listen to Jane and mind my own business. Yes, tonight that seems like very good advice. Stop watching, stop wondering, stop asking questions. That, I think, is what I will do.

And then I hear the gunshot.

TWENTY-NINE

JANE

B Y 7:35 IT WAS ALMOST A FULL HOUSE. Jane watched in
amazement as the last arrivals scavenged for open
seats in the high school auditorium. Who knew that
classical music played by an orchestra of amateurs
would draw such a crowd? She certainly never expected
to be sitting shoulder to shoulder with eight hundred
people who all seemed to be studiously reading the program notes. Unfortunately, the last person Jane wanted
to sit next to was right beside her.

"It's always been one of my favorite concertos, ever
since I heard the Boston Symphony Orchestra perform
it when I was thirteen years old," said Alice Frost. "Not
everyone can be Yo-Yo Ma, but it's nice that amateurs
are making the effort, don't you think?"

"Yeah. Sure," said Jane.

"Good for them, making the *attempt*. So few people
try to stretch themselves. That's why Barry and I had to
come tonight, to cheer them on. Amateurs or not."

"Hey, Maura's gonna be playing tonight," said Frost,
sitting on the other side of his wife. "I can't imagine
she'll be anything less than amazing."

"Have you ever heard her play the piano?" Alice
asked.

"No."

"Then how would you know?"

"Because she's amazing at everything she does."

"Oh." Alice sniffed. "We'll have to see, won't we?"

It's going to be a very long night. Jane grabbed Gabriel's hand and whispered to him: "You wanna switch seats with me?"

"And deprive you of the commentary?"

"I'll make it up to you."

"Intermission," he said. "I'll switch with you then."

I won't last that long.

"Why do you suppose she didn't tell you about this concert?" Alice asked.

Reluctantly Jane turned her attention back to Alice. "Are you talking about Maura?"

"Barry said you found out about it from someone else. Here she's been rehearsing for weeks and she never even mentioned it."

That comment grated on Jane, not only because it made her question how close her friendship was with Maura, but also because it came from Alice. She wondered what other secrets Maura kept from her.

"Maybe she's afraid it won't go well tonight," said Alice, "and she doesn't want you to witness it." Alice turned her attention to the stage. "Here they come," she said as the musicians walked out to take their seats. There was no sign of Maura yet, but Jane saw Dr. Antrim settling into his chair in the violin section.

"Did you know violins didn't always tune to four-forty?" asked Alice.

Jane turned to her. "Four-forty what?"

"Hertz. That's a fun little factoid I read a few years ago. In the eighteen hundreds, violins tuned their A strings to four thirty-five hertz. Isn't it interesting that even classical music isn't static? It adapts to the modern ear. Ah, here's the conductor."

A silver-haired man in a tuxedo walked onstage and the audience applauded.

"That's Claude Ellison, and he's actually a real conductor, not a doctor," said Alice. "I looked up his name just now, on my phone. I guess it takes a real professional to whip amateurs into shape."

There was a fresh burst of applause and Jane turned back to the stage to see Maura walk out. She looked especially elegant tonight in a black dress of gleaming silk, and as she stood beside the grand piano, she smiled down at the first row where Daniel Brophy was sitting. Gracefully she swept her skirt to the side and sat down at the keyboard.

Make us proud, Maura. And annoy Alice while you're at it.

The conductor raised his baton. The violinists lifted their bows and began to play.

Jane's cell phone buzzed; thank god she'd remembered to mute it. She glanced at caller ID, saw it was her mother, and shoved the phone back into her purse. *Not now, Mom.*

"I have to admit, they're not half bad," said Alice. "For amateurs."

As the whole orchestra joined in and the music swelled toward the piano solo, Maura raised her hands to the keyboard. Jane tensed, dreading any mistakes to come. She dreaded it for Maura's sake, and also because if Alice kept up her snarky comments, Jane might have to strangle her. But from her very first notes,

Maura was clearly in control, her fingers racing effortlessly across the keys.

"Not bad at all," Alice admitted.

Not bad? My friend is freaking amazing.

Jane's phone buzzed again. A text message this time.
She ignored it; nothing was going to distract her. She
tilted forward in her seat, pulled by the magnetic force
of Maura's performance. *What other superpowers have
you not told me about?* All her attention was riveted to
the stage, to the woman weaving her spell at the piano.

She never heard the buzz of the next text message.

THIRTY

ANGELA

M Y DAUGHTER STILL ISN'T ANSWERING ME. I've sent her three text messages and tried calling her twice but both times it went straight to voicemail. She's ignoring me because she's tired of all my phone calls, all my dispatches from the neighborhood. I'm the mom who cried wolf too many times and this is the result. When there really *is* a wolf at the door, she pays no attention.

So I call the Revere Police Department instead.

"This is Angela Rizzoli, on Mill Street. I just heard—"

"Hello again, Mrs. Rizzoli." The dispatcher sighs, and I recognize the note of resignation in her voice.

"I just heard a gunshot. Outside my house."

"Are you sure it was really a gunshot, Mrs. Rizzoli? That it wasn't just a car backfiring or something?"

"I know what a gunshot sounds like! And I also know the people across the street own a gun!"

"This would be about the Greens again."

"I don't know if *they're* the ones who did the shooting. I'm just pointing out they have a gun and *someone* in the neighborhood is shooting one."

"Can you give me any more information about this gunshot?"

"Wait. Let me turn off the lights. I don't want anyone to see me in the window."

I scurry around the living room, flicking off light switches. Only when the room is completely dark do I go to the window and peer outside. The first thing I notice is that the Greens' lights are off as well. Are they home? Or are they also peeking out from one of those dark windows, trying to size up the situation? Jonas's lights are on and he's standing in his living room, fully visible as he peers out. For a Navy SEAL, you'd think he'd try to avoid being such an easy target for a sniper. The lights are also on at the Leopolds' house, but no one there is standing in any windows.

"Mrs. Rizzoli?" the police dispatcher says. I'd almost forgotten I still had her on the line. "Do you know where the shot came from?"

"It's hard to tell. I just know I heard it." I pause, suddenly focusing on a vehicle parked in the Leopolds' driveway. It's not their car, but it looks just like Rick Talley's Camaro. Why would Rick be visiting the Leopolds at this time of night? Just as unusual is the fact the Leopolds' front door is wide open, the lights from their foyer spilling out onto the porch. Larry's a security freak. He would never leave his door unlocked, much less hanging wide open on a Friday night, so anyone could just walk in.

"Something's wrong," I tell the dispatcher. "You have to send someone."

"Okay." She sighs. "I'll have a patrol car check out the situation. But you stay out of it, okay? Stay in your house."

I hang up and remain glued to my window, watching what happens next. Across the street, Jonas emerges from his house and stands on the sidewalk, looking up and down the street. Now Agnes Kaminsky comes out of her house and she has the nerve to stand smoking a cigarette right in front of my window, no doubt spying on me at the same time.

I can't stand not being part of the action. The dispatcher told me to stay inside, which is exactly what Jane would tell me to do, but when even my seventy-eight-year-old neighbor is brave enough to be out there, staying inside makes me look like a coward.

I step out of the house.

Agnes greets me with a scowl. "Angela," she says coolly.

"What's going on?"

"Why don't you ask Mr. Universe over there?"

I look across the street at Jonas, who waves at me and calls out: "You want another martini?"

"We're only friends," I tell Agnes.

"Does *he* know that?"

Jonas crosses the street to join us. "Ladies," he says. "A little excitement in the neighborhood, hey?"

"You heard the gunshot too?" I ask him.

"I had my workout music at full blast, so I can't be certain what it was I heard."

"I think that's Rick Talley's Camaro over there," I say. "What the heck is he doing at the Leopolds'?"

Jonas sighs. "And here come the consequences."

"Of what?" I frown at Jonas, who earlier tonight was so cagey about the Leopolds and their marriage. "Oh my god. Are you telling me Jackie *Talley*'s the one?"

"The one what?" Agnes says.

"The one Larry's been banging!"

"I'm not at liberty to confirm or deny," says Jonas.

"You don't have to! The situation's clear enough to—"

The crack of another gunshot makes us all freeze. We stand there paralyzed, even as we hear Lorelei screaming: "Stop! Oh my god, please *stop*!" It's a shriek of sheer terror, the shriek of a woman desperate for someone, anyone, to save her.

I don't even pause to think about it; I run toward the Leopolds' house. It's not like I'm entirely on my own; I have backup in this fight. *Someone* has to save Lorelei, and right now we're the only ones who can do it.

I scramble up the porch steps and the first thing I see through the open doorway is broken glass littering the foyer. A few steps inside, I spot where the glass came from: a shattered picture frame, now hanging askew on the foyer wall.

I move into the living room, my shoes crunching over glass shards, and the sight of blood makes me freeze. It's just a few spatters, but they stand out shockingly bright on Lorelei's white leather sofa, the sofa she once proudly informed me cost two thousand dollars. Slowly my gaze pivots to the source of that blood: Larry, who's now lying on the floor, clutching his left shoulder. He's very much alive and moaning.

"You son of a bitch, you shot me! You fucking *shot* me!"

Rick Talley stands over him, clutching his weapon in both hands. His arms tremble, the barrel of the gun bobbing in his unsteady grip.

"Why?" cries Lorelei, who cowers behind her blood-stained sofa. "Why are you doing this, Rick?"

"Tell her, Larry," Rick says. "Go on, tell her."

"Get out of my house," says Larry.

"Tell her!" Rick's arms snap taut, his aim suddenly straight and true, the barrel pointed directly at Larry's head.

In panic, I turn to Jonas for help.

Only he isn't there. The only person behind me is Agnes, who's doubled over in the foyer, hacking up phlegm. I'm the one person who can stop this.

"Rick," I say quietly. "This doesn't solve anything."

He looks at me, clearly surprised to see me. His attention was so fixed on Larry, he wasn't even aware that I'd come into the house. "Go away, Angie," he says.

"Not until you put down the gun."

"Jesus, do you *ever* stop sticking your nose into other people's business?"

"This is my neighborhood. It *is* my business. Put down the gun."

Lorelei pleads: "Listen to her, Rick. Please!"

"I have every right," he says, his gun swinging back toward Larry.

"No one has a right to kill anyone," I say.

"He ruined my life! He took what wasn't his."

Larry snorts. "Jackie sure didn't object."

Not helping, Larry. Not helping at all.

"What are you saying, Larry?" asks Lorelei, her head popping up from behind the sofa. "You mean it's *true*?"

Larry groans and tries to sit up but falls back again, clutching his wounded shoulder. "Will somebody here just call a fucking ambulance?"

"You and Jackie Talley? You two *did it*?" says Lorelei.

"It didn't last. And it was a long time ago."

"How long ago?"

"Way back. When she started working at the high school."

"When did it end?" Lorelei rises to her feet, so angry now that she no longer cares that there's a man with a gun in her house and she's out in the open. "Tell me."

"Why does it matter?"

"It matters!"

"Years ago. Fifteen, sixteen, I don't remember. After all this time, I don't know why the hell it's coming up now."

"Who else, Larry? I need to know who else you've slept with!"

"I don't," says Rick. "I know all I need to." Once again he raises the gun.

Again I jump into the conversation. "What good does killing him do, Rick?" I ask, and I'm surprised by the sound of my own voice. I sound so calm, so steady. I'm surprised I'm standing here at all, facing a man who's holding a loaded gun. It is an out-of-body experience, as if I'm floating above, watching myself—a braver, crazier version of Angela Rizzoli—confronting this angry man. "It won't solve anything."

"It'll make *me* feel better."

"Will it, though? Really?"

Rick goes silent, thinking about it.

"Yes, they betrayed you and that sucks. But Rick, honey, you'll move on from this. I know you will because the same thing happened to me. When I found out my Frank was banging that bimbo, you can bet I was pissed. I thought my life was over. If I'd had a gun, I might've thought about using it, just like you. Instead I picked myself up, dusted myself off, and I found Vince.

Now look at me! I'm happier than I've ever been. You will be too."

"No, I won't." Rick's voice breaks and his shoulders slump. He seems to be melting before my eyes, his whole body drooping like candle wax toward the floor. "There's no one else for me."

"Of course there is."

"How would *you* know, Angie? Of course you had no trouble moving on. *You've* still got your looks."

Even in the midst of crisis, with a loaded gun poised to go off, I'm shallow enough to appreciate the compliment, but I can't take the time to enjoy it. Larry's life is at stake.

In the distance a siren wails. The police are on their way. I just have to keep Rick talking until they get here.

"What about Tricia?" I ask. "Do you want your daughter to suffer, having to live with what her father did?"

"Her father?" Instead of calming him down, my words seem to inflame him. He looks at me with wild eyes, his gun waving in an uncontrolled arc that sweeps past Lorelei and me and the wall and back to Larry. "I *thought* I was her father!"

I look at Larry, lying on the floor, then look back at Rick. Oh my, this is even more complicated than I realized. Suddenly it hits me, the reason why Tricia is so angry at her mother. Why she ran away and now refuses to speak to Jackie. Tricia knows that her mother cheated on Rick. Of course she knows.

The siren is closer. *Just keep him talking a little longer.*

"You love Tricia, don't you?" I say to Rick.

"Of course I do."

"You raised her. In all the ways that really matter, she's your real daughter."

"Not *his*." Rick looks bitterly at Larry. "She'll *never* be his."

"Wait," says Lorelei. "*Larry*'s her father?"

We all ignore her. I keep my attention where it belongs, on the man holding the gun. "Think about her future, Rick," I say. "You need to be here for Tricia. You need to see her graduate. Get married. Have a baby . . ."

He sobs. "It's already too late. I'm gonna go to jail for this."

Larry grunts. "Damn right you are."

"Shut up, Larry," Lorelei snaps.

"It's only a wounding!" I point out. "You'll serve a little time and then you'll be out. You'll be here for her. But you have to let Larry live."

Rick rocks forward, his whole body shaking with sobs.

Slowly I move toward him. The gun dangles from his hand, the barrel drooping toward the floor. I wrap one arm around his shoulder to hug him, and with my free hand, I reach down and gently take his gun. He surrenders it without a fight and drops to his knees, crying. The sound is heart-wrenching. All I can do is keep hugging him as his face presses against my shoulder, as his tears soak through my blouse. I forget I am still holding the gun. I can focus only on this broken man shuddering in my arms and I think about what lies ahead for him. Even though he's shot Larry, at least he hasn't killed him. He will go to jail for a while, I suppose. He will lose his job, and Jackie will probably divorce him. But one day he will walk out of prison a free man, and if his daughter, Tricia, isn't the little snot she sometimes seems to be, then she will be waiting there to help him get on with his life.

And I'll try to be there as well. I know all about heartbreak and I know how to survive it. He'll need a friend, and that I can be.

Footsteps thud into the house. A voice screams: "Drop it, lady! Drop the gun!"

I turn to see two Revere police officers, their weapons pointed at me. They are young, nervous. Dangerous.

I'd forgotten I was holding the gun. Slowly I place it on the floor.

"Now get away from it! Lie down, face on the floor!" the cop yells.

Really? I think. You're really gonna make this grandmother lie down?

That's when Agnes steps in. She clomps into the room on her orthopedic shoes and plants all 110 pounds of herself between the cops and me. "Don't you boys *dare* point your guns at her!" she croaks in her cigarette voice. "Can't you see she's a fucking hero?"

THIRTY-ONE

A WEEK AGO, AGNES KAMINSKY AND I weren't speaking to each other. Now she stands beside me in the Leopolds' front yard, stroking my back as we watch the ambulance drive away with Larry. Judging by the way he cussed at the paramedics when he was poked for the IV, he's going to be absolutely fine. I can't say the same about his marriage.

Lorelei backs her car out of the garage and says to us through the car window: "The son of a bitch is gonna want his wallet and glasses, so I'm going to the hospital too. Though I don't know why I bother."

We watch Lorelei drive away after the ambulance and Agnes snorts. "Maybe you should've just let Rick finish off the asshole."

But I'm glad I did what I did. As the police escort a handcuffed Rick out of the house, he nods at me. It's a gesture of thanks for stopping him from making an even bigger mistake than he already has. Humans are such flawed creatures, prone to doing reckless things, and sometimes it's only by the grace of god—or a neighbor—that we are saved. I raise my hand to say goodbye, and then Rick disappears into the glare of flashing rack lights.

It's over. And we are all alive.

Suddenly the impact of what happened tonight hits me, and my legs go wobbly. I stagger over to the Leopolds' porch and drop down onto the steps. I can't believe everything that happened. I can't believe I ran into that house without even thinking about it. But that was when I thought I had my neighbors as backup, when I thought my posse would come charging in right behind me. My only posse now stands beside me, hacking up smoker's phlegm.

"That Jonas," I mutter.

"What about him?"

"What kind of Navy SEAL lets a woman face the enemy all by herself?"

"A chickenshit one." Agnes sits down on the step beside me. "Did you really believe that Navy SEAL crap?"

"You mean it's not true?"

"Oh, I had my suspicions. Tonight, he confirmed them." Her laugh sounds like the bark of a seal. A *real* seal, not a fake one. "All that lifting weights, all that bragging about his dangerous missions. Who needs to brag if you've actually walked the walk?"

She's right. Of course she's right, and I feel like a sucker for ever believing his war stories. But that's always been my problem, I take people at their word, and tonight I could've gotten killed because of it.

A light comes on in the Greens' house right next door, spilling through the slits in the lowered blinds. So they were home after all, holed up in their house with all the lights turned off, while the crisis was playing out right next door. They would have heard the gunshots and Lorelei's screams. They would've known I was running unarmed into danger. Even though Matthew

Green owns a gun, he didn't even bother to step out of his house to help me. Even now, with all these cop cars parked on the street, he won't come out.

Yet another coward. It seems this neighborhood is full of them.

A voice calls out to me, from beyond the flashing rack lights. "Ma?"

I look up, squinting, but I can barely make out my daughter's silhouette as she emerges from the darkness into the glare of the lights.

"I tried calling you, but you didn't answer," she says.

I look around at the cruisers and shrug. "Things got kind of crazy around here."

"Detective Saldana filled me in on what happened here. Jesus, Ma, I'm so sorry I didn't know all this was going on. I was at Maura's concert and—"

Agnes cuts in: "You should've seen her, Janie! Your ma was like a superhero!"

Jane knows that Agnes and I have been at odds for months, and now she looks back and forth at the two of us, trying to absorb this new state of affairs between my neighbor and me.

"She disarmed that man with her bare hands!" Agnes says, punching the air in emphasis. "Didn't need any gun, no siree. She just marched in there and told him to hand it over. Now we know where you get *your* moxie, Jane."

"Oh, Ma," Jane sighs. "What were you thinking?"

"*Someone* had to do it."

"Did it have to be you?"

"Well, Mr. Navy SEAL was a no-show. So was Mr. Green-with-the-gun. I was the only one left."

She sits down too, and now there are three of us,

lined up like bowling pins on the porch steps. "I'm so sorry."

I shrug. "You were at the concert. Was it good?"

"I left early, after I finally read your text. I'm sorry for not taking you seriously. All those things you tried to tell me about the neighborhood."

"But none of those things turned out to be the problem. They were just distractions. The Greens. Tricia running away. When the *real* trouble was something else entirely, something that happened a long time ago."

"What?"

"Jackie was banging Larry Leopold," says Agnes.

"Thank you for that summary, Mrs. Kaminsky," says Jane.

"Well, that's what your mother told me."

"And the strange thing is, it was news to Rick," I tell Jane. "He never knew about it. All these years later, you'd think it'd be long buried and forgotten."

"So how did it come out now?" Jane asks.

"I don't know. But I think Rick hired that guy in the white van to investigate Larry. That must be how he found out the truth."

"What guy?"

"Didn't I tell you about him? There's been a white van surveilling the Leopolds' house. I'm guessing he's a private detective. I think he must've confirmed Rick's suspicions and that's why Rick showed up here tonight, to finally have it out with Larry."

"What about Jackie? Has anyone talked to her yet, made sure she's okay?"

"Yeah, yeah. I called her and she's fine. But she says Tricia still refuses to come home." I shake my head. "What a mess."

"Come on, Ma. I'll walk you home. You want me to stay and spend the night with you?"

"Why?"

"For the company? This must've been a pretty traumatic experience."

Agnes laughs, "Does your ma *look* traumatized?"

Jane pauses and for the first time in a long time, my daughter looks at me. I mean, really *looks* at me. All her life I've just been Mom to her, the woman who cooked and cleaned, who bandaged her scrapes and cheered at her T-ball games. Does anyone *really* look at their own mother? We're just *there,* as reliable as gravity. But tonight, Jane seems to see something else, someone else, and she reaches down to help me to my feet.

"No, you don't look traumatized," she says. "But you do look like you could use a drink."

"I'll have one with her," says Agnes. "I got scotch at home. The good stuff."

"Jane, I'll be fine," I say. "I'm just gonna go home."

"You sure?"

"You heard Agnes. I'm a superhero now." I look at my neighbor. "You said you've got the good stuff?"

"The very best."

"Well, okay then," I say.

We start walking back toward her house and Agnes says to me: "You know what, Angie?"

"What?"

"It's good to be talking again."

THIRTY-TWO

MAURA

"A TOAST, EVERYONE! TO OUR BRILLIANT PIANIST!" said
Mike Antrim.

Maura managed a game smile as her fellow musicians hoisted their champagne flutes. She'd never been comfortable being the center of attention, but this was not a night she could hide modestly in a corner—not after her flawless performance.

"To our brilliant pianist!" everyone echoed.

Daniel leaned in close and whispered, "You earned the applause. Enjoy the moment."

She raised her glass to toast the gathering. "And thank *you*. We may be amateurs, but I think we all sounded pretty damn good tonight."

"Hey, I'm ready to hang up my stethoscope," someone called out. "When do we take this show on the road?"

"First," said Antrim, "everyone please grab some of that food in the dining room. If you don't help us finish it, we'll be eating leftovers for the next month."

Before the performance, Maura had been too nervous to eat anything and now she was ravenous. She made her way into the dining room where she filled her plate with crab cakes and beef tenderloin and crisp spears of asparagus. She also picked up another glass of wine, this time a rich and hearty red, which she happily sipped as she moved into the Antrims' spacious living room to mingle with the other guests.

Antrim waved her over to his conversational circle. "Maura, come join us! We're talking about which music to put on the next program."

"The *next* program? I'm still recovering from this one."

"I think you should choose something dramatic. Or wildly romantic," said Julianne. "I was listening to a concerto by Rachmaninoff on the radio. What do you think?"

All the musicians in the circle groaned.

"Julianne, sweetie," her husband said, "we're just amateurs."

"But I think it'd be a real crowd-pleaser."

One of the violinists turned to Maura. "Rachmaninoff? Up for the challenge?"

"Never in a million years," she said. "Just the thought of playing it makes my hands sweat."

Antrim laughed. "I didn't think anything could make our cool ME break a sweat."

If only you knew, thought Maura. Icy Dr. Isles, Queen of the Dead, was merely a facade. The woman who was never rattled and always sure of her facts. It was the mask she wore to crime scenes and into courtrooms, and she'd assumed the role for so long that most people believed it was real.

Most people.

She glanced around the room, searching for Daniel, but he was standing on the other side of the room with the Antrims' daughter, Amy, both of them focused on one of the paintings on the wall.

"Did your friends enjoy the concert?" asked Julianne.

"I didn't get the chance to talk to them afterward. There were so many people there, it was pretty chaotic."

"A full house!" said Antrim. "I heard every seat was sold."

"I noticed Detective Rizzoli left halfway through the performance," said Julianne. "What a shame she didn't stay to hear the whole thing."

"Detectives are probably like us doctors," said Antrim. "Always getting called away."

"We all know what that's like," said a cellist. "Birthdays interrupted, kids' recitals missed. At least our star pianist didn't get yanked away to some crime scene."

"My calls, at least, are never emergencies," said Maura.

"Well, I spot an emergency right now," said Antrim. "Your glass is empty!" He reached for the bottle of red wine, but paused before pouring any. "More?"

"Yes, please. Daniel's driving tonight."

Antrim refilled her glass, then glanced across the room at Daniel and Amy, who were still focused on the painting. "I see he's interested in art."

"Yes. Sacred art in particular."

"Then he should take a look at the triptych in my office. I bought it in Greece a few years ago. The dealer swore it's antique, but Julianne has her doubts."

"Is Daniel also in the medical field?" Julianne asked.

"No," said Maura.

There was a conversational pause, during which it would have been natural for her to fill in the blank, to answer Julianne's unspoken question, a question she always dreaded hearing: *What is Daniel's job?* The truth was too complicated and it invariably raised eyebrows, so she deftly pivoted toward the glass-fronted cabinet of violins.

"Tell me the story about these instruments, Mike," she said. "How did you end up with five violins?"

"The truth?" Antrim laughed. "I keep buying them because I think one of these days I'll *finally* find one that makes me sound like Heifetz. Instead I sound equally bad on all of them."

"At least you can play an instrument," said Julianne. "I can't even read music." She looked around at their guests. "All these talented doctors! I feel like an under-achiever in this room."

Antrim wrapped his arm around his wife's waist. "Ah, but you cook like an angel."

"If angels could cook."

"That's how we met, did you know that? Julianne managed the little café across from the hospital. I used to drop in there every day, to order lunch and to chat up this pretty gal."

"Turkey-and-bacon sandwich with a double cappuccino," said Julianne. "He ordered the same lunch every day."

"You see?" Antrim laughed. "How could I resist a woman who knows her way to a man's stomach?"

"Speaking of which, we should refill those trays. I've got more crab cakes warming in the oven."

As the Antrims headed off to the kitchen, Maura looked around for Daniel, and when she didn't see him, she crossed the room to the painting where he and Amy had last been standing. She could see why he'd been so interested in it. It was a cubist image of Madonna and child, rendered in blocky oranges and reds. A stark departure from the sacred paintings Daniel was so fond of, even if it featured the same beloved icons.

Faintly she heard his voice and she followed the sound into the hallway, where he and Amy were standing before a black-and-white photograph.

"Maura, come look at this," said Daniel. "It's the Piazza San Marco as most people have never seen it. Deserted!"

"I woke up at four A.M. to take that shot," said Amy. "It was the only time tourists weren't mobbing it."

"You took the photo, Amy?" asked Maura.

"We were in Venice for my sixteenth birthday." She smiled at the image. "That's the trip that made me love art history. I can't wait to go back to Italy. Dad says next time, we'll visit the Uffizi Gallery. I wrote my senior thesis about a painting there, and I've never seen it in person."

"Your dad said there's a triptych in his study that Daniel might like to see."

"Oh, that's a good idea. Mom thinks it's a fake. Maybe Daniel can tell if it's real or not."

Amy led them down the hallway and flicked on the light. It took only a glance to see that this study belonged to a doctor. The bookcase was filled with many of the same medical texts that Maura had in her own home office: Harrison's and Schwartz, Sabiston and Zollinger. The volumes flanked a framed photo of Mike and Julianne in their wedding finery, with little Amy standing between them. She looked about ten years old, a fairy princess with a crown of roses on her short black hair.

"Here's the notorious triptych," said Amy, pointing to the painting on the wall. "Mom thinks Dad got ripped off, but the antique dealer in Athens swore it's a hundred years old. What do you think, Daniel?"

"I'm not expert enough to speak to its age or authenticity," said Daniel, bending in close to examine it. "But I can identify these saints. They're iconic figures in the Greek Orthodox church. The female at the center is Theotokos, whom we know as Mary, mother of Jesus. On the left panel, that's clearly John the Baptist. And on the right panel, based on the design of his robe and collar, it would have to be Saint Nicholas."

"The Bishop of Myra," said Amy.

Daniel smiled. "Not everyone knows that the real Santa Claus was Turkish." He pointed to the bottom corner. "There's a fragment of text here. Maura, come take a look. You know a little Greek, maybe you can read this."

Maura moved in for a closer look. "It's so small. I need a magnifying glass."

"My dad has one here somewhere," said Amy, and she turned to the desk. "I think he keeps it in the top—"

Maura heard a loud gasp and turned. Amy stood frozen, her hand pressed to her mouth, staring through the window.

"What is it?" said Maura.

"He's here." Amy backed away from the window. "He found me."

"What?"

Amy turned, wild-eyed, to Maura. "The man from the cemetery!"

Daniel crossed to the window and peered out at the backyard. "I don't see anyone out there."

"He was by the tree, looking at me!"

Daniel headed for the door. "I'm going outside."

"Wait," Maura called. "Daniel?"

She was right behind him as he ran out the back door, into a night so thick with humidity it was like walking into a wall of steam. Together they stood on the lawn, scanning the darkness. From inside the house came the sound of jazz and the muffled voices of the Antrims' guests, but outside there was only the chirp of crickets. Maura turned and saw Amy standing in the study window, anxiously watching them.

"There's no one here," said Daniel.

"He had time to run."

"If anyone was here at all."

She looked at him and said quietly: "You think she imagined it?"

"Maybe she saw her own reflection. Thought she saw someone out here."

Maura walked across the damp grass and crouched beneath the tree. "Daniel," she said quietly. "She didn't imagine it. There *was* someone here."

He dropped down beside her and stared at what was clearly pressed into the soil: shoe prints.

She pulled out her cell phone and called Jane.

"A FITTING END TO A CRAZY NIGHT," said Jane. "First my mom disarms a man with a gun. And now Amy's stalker seems to be back."

"You neglected to mention my triumphant debut on the piano," said Maura.

"Oh. Yeah." Jane sighed. "I'm sorry about cutting

out of your concert early, Maura. But when I read that text from my mom—"

"I'm just kidding. Mom emergencies always take precedence."

They crouched side by side in the semidarkness of the Antrims' backyard. It was now midnight, the other guests had left except for her and Daniel, and the neighborhood had fallen silent. Maura looked down at the hem of her silk skirt, which was now damp and probably stained from the wet grass. Every investigation had its price, but this one was more expensive than most.

Maura rose back to her feet and her thighs ached from crouching so long. "He knows where she lives. He could show up again at any time."

Jane stood up as well. "Her parents are scared. And pissed as hell."

"Surely they don't blame you."

"Who else are they going to blame? Their daughter's got a stalker and I can't seem to catch him." Jane turned to look at the flashing lights of the police cruiser parked on the street. "You and Daniel didn't see anyone at all?"

"No. Amy's the only one who saw him. By the time we got outside, he was gone. With all the guests, there were at least a dozen cars parked on the street, so his car wouldn't have been noticed. From here, he would have had a clear view into the study." Maura turned to the window, where the lights were still on inside. "While we were there, looking at the painting, he was right here in the yard. Watching her."

"Detective Rizzoli?"

They turned to see Julianne emerge from the back door and walk toward them across the lawn. The night was warm but she hugged herself as though chilled as she stood half in darkness, her face eclipsed by the shadow of a lilac bush.

"What should we be doing?" she asked.

"You have a security system. Keep it armed."

"But it doesn't feel safe, having her stay at home. Knowing that *he* could show up here at any time. Mike has to work, so he can't be here all the time to protect us."

"The police are ten minutes away, Mrs. Antrim."

"What if it takes them longer? By the time they get here, he could be inside our house, attacking us. Attacking *her*." She hugged herself tighter and looked over her shoulder toward the street, as if someone were watching them even now. "Until you catch this man, I want to get Amy out of here. I know where to take her."

"Where are you thinking?"

"We have this lake house, out near Douglas State Forest. It's in the middle of nowhere and he'd never be able to find us there. Mike agrees it's the perfect place for us to go. He has to stay in the city to work, but he'll join us on Saturday. Right now, I don't want Amy here."

Maura looked at the house, every room so glaringly exposed. How easy it is to peer into a stranger's house at night, to observe the details of their lives. To watch them cook dinner, sit down at the table. To see what is playing on their televisions, to know what time they go upstairs and turn off their lights. At night, every house invites the gaze of strangers whose interest may or may not be benign.

"If you're going to take her anywhere," said Jane, "then go to a hotel or a friend's house. But your lake house? I can't protect her."

"Can you protect her *here*?"

"I'm just trying to keep her safe, Mrs. Antrim."

"So am I," said Julianne. Her face was obscured by shadow, but there was no missing the coldly metallic edge in her voice. "You do your job, Detective. And let me do mine."

THIRTY-THREE

AMY

S HE DID NOT KNOW WHY it was called Lantern Lake, but the name always made her think of magical nights and fireflies and golden ripples on the water. Every summer since she was ten years old, when the heat in the city became too stifling to bear, this lake was where her family escaped to. Here they'd while away the weekends paddling the canoe or splashing among the reeds. Amy heard there was good fishing here, and her father sometimes took his pole out onto the water, but Amy never understood the attraction of fussing with hooks and line and tackle. No, this was where she could simply be, not do, a place where both she and her mother felt safe. They hadn't bothered to ask Detective Rizzoli for permission; they'd simply packed up and left, and now that they were here, Amy knew it was the right decision.

She only wished they'd given more thought to what to bring. In the rush to leave the city this morning, her mother had filled grocery bags with random items from the kitchen. Still, the two of them would make do. They always managed to.

The far-off growl of an engine drew Amy's gaze to a motorboat skimming across the water, a noisy annoyance on the otherwise peaceful lake, but to be expected on a warm afternoon. By tonight, all the boats would be gone and the ducks and loons would reclaim their kingdom.

"Amy, are you hungry yet?" her mother called from the back porch.

"Not really."

"When do you want to have dinner?"

"Whenever you want."

Julianne came down the path to join her at the water's edge. For a moment they just stood side by side, not speaking, listening to the leaves rustle in the trees.

"We should pull out the canoe tomorrow," Julianne said. "First thing in the morning, before the motorboats show up, let's get out on the water."

"Okay."

Her mother looked at her. "Are you scared, sweetheart?"

"Aren't you?"

Julianne peered out at the lake. "We've gone through worse. We can get through this too. For now, let's take it one day at a time." She turned back to the house. "I'll finish unpacking, then let's open a bottle of wine."

"Are you sure we should?"

"I think we could both use a glass right now."

It was almost nine that evening when they finally sat down to eat dinner. The meal was uncharacteristic of Julianne, who prided herself on her cooking and usually spared no effort in the kitchen. Tonight it was spaghetti with marinara sauce straight out of a jar, and a salad dressed only with olive oil and salt. An indication that Julianne was more preoccupied than she admitted. The motorboats had finally quieted for the day, and except for the ghostly cry of a loon, the night had gone still. They were both still rattled by the turn of events and they ate in silence, sipping sparingly from their wineglasses. This cabin might be their safe place, but the gathering darkness made them both nervous again and they could not help listening for any warning sounds. The snap of a twig, the rattle of a bush.

The ringing cell phone was such a shock, Amy tipped over her glass and cabernet splashed onto the table. Heart pounding, she tossed down a napkin to mop it up as Julianne answered the phone.

"Yes, we're fine here. Everything's fine."

Amy shot her mother a questioning look and Julianne mouthed the word *Daddy*. Of course he must be feeling guilty that he wasn't there with them, but Julianne insisted he should go to the hospital as scheduled. Someone needed to be in the house and make it obvious it was occupied so the stalker would assume that Amy was still there. That was the best way to keep their daughter safe, Julianne told him: Divert the stalker's attention away from Amy.

"Yes, I've called Detective Rizzoli," Julianne said. "She's not happy we're here, but at least she knows where we are. She's been in touch with the Douglas Police Department, so they know the situation. There's no need to worry, Mike. Really."

She was using her *Mommy's in charge* voice, which Amy knew so well, a voice that worked on Daddy too. He might be a doctor, accustomed to giving orders in the ICU, but at home he was happy to defer to his wife because she really was on top of things, whether it was the checkbook or the kitchen.

When at last Julianne hung up, she looked frazzled from all the expended effort to calm her husband, and she gave Amy a weary smile. "He wishes he were here."

"Is he still coming on Saturday?"

"Yes. He'll leave straight from the hospital."

"Tell him to bring a few more bottles of wine."

Julianne laughed. "Poor you. Stuck out here in the middle of nowhere with just your boring parents."

"Boring is good. Right now, it's what we both need." Amy carried the plates to the sink and turned to look at her mother, who sat staring off into the distance, her fingers drumming the table. Julianne never admitted when she was afraid. She never admitted to anything that might rattle her daughter, but Amy didn't need to be told. She could see it in those fingers, relentlessly tapping out a Morse code of fear.

Julianne stood up. "I'm going out to check the car again. I can't find my flip-flops anywhere, and I *know* I packed them."

"Maybe on the floor of the back seat?"

"Or the trunk. They might be under all those grocery sacks." Julianne grabbed a flashlight out of the kitchen drawer and stepped outside, the screen door squealing shut behind her. Amy listened to her mother's footsteps thumping down the porch stairs, and from the window she saw Julianne's silhouette moving through the trees, toward the driveway.

Amy went back to the sink and tackled the dirty dishes from dinner. Neither one of them had eaten very much tonight, and she scraped congealed spaghetti into the trash, washed and dried the dishes, and set them back in the cabinet.

Julianne hadn't returned.

Amy looked out the window but didn't see Julianne or any flicker of the flashlight. Where had her mother gone? She hovered between going outside to find Julianne and staying here, in the cheery light of the kitchen. The moments ticked by. She heard no cries, nothing to alarm her, only the chirp of crickets. Yet something was not quite right.

She stepped outside onto the porch. "Mom?" she called out.

There was no answer.

She saw no other house lights on the lake. Theirs was the only cabin occupied tonight. They were alone here, tucked into these woods and far from the main road. It was exactly where they'd wanted to be, but now Amy was having second thoughts. Wondering if coming here had been a mistake.

"Mom?"

Something splashed in the lake and she saw ripples disturb the reflection of moonlight on the water. Just a duck or a loon. Nothing to worry about. She went back into the cabin, but just as the screen door slapped shut behind her, she heard another sound. This one did not come from the lake; this was much closer. A rustling. A snap of a twig.

Footsteps.

She stared through the screen door, trying to make out who or what was approaching. Was it Julianne, returning from the car?

Then she saw the figure emerge from the shadow of the trees. It loomed on the path, silhouetted by the glow from the lake. Not Julianne. It was a man, and he was coming toward her.

That's when she began to scream.

THIRTY-FOUR

JANE

EVEN BEFORE JANE STEPPED INTO THE CABIN, she could see the blood. It was splattered across the floor and up the opposite wall in a machine-gun spurt of arterial spray. Wordlessly she paused on the porch and bent down to pull on paper shoe covers. As she straightened again she took a breath, steeling herself for what waited inside the cabin. Outside, the air smelled of damp earth and pine needles, but inside it would be a different matter, a different scent. Something she had smelled too many times before.

"As you can see, the attack started in the kitchen," said Detective Sergeant Goode. He had been the first detective to arrive on the scene and his eyes were puffy and bloodshot from a night without sleep. In this rural county, homicide investigations were few and far between, and last night he'd walked into one that had clearly left him shaken. As though reluctant to revisit the horror, he paused outside on the porch before finally pulling open the screen door and stepping inside the cabin.

"It's pretty obvious what happened," he said.

The blood told the story. Streamers of it had dried on the walls, on the kitchen cabinets, pumped out in bursts by a frantically beating heart. A chair lay toppled on its side, and on the floor was shattered glass and smeared shoe prints marking the chaotic dance steps of attacker and victim.

"It goes into the hallway," said Det. Sgt. Goode.

He led her out of the kitchen, following the trail of blood. Only weeks ago, Jane had followed just such a trail, in the home of Sofia Suarez. This felt like a nightmare, on repeat. She halted, staring at the single smeared handprint on the wall. It was left by the victim, who had been dizzy and weak, desperately reaching out for support before stumbling forward.

In the bedroom, the trail finally ended.

Here there were no more arcs of arterial spray on the walls. Too much blood had already been lost and there was little left for the heart to pump. What remained in the dying victim's body had simply seeped out in a slowly weakening stream and collected in the congealed pool that now lay at Jane's feet. The ME's office had already removed the body, but the impression of where it had been lying was still there, left behind by the blood-soaked clothes.

"We had the body transported to Boston, as you requested," said Goode, "since this seems to be connected to the case you're already investigating."

Jane nodded. "I'd like our ME to do the autopsy."

"Well then, that makes it simpler for us. Simpler all around, actually, since you already have the background on this. The witness statements are pretty clear about what happened." He looked at Jane. "Is there anything else you need to see?"

"The vehicle."

"It's parked a ways down the main road. Either he got lost on the way here or—"

"He didn't want to alert them that he was in the area."

Goode nodded. "Which is the explanation I'm going with."

They left the cabin and tramped up the dirt driveway toward the paved road that skirted the southern end of Lantern Lake. They reached the paved road and Goode said: "There. That's the vehicle."

The car he pointed to sat just a dozen yards beyond the entrance to the Antrims' driveway. It was a dark green Honda Civic with Maine plates and an expired safety sticker. It had clearly seen years of use, with rust staining the undercarriage and more than a few dents in the driver's door.

"We ran the plates, confirmed it's registered to a James Creighton, Portland, Maine, but that address is no longer current. The landlord says Creighton got behind on his rent and had to be kicked out about four months ago. The fingerprints are a match, so we know it *is* him. We went through the vehicle, found a sleeping bag and pillow in the back seat, plus half a dozen empty bottles of coffee brandy. Looks like he was living in his car for some time."

"Where's his cell phone?"

"Didn't find one."

Jane frowned. "We're pretty sure he had a burner phone."

"No idea what happened to it. But you'll be interested in what we *did* find." He pulled out his cell phone and pulled up an image. "It's at the state lab now. I took a photo because I figured you'd want to see it."

Jane stared at the image on his phone. It was a hammer.

"Found it tucked under the carpet in the trunk, next to the spare tire. It's not that unusual that he'd have a hammer, but you *did* ask about one."

"Was there blood on it?"

"Not to my naked eye, but the crime lab just texted me. They found occult blood on the hammerhead." The afternoon sun was now shining right into his eyes and he squinted against the glare. The harsh light brought out every wrinkle, every flaw on his face. "If it matches your victim in Boston, this might solve all your problems."

"So it would seem."

He regarded her for a moment. "The stalker's dead, the ladies are safe. Yet you don't look satisfied."

She sighed, looked up at the trees. "I'd like to walk through the cabin again."

"Sure. Crime scene unit's already been through it, so be my guest. I've got to head back to town now. Any questions, just give me a call."

Jane walked alone back down the driveway to the cabin. Stood outside for a moment in the yard, listening to the chirping of birds, the wind rustling the trees. Early this morning, she and Frost had interviewed Amy and Julianne about what happened here last night, and their statements played in her head as she again mounted the porch steps.

Amy: *He came out of the woods—came straight toward me. I tried to close the door on him to keep him out, but he shoved his way inside. I knew he was going to kill me . . .*

Julianne: *I was down by the lake, looking at the water,*

and I heard her screaming. I heard my baby screaming and I just ran toward the cabin . . .

Jane stepped inside and stood in the kitchen, once again surveying the blood-splattered cabinets, the broken glass, the toppled chair. She turned to the countertop and stared at the butcher block knife holder. One of the slots was vacant. It was a wide slot, large enough to hold a chef's knife.

Julianne: *I ran into the kitchen. He was there with Amy and he had her shoved up against the wall with his hands around her throat. I did it without thinking. I did what any mother would do. I grabbed a knife from the counter . . .*

The evidence of what happened next was splashed across the cabinets, smeared on the floor, and Jane could see it unfolding as if it were happening right here, right now. Julianne plunges the knife into the attacker's back. Wounded and howling, he turns to face her. Lunges at her. In desperation she blindly slashes at him and the blade slices across his neck. This time the wound is mortal, but not immediately. He has enough strength to try and wrestle the knife away from her, and in the struggle, she cuts her hand. But now his vision is fading . . .

Blindly, he staggers into the hallway where he reaches out to steady himself, leaving his smeared handprint on the wall. By now he has lost so much blood that everything is starting to go dark. He stumbles into a bedroom—a dead end. And here his legs can carry him no further.

Jane halted, looking down at the spot where James Creighton's body at last came to rest. Here he had taken his final breaths as the bleeding slowed to a trickle, as his heart stuttered and stopped.

Julianne: *When I called 911, he was still alive. I'm sure he was. He never said anything. He never told us why he attacked. By the time the police arrived, he was dead, so we'll never know why he chose Amy. Why he wouldn't leave her alone . . .*

Amy. Jane looked around the bedroom, at the lace curtains, the row of stuffed animals on the shelf. This must be Amy's bedroom. After their terrifying night, she and her mother had been escorted back home to Boston and they'd left everything behind in the cabin. Amy's empty suitcase was still in the closet and the dresser drawers contained her underwear and socks and T-shirts. Both their toothbrushes were still in the shared bathroom cabinet, along with a prescription bottle of Julianne's high blood pressure pills and a box of Clairol hair color.

Jane walked out of the cabin to the front porch where she pulled out her cell phone to call Frost. "You still at their house?" she asked. "How are they?"

"Pretty shaken up, but doing okay, considering," he said. "Dr. Antrim's home with them and Julianne's gone upstairs to take a nap. Any surprises at the lake?"

"Maybe. The crime scene unit found a hammer in Creighton's vehicle. State lab says it's got trace blood on it. If it's Sofia Suarez's blood—"

"That would really wrap this all up."

"Except for the question of *why*? We still don't know his motive. Why did he kill Sofia? Why did he stalk Amy?"

"Why *any* of this? I know you hate me saying this but, well, it's a mystery."

"Yeah, I do hate when you say that." She looked off toward the lake, where a couple paddled by in their red canoe. The afternoon was windless, the water as flat as glass. "It's really beautiful here. Makes me want to buy a house on a lake."

"This calls for a celebration, right? Alice has been wanting to try this new Italian restaurant out past Newton. Everyone in her office is raving about it. What do you think?"

"Maybe. Right now, I've got one more detail to check on."

"What?"

"The autopsy."

ALTHOUGH SHE WAS GOWNED AND MASKED and her hair was hidden beneath a paper cap, the figure standing at the autopsy table was unmistakably Maura. Watching her through the morgue's anteroom window, Jane wondered what made Maura so recognizable. Her regal bearing as she reached for a scalpel? Her relentless focus as she stared down at the body laid out on the table? Even as Jane pushed through the door and walked into the autopsy room, Maura did not look up from the cadaver as she completed her Y incision and began snapping through ribs.

"Do you have a time of death?" Jane asked, joining Maura at the table.

"My estimate doesn't contradict what the witnesses said." Maura lifted off the sternum, revealing a jewelry box of organs contained within the thorax. "Death was around ten to eleven P.M. I've already examined the stab wound in the back. It penetrated the intercostal space between T5 and T6 and it's consistent with the dimensions of the chef's knife they have in evidence." Maura pointed to the neck where the wound, now washed clean of blood, gaped open like a second mouth, pink and smiling. "And as you can see, that second wound incised the left carotid artery. I spoke to the ME in Worcester. He was at the scene last night and described it as a bloody mess."

"It was," said Jane.

"They could have done this autopsy in Worcester. You didn't need to transport the body to Boston."

"But I know *you* won't miss anything. And you've been on this investigation from the beginning. I thought you'd appreciate the follow-through."

"Thank you."

Was that sarcasm? With Maura it was sometimes hard to tell and Maura's expression did not offer any clues as she resected heart and lungs and laid open the coronary arteries. No wasted motions, every slice efficient and precise.

"Coronaries are clean," said Maura. She glanced at the gaunt face. "Even if nothing else about him looks healthy."

"Yeah, death does that to a body."

"I mean his cachexia. His clothes were several sizes too big, and see how wasted his temples are? He's lost a great deal of weight."

Jane thought about the empty bottles of coffee brandy in the car. "Alcoholic?"

"That could be part of it." Maura moved aside loops of small bowel. "But I think this was the real reason." She pointed to a bulging mass. "Pancreas. It's already metastasized to the liver."

"Cancer, then?"

"Advanced. He was dying."

Jane looked down at James Creighton's sunken eyes. "You think he knew?"

"All he had to do was look in a mirror."

Jane shook her head. "This makes no sense. The man had cancer and he must have known he was dying. Why would he stalk a woman? Why follow her to the lake and attack her?"

Maura looked up. "Did you actually see the bruises on Amy's neck?"

"Yeah."

"Obvious ones?"

"You don't believe the victim?"

"It's just in my nature to question. You know that."

"The bruises were faint," said Jane. "But Amy *did* have them. And remember, his ex-wife was strangled too."

"It was never proven that Creighton did it."

"After this attack, it looks more likely."

"*Likely* is not proof." Just the sort of thing that Maura would say. The sort of thing that irritated Jane, even though she knew it was true.

Maura set down the scalpel. "What I *can* give you is a time of death, a cause of death, and an ID. This man's fingerprints and his blood type match James Creighton, age fifty-six."

Jane's cell phone rang. She reached under the surgical gown and fished it out of her pocket. "Detective Rizzoli."

"I have some news that'll make you happy," said Det. Sgt. Goode.

"Make me happy."

"You know that hammer we found in James Creighton's car? The state lab just confirmed the blood on it is human and it matches Sofia Suarez's. Congratulations. You've got your man."

Jane looked down at the hollowed-out body. She should be feeling happy that the last piece of the puzzle had just fallen into place, relieved that she could now close the file on Sofia Suarez's murder. Instead, as she stared at the face of James Creighton, she thought: *Why do I feel like I'm missing something?*

THIRTY-FIVE

ANGELA

TONIGHT I'M BEING CELEBRATED AS A HERO. That's what everyone around the table is calling me anyway, and you bet I'm gonna bask in it because it's not often that plain old Mom gets a round of toasts and a dinner out. A really nice dinner too, not one I had to cook myself, but a meal at one of the most expensive restaurants I've ever eaten in. Alice Frost was the one who chose it, so I guess I have to give her credit for that at least, even if we had to drive halfway to Framingham to get here. Alice knows all the best places to dine, and when you're a lawyer at a high-flying firm like she is, you get tipped off to the hottest new chefs.

I guess I could learn to like her. One of these days.

She's ordered the wine for the table tonight, and that's another thing she's darn good at. I've already had two glasses, and now the waiter swoops in to refill my glass. He pauses, bottle poised to pour, and tilts his head in a question.

"Go ahead, Ma," says Jane. "I'm driving you home, so drink up."

I flash the waiter a giddy smile and he fills my glass. As I sip and look around the table, I wish Vince were here tonight. He loves a good party. When he gets home from California, I'm going to bring him to this restaurant to celebrate.

All of us have something to celebrate tonight. Jane and Barry have closed their case, Alice has been promoted to partner, and my little Regina has just graduated from her first year in preschool. I look around the table at Alice and Barry, at Gabriel and Jane and Regina, and I think: I am such a lucky woman.

When Vince comes home, life will be perfect.

"Here's to Angela Rizzoli, superhero!" says Gabriel, lifting his glass of tonic water. "Who single-handedly disarmed a man with a gun."

"Well, not single-handedly," I admit. "I had Agnes Kaminsky as backup. So even though she's not here, we really should toast her too."

"To Agnes!" they all say, which makes me feel a little bad that I didn't invite her, but I know that if I had, she'd be complaining that the food's too salty and the music's too loud and what fool pays thirty bucks for an entrée?

Now I raise my glass of wine to make a toast. "And congratulations to Jane and Barry. All these weeks, after all that hard work, you got your man!"

"Technically, Ma, we didn't," Jane says.

"But you solved the case and now he'll never hurt anyone else. So here's to the best detectives in Boston!"

Jane looks a little reluctant to acknowledge the toast, even if everyone else takes a hearty gulp. I know my daughter too well and I can see something is bothering her. Which bothers me. That's the burden of motherhood: No matter how old your kids get, their problems are always your problems.

I lean toward my daughter and ask quietly: "What is it, Janie?"

"It's just been a long, frustrating investigation."

"Want to talk about it?"

"No, it's nothing. Just annoying details."

I put down my wineglass. "I raised the smartest cop in the world . . ." I pause, suddenly aware that her partner Barry is also listening, but he takes no offense and merely gives a good-natured salute.

"No argument there, Mrs. Rizzoli."

"Okay, I raised one of the *two* smartest cops in the world," I correct myself. "You inherited those detective chops from someone, and I don't think it was your father."

Jane snorts. "I don't think so either."

"So maybe you got it from me. Maybe I can shed a little light on your case. Give a fresh perspective on things, what do you think?"

"I'm not so sure, Ma."

"I may not be a cop, and I know it's easy to underestimate me because I'm an older woman and all, but—"

"*That,*" Alice interjects, waving her wineglass in the air, "is society's fault. We women lose all our value when we age beyond our reproductive prime."

"Yeah, okay. I don't know about that reproductive prime stuff. I just like being listened to." I look at Jane. "If something's bothering you, I might be able to help."

Jane sighs. "I don't know *what's* bothering me."

"But you know something's not right, is that it? Yeah, I get that. The same way I knew something wasn't right when your brother Frankie told me he was spending the night at Mike Popovich's house and he was really down by the quarry smoking pot. I knew it because I have instincts."

"I just have to think about it," she says.

And I can see her doing just that as we move on to tiramisu for dessert and I polish off a fourth glass of wine. She's had only one glass all evening because she's my designated driver. That's the public servant in her. She's dedicated to enforcing the law, which means she hasn't really relaxed all evening. And her mind is clearly somewhere else.

She's still distracted when we climb into her car and buckle up. She and Gabriel drove here separately, and he's taking Regina straight home to bed, so it's just me and Jane sitting together. I wish I had more time alone with my daughter. Life moves too fast, she is too busy, and when I do have Jane to myself, she always seems in a rush to be somewhere else.

"That was some dinner, hey, Ma?" she says.

"Alice picked a good one." I pat the precious box of leftovers on my lap. "I guess that woman isn't all hot air."

"That sounds suspiciously like a compliment."

"I wouldn't go that far." I look out the window at Alice and Barry, climbing into their car. A man as nice as Barry deserves a kinder woman, but when it comes to love, there's no accounting for taste.

Jane starts the car and we pull out of the restaurant parking lot.

Up ahead, there's a cruiser with flashing lights that's just pulled over a pickup truck and they've both stopped at the side of the road. Naturally, Jane slows down to scope out the situation, to see if it's something requiring her intervention. That's my daughter, always sniffing for trouble.

The way I do.

"I think the Greens must have moved out," I say.

"Yeah?" she asks. She's not really listening to me because her attention is still focused on the stopped cruiser.

"I haven't seen either one of them for a few days. But I have seen lights on inside the house, so I think they must have one of those automatic timers. The ones that turn on your lights when it gets dark, to scare away burglars."

"Ma, with you watching that house all the time, a burglar doesn't have a chance."

That makes me laugh. "Yeah. I think you're right."

"*When you see something, say something.* You take that to a whole new level." Satisfied that the cruiser has things under control, she drives past it. "The Greens probably got fed up with you spying on them."

"I'm just keeping an eye on my neighborhood. If I didn't, Larry Leopold would be dead now and Rick Talley would be facing a murder charge."

"Have you spoken to Jackie yet?"

"I think she's too embarrassed to talk to me."

"Because of her affair, you mean?"

"No, I think it's more because of *who* she had the affair with. Larry *Leopold*? Really?" I snort.

"You just never know, Ma. He might be a tiger in bed."

Just for an instant I think about Jonas and his sculpted pectorals. I admit, he did catch my eye. I also admit that in a weak moment, with a few too many martinis under my belt, I *might* have entertained some carnal thoughts. Luckily, Agnes has set me straight. From the beginning, Agnes saw right through him.

Now I feel guilty for not inviting her to dinner tonight. As annoying as Agnes can be, she stood by me in my time of crisis. Gasping for breath, to be sure, but she *did* stand by me.

When Jane drops me off at home, I notice that Agnes's lights are still on. I know she keeps late hours and she's probably sitting in front of her TV right now, smoking her beloved Virginia Slims. She'd probably welcome my company. And my precious leftovers.

I go next door and ring the bell.

"Angie!" she croaks when she sees me on her doorstep. I take a step back, overwhelmed by the cloud of cigarette smoke pouring out of her house like a five-alarm fire. "I just poured myself a glass! Come in and join me."

"I brought the snacks," I say and hold up my box of leftovers.

"I could use some snacks about now." She reaches for a bottle of whiskey on her coffee table. "Want me to pour you a double?"

"Why not?"

The next morning, I pay for it.

I wake up with a pounding headache and a vague memory of our finishing off her bottle of Jameson. The sun is up, the light in my bedroom is blinding, and I can barely open my eyes in the glare. I look at the clock and groan when I see it's already noon. Never again will I try to keep up with Agnes. Some superhero I am, when a seventy-eight-year-old woman can drink me under the table.

I sit up, rubbing my temples. Through the pounding in my head I hear the chime of the doorbell.

The last thing I want is visitors, but I'm expecting a package from Vince so I slide my feet into slippers and shuffle to the foyer. I'm taken aback when I open the front door and find Tricia Talley standing outside instead of the UPS guy. These past few weeks she's put her parents through hell; now she's standing on my porch, her eyes downcast, her shoulders slumped.

"I found this wedged in your door," she says and hands me an advertising circular for the local pizza joint.

"Tricia." I sigh. "I know you're not here just to hand me coupons."

"No."

"You want to come in?"

"Yeah. I guess."

"Look, can you just wait in the living room for a few minutes? I had a really late night, so give me a chance to get dressed, and I'll be right out."

I go back to my bedroom to splash water on my face and comb my hair. As I pull on jeans and a fresh blouse, I wonder why on earth that girl has suddenly turned up to talk to me. *Is* that why she's here, just to talk? Or will I walk out to discover she's made off with my silver or something? With teenagers, you just never know.

When I come back out, she's not in the living room where I left her. I smell coffee brewing and I follow the scent to the kitchen, where Tricia is standing at the counter, pouring coffee for both of us. She sets the cups on the table and sits, looking at me expectantly. I don't remember my kids drinking coffee at age sixteen, but obviously she not only drinks it, she knows how to brew it.

Point for Tricia.

As I sit down, I see her hands clenching and unclenching, as if she can't decide whether fists are necessary for this particular conversation.

"It's my fault, what happened," she says. "I mean, I'm not the one who screwed up everything in the first place, but I *did* make it all worse."

"I'm not quite following this conversation."

"It's all because of biology class."

"Now I'm *really* not following it."

"See, just before the school year ended, we did this lab about genetics. We had to poke ourselves in the finger and collect our own blood." She winces at the memory. "I hated that. Sticking myself."

I nod in sympathy. "I could never do it myself. My lab partner had to poke me."

She frowns. "*You* did biology?"

"Yes, Tricia. Believe it or not, I was in high school once. I got in fights with my parents too. And by the way, I was a very popular girl. What does all this stuff about biology class have to do with anything?"

"We were studying blood types. You know, A, B, O. And after we poked ourselves, we were supposed to type our own blood. I found out I'm B positive. Which is, like, nine percent of the population. Not that unusual."

"Okay."

"So then, 'cause we're learning about principles of genetics and how blood types are inherited, I wanted to find out my mom's and dad's blood types, for an extra-credit paper."

Uh-oh. And that is where our education system fails us. It doesn't foresee disasters. It doesn't plan for the consequences of too much knowledge.

"My mom keeps her blood donor card in her wallet, so I already knew she was A positive. Then I asked my dad, and he told me he was O positive. That's when I knew." She took a deep breath. "There is *no* possible way you can cross an A positive mother with an O positive dad and end up with a B positive kid, okay?" With an angry swipe of her hand, she dashed away tears. "My mom denied it, but I knew she was lying. I couldn't stand to look at her. I couldn't stand to see her and my dad together, pretending everything was fine, while all the time I knew." She looks straight at me. "That's why I took off. I had to get away from them for a while. But I *did* call my dad, to let him know I was okay. He tracked me down at my friend's house and started yelling at me about how ungrateful I am and what a little shit I am, and I just couldn't hold it in. I told him he isn't even my dad. I told him we've all been living a lie."

"*You're* the one who told him?"

Her head drooped. "That was a mistake."

"Then he didn't hear this from any private detective."

"What private detective?"

"The man in the white van."

"I don't know about any white van. I just know that I shouldn't have told him. I should have kept the secret, let him go on thinking nothing was wrong. Let him believe that we're just one big fake happy family. But I couldn't keep it in."

"Did you also tell him Larry is your dad?"

"No, I didn't know it was *him*." She makes a face, a

look of disgust that is absolutely appropriate. What other face would you make when you discover you share genes with Larry Leopold? "I can't believe my mom—and *him* . . ." She shudders.

"Then how did Rick find out?"

"My mom finally confessed. That evening, she told him who the man was. And that's why all this happened. Why my dad drove to Larry's house."

"Oh, Tricia. What a mess."

"I know. I know." She sighs. "And it could've been worse, so much worse, if you hadn't been there to stop him, Mrs. Rizzoli. He might've *killed* Larry. Then he would've ended up in jail for the rest of his life. All because of me."

"No, honey. It's not because of you. Don't ever blame yourself for this. It's the grown-ups who messed up here." I pause. "It's usually the grown-ups."

She drops her head into her hands and cries silent tears. She is so unlike my own daughter when she was a teenager. My Janie didn't cry silent tears. If she got punched, she didn't cry; she punched right back. But Tricia is a far more sensitive girl, and she is going to need her mother's help to get through this.

I need to call Jackie. It's going to be an uncomfortable conversation because she doesn't know how much I know about her family, but she and Tricia need each other, and I may have to be the one to shove them back into each other's arms.

I walk Tricia to the front door and as she walks away down the street, I think about what I will say to Jackie on the phone. Nothing judgmental; she already knows she screwed up (and with *Larry Leopold*!) but now she needs a friend. For a moment I pause on my porch, surveying the neighborhood, girding myself to make the dreaded phone call. Even though everything looks the same, somehow the street seems different. The Leopolds' garden is as well-tended as it's always been, but inside that house is a marriage in crisis. Jonas, the man formerly known as our neighborhood Navy SEAL, is not at his usual spot in the window lifting weights. He's probably afraid to show his face, now that he's been exposed as the fraud he is. And the Greens? Even on this bright and beautiful Sunday, their blinds are closed, their secrets tucked away.

I'm about to step back into my house when I spot a familiar white van approaching. It's the same van that keeps driving down my street, the one I saw a few nights ago parked outside the Leopolds' house. I had assumed it belonged to some private investigator that Rick hired, but now I know that isn't true. So who is driving the van, and why is it back in my neighborhood?

Slowly it cruises past my house and pulls over to the curb a few houses down. There it just sits, its engine turned off. Why isn't the driver getting out? What is he waiting for?

I can't stand the uncertainty any longer. I'm the woman who faced down a gunman, who saved Larry Leopold's life. Surely I can solve this little mystery.

I grab my cell phone and step outside. It's the first time the van has stopped here long enough in the daytime for me to get a good look at it. I snap a photo of the rear license plate, then I go to the driver's door and tap on his window.

"Hello?" I call out. "Hello?"

He glances up from his cell phone and stares at me.

He's a blond man in his thirties with bulked-up shoulders and no smile. Absolutely no smile.

"Who do you work for?" I ask.

He just keeps staring at me, as if I'm speaking a foreign language.

"Because it's my job to keep an eye on this neighborhood. I've seen you on this street a number of times now, and I'd like to know your business here."

I don't think I'm getting through to him, because he still doesn't answer me. Maybe it's because all he sees is a middle-aged housewife, someone he can simply ignore. I've been ignored too long and I'm tired of it. I stand up straight. It's time to channel my daughter's voice, my daughter's authority. What would a cop say?

"I'm going to have to call this in," I tell him.

That does the trick. "I have a delivery," he finally says. "Flowers."

"For who?"

"Let me check the name again. It's on the clipboard in back."

He steps out of the van. He's even bigger than he looked in the driver's seat, and as I follow him to the rear of the van, I feel like I'm walking behind Hercules.

"Maybe you can take a look at the name on the card," he says. "Tell me if I'm at the right address?"

"Show me."

He opens the rear door and steps aside so I can look in at the flowers.

Only there are no flowers. There's just an empty van.

A hand clamps over my mouth. I try to twist free, try to fight back, but I'm wrestling with a wall of muscle. My phone clatters to the ground as he lifts me off my feet and heaves me into the back. He climbs in and yanks the door shut, trapping me inside with him. After the glare of sunshine, the van seems so dark I can barely make out his figure bent over me. I hear the screech of duct tape.

Just as I draw in a breath to scream, he slaps the tape over my mouth. Rolls me over onto my belly, and savagely yanks my hands together behind my back. In seconds he binds my wrists and ankles, working with swift and brutal efficiency.

A professional. Which means I'm going to die.

THIRTY-SIX

JANE

"I KNEW SOMETHING WASN'T RIGHT AS SOON as I saw that cell phone lying out here in the street," said Agnes Kaminsky. "I knocked on her door and she didn't answer, but the door wasn't locked. Your mother *always* locks her door because of all the horror stories you tell her. That's why I called you."

With a mounting sense of alarm, Jane examined her mother's cell phone. There was a photo of Regina on the cell phone case, which left no doubt this was indeed Angela's phone. She wanted to believe there was a perfectly benign reason for why it had been lying in the street, that perhaps her mother had gone out for a walk and simply dropped it, but that did not explain why she'd left her front door unlocked. When your daughter is a homicide cop, when your boyfriend is a retired cop, and you've heard all their stories about predators in the big city, you never fail to lock your door.

"Her house is fine inside," said Agnes. "Nobody's robbed it."

"You've already been inside?"

"Well, I had to check. We ladies living alone have to keep an eye on each other."

Just a few weeks ago, Agnes and Angela weren't even

speaking to each other. Now it seemed they were best buddies. Life moved fast.

"She didn't make her bed but she *did* make coffee and the pot's still warm," said Agnes. "And there are two cups on the kitchen table, so she had a visitor. If that means anything."

Jane stepped into the house with Agnes tagging along, trailing her usual miasma of cigarette smoke. There on the foyer table, in its regular place, was Angela's purse and her house keys. Another bad sign. They headed into the kitchen, where the carafe was indeed still warm. And on the table were two empty coffee mugs, just as Agnes had described.

Someone visited this morning. Someone who'd sat down at this table and sipped coffee with Angela.

"You see?" said Agnes. "It's just like I told you."

Jane turned to her. "Did you see who was visiting?"

"No. I was busy watching QVC. They're selling these newfangled vacuum cleaners and I think I might want one." She pointed to the cell phone. "Don't you know how to unlock that thing? Maybe she called someone or someone called her. Maybe that's the vital clue."

Jane frowned at her mother's phone. It required a six-digit code to unlock it. *She's my mother. I should know this.* She typed in her mother's birthdate. Wrong code. She typed her own birthdate. Wrong code.

"That's your little girl, right?" said Agnes.

"What?"

"On the phone case. That's her picture. Before she started going to preschool, she was here with your mother almost every day. Angie misses her something awful."

Of course, thought Jane, and she typed in Regina's birthdate.

The phone magically unlocked and opened to the screen that had last been in use: the camera. She clicked on the most recent image. The photo was the back of a white van, and it was taken two hours ago, at 1:12 P.M.

"That's our street," said Agnes, leaning in to look at the screen. "It's right out front."

Jane went outside to the sidewalk and stood at about the same spot her mother had been standing when the photo was taken. There was no van there now, only an empty curb. She zoomed in on the image and the license number filled the screen. A Massachusetts plate. *Why did you take this photo, Mom? Is this why you've vanished?*

"Oh my god," said Agnes, staring across the street. "It's him."

The mysterious Matthew Green had just stepped out of his house. He walked straight toward them, moving like a man primed for battle, his stride deliberate, his shoulders squared. Mirrored sunglasses hid his eyes and Jane could not read his expression, but she had no trouble spotting the telltale outline of the concealed weapon under his shirt. As he approached, Jane resisted the impulse to reach for her own gun. This was broad daylight, after all, and standing right beside her was a witness, even if it was only Agnes Kaminsky.

"Detective Jane Rizzoli?" he said.

"Yes."

"I gather you're searching for your mother."

"Yes, I am. Do you know where she is, Mr. Green?"

"I'm not entirely certain." He pulled off his sunglasses and stared straight at her, his face as unreadable as a cyborg's. "But I think I can help you find her."

THIRTY-SEVEN

ANGELA

WHENEVER I USED TO THINK OF MY DEATH, I assumed it would be many years from now. I imagined myself lying at home in my own bed, surrounded by my loving family. Or maybe in a hospital room, tended by nurses. Or best of all, I would go suddenly and painlessly, killed by a stroke while lying on a warm beach with a mai tai in my hand. Never in my imagination did duct tape ever come into the picture.

Yet this is how it's going to end, with my hands and feet bound, strangled in the back of this van. Or maybe he'll drag me out to some remote location and put a bullet in my head. That's how professionals do it, and I believe that's who's now in the driver's seat, delivering me to my grave. A professional.

How did I get this so wrong? While I was focused on Tricia and the Leopolds and the mysterious Greens, something entirely different was going on right under my nose, something that drew this van back again and again to our neighborhood. It wasn't there to spy on Larry Leopold; it was there for another reason, which I still haven't figured out. Not that it makes a difference, not now.

I keep trying to twist myself free but duct tape is unyielding, the strongest material in the universe. Exhausted, I give in to despair. This is what I get for poking my nose into other people's business. I got lucky with the Leopolds when I didn't get shot. It made me cocky, and now I'm going to pay for it.

The van swerves around a corner and the momentum sends me rolling sideways, slamming my head against the side. Pain shoots down my neck, as excruciating as a jolt of electricity. It leaves me whimpering, weak and defeated. How can I fight back when I can't even move my arms?

The van rolls to a stop.

Through the pounding of my heart, I hear the driver's door open and slam shut. The thud reverberates, which tells me we are not in the outdoors but enclosed in a building. Maybe a warehouse? The driver doesn't open the rear door; he simply walks away, his footsteps echoing on concrete, and leaves me tied up in the vehicle. Faintly I hear him talking to someone, but there's no other voice. He must be on the phone and he sounds agitated, upset. Are they talking about what to do with me?

His voice fades away and there's silence. For the moment it seems I've been forgotten.

Now that I'm not being tossed side to side in traffic, I can finally sit up, but middle age and stiff joints make it a struggle just to right myself. Sitting up is about all I can manage. I can't scream, I can't free my hands or feet, and I'm trapped in a locked metal box.

Eventually *someone* will notice I've gone missing, but how long will it take? Will Vince wonder why I'm not answering the phone and will he call Jane? Will Agnes pop by to thank me for the leftovers? I run through all the possible scenarios that end with me staying alive, but I keep crashing into the insurmountable barrier that even if they *did* go looking for me, no one knows where I am.

Oh, Angie, you really are dead.

Panic makes me twist again at the duct tape. Sobbing and sweating, I twist so hard, so desperately, that my fingers go numb. I've lost track of the time, but it feels like hours. Maybe he's not coming back. Maybe *this* is how it ends, with me mummified in an abandoned van.

And I never even ate breakfast.

I slump back in exhaustion. Janie, I know you expect more of me but I can't do this. I can't save myself.

The air has grown hot and stale and I fight to catch my breath. Or maybe it's just panic. Calm down, calm down. I close my eyes and try to slow my breathing.

Then a second vehicle arrives and I jerk up straight.

I hear the growl of its engine, the squeal of its tires braking on concrete as it rolls into the building. The engine shuts off and car doors slam shut.

The van's rear door swings open and a man stands looking in at me. His face is backlit so I can't read his expression, but I can make out a silhouette of a thick waist and short, fat neck.

"Get her out of there. I want to talk to her," he says.

A second man reaches in with a knife, slashes the duct tape that binds my ankles and wrists, and drags me out feetfirst. I've been tied up for so long that my legs are stiff and I wobble as I stand facing three men. One is the van driver who snatched me off my street. The other two have just arrived in a black Escalade SUV that's now parked next to the van. No one is smiling. It's easy to tell that the older, fatter man is the one in charge. As the younger men stand flanking him, the boss steps toward me until we're almost nose to nose. He's in his fifties, with pale blue eyes and close-cropped blond hair and he reeks of aftershave. An expensive scent, I imagine, but he's slapped it on with an undiscriminating hand.

"So where is she?" he asks.

I mumble behind the duct tape that still covers my mouth. With no warning he yanks off the tape and I'm so startled that I jerk away and the backs of my knees collide with the van's rear bumper. There's no room for me to retreat. I'm trapped between the vehicle and this aftershave-drenched man.

"Where is she?" he repeats.

"Who?" I ask.

"Nina."

"I don't know anyone named Nina."

To my surprise he laughs and looks at the other two men. "This must be the new strategy they're teaching them now. How to play dumb."

"I'm not playing dumb." *I really am dumb.*

He turns to the van driver. "You got her ID?"

The driver shakes his head. "Didn't have any on her."

"Then she'll just have to tell us herself." The big man turns back to me. "Who do you work for?"

"What? No one. I'm just a—"

"Which agency?"

Agency? Slowly it's starting to sink in. They think I'm someone else. Or something other than what I am, a housewife.

"Where are you people hiding her?"

If I tell them the truth, that I have no idea, then I'm

worthless to them. As long as they think I know something valuable, they'll let me live. They may break my bones and yank out my fingernails but they won't kill me. Which is good news, I suppose.

I don't see the blow coming. He hits me so fast, so unexpectedly, that I have no chance to brace myself. His fist thuds into my cheek and I stagger sideways, lights exploding in my head. When I'm able to focus again, I see him looming over me, his lip curled in a sneer.

"Aren't you too old for this business, lady?" he says.

"Aren't you?" The words are out of my mouth before I can stop myself and I cringe as his hand comes up to deliver another blow. Then he stops, lowers his fist.

"Maybe we got off on the wrong foot," he says. He grabs my hand and hauls me back to my feet. "You know, a little cooperation on your part will make things a lot easier. It may even be worth your while, in a monetary sense. I can't imagine retirement on a government salary is anything to crow about."

Gingerly I touch my cheek where he hit me. There's no blood but I can feel the tissues already ballooning up. I'm going to have a hell of a shiner. If I live long enough.

"Tell me where you moved Nina," he says.

We're back to this mysterious Nina again. I can't let him know that I have no idea who she is. I have to bluff my way through this.

"Nina doesn't want to be found," I say.

"Tell me something I don't know."

"She's terrified, in fact."

"She ought to be. I expect loyalty from my employees and talking to the feds is the *height* of disloyalty." He glances at the men standing beside him. "*They* understand."

"But Nina didn't."

"She'll never make it to that courtroom. No matter how many times you people move her, I'm gonna find her. But you know, it does get wearisome." His voice softens, becomes friendly, almost intimate. "Devoting so many of my resources to tracking down the bitch. This time it took me four entire weeks to track her down. Forced me to call in a favor from Revere PD."

Four weeks. It all becomes clear. Four weeks ago was when the Greens moved into the house across the street. The Greens, who kept their window blinds closed and their garage door shut. Who never said boo to me. I think of the nervous woman who called herself Carrie Green, but that's not her real name.

It's Nina, and clearly she knows enough to send this man to prison. If he doesn't kill her first.

"Let's make this nice and easy," the man says, once again leaning in, his voice low and coaxing. "You help me, I help you."

"And if I don't?"

He glances at his men. "What do you think, boys? Bury her alive? Trash compactor?"

A bullet in the head is starting to sound good.

He turns back to me. "Let's try this again. Tell me where you've got her and I'll let you live. I might even keep you on retainer. I could use another set of eyes and ears on the inside. Who did you say you work for?"

"She didn't say," the van driver says. "But I could smell a cop. The way she spoke to me. The way she came at me, like she fucking owned the street."

And that was my mistake, thinking that I'm a genuine action hero when really, I'm just a housewife in Revere. It's too bad I was so convincing. Now I'm going to die because I have no idea where Nina/Carrie is.

But they don't have to know that.

"Let me guess. FBI?" the big man asks me.

I don't answer. This time I see his hand coming, but even though I'm ready for it, the blow is every bit as stunning as the first one. I stagger sideways, my jaw throbbing. My lip stings and when I touch it, I see blood on my fingers.

"I'll ask again. Are you FBI?" he says.

I draw in a breath. Whisper: "Boston PD."

"Now we're getting somewhere."

I'm too demoralized to say a word. I stare down at my blood dripping onto the concrete, blood that will be silent testimony long after I'm dead. I imagine crime scene technicians scouring this warehouse days or weeks or even years from now, staring at the evidence of my demise glowing at their feet. I won't be able to tell them what happened, but my blood will.

And Jane will take it from there. That is one thing I know I can count on: My daughter will see that justice is done.

"Let's try this again," he says. "Where is Nina?"

I merely shake my head.

"Kill her," he says and turns to walk away.

One of the men pulls out his gun and steps forward.

"Wait," I say.

The big man turns back.

"The Colonnade Hotel," I blurt. The name pops into my head only because it's where Agnes Kaminsky's grandniece had her wedding reception. I remember the three-tiered cake and champagne and the startlingly short groom. It's just a Hail Mary answer, one that they'll be able to knock down with a quick visit to the hotel, but it's all I can come up with to delay the inevitable.

"What name is she registered under?"

"Kaminsky," I answer, hoping there isn't really anyone named Kaminsky staying there.

He glances at the van driver. "Get over there. Check it out."

And that will be the end of this charade, I think. When he finds out I've been bluffing and the woman they're hunting for isn't there. I can't think of anything else I can say or do to save myself. I can think only of the people I love and how I'll never see them again.

The driver climbs into the van and pulls out of the warehouse. A half hour, an hour at the most, I think. That's all it will take to expose me as a liar. I glance around, looking for an escape route. I see construction equipment—a cement truck, an earthmover—but there is no exit except for the open bay door which is now blocked by the men.

The big man drags over a crate and sits down. He looks at his knuckles and gives his hand a shake. The asshole bruised himself hitting me. Good. He looks at his watch, scratches his nose, ordinary gestures by an ordinary-looking man. He doesn't look like a monster but he is, and I think about how courageous Nina is, to go up against him. I remember her nervous face and the note she left on my porch, asking me to leave them alone. All this time I thought she was afraid of her husband, when she was really afraid of these men.

I flinch at the sound of his ringing cell phone. He pulls it from his pocket and says: "Yeah?"

And now it ends. He's going to hear there's no Ka-

minsky registered at the Colonnade. He'll know I'm
lying.

"Who is this?" he snaps. "How did you get this
number?"

The roar of an engine makes both men whip around
toward the open bay door as a black SUV comes hurtling into the warehouse. It screeches to a stop just
inches from the men.

This is my chance. Maybe my only chance. I take it.

I'm blocked from fleeing through the bay door, so I
slip around behind the Escalade and dart toward the
cement truck.

"What the fuck?" yells the man.

I'm crouched behind the cement truck so I can't see
what's going on, but I hear other tires screeching to a
stop as more vehicles skid into the building. I hear
shouts and the thud of boots landing on concrete.

And gunfire. Oh Jesus, it's a mob execution. And I'm
right in the middle of it.

I scramble further into the warehouse and dive un-
derneath an earthmover. They're too busy fighting for
their own lives; maybe they'll forget I'm here. And after
they've finished shooting one another, after all the bodies have fallen, I can creep out and slip away. Escape the
carnage. I curl into a tight ball, cover my head, and si-
lently chant the mantra: They can't see me. I'm invisible. I'm invisible.

My arms are so tightly wrapped around my head that
it takes a moment for me to realize the shooting has
stopped. That no one's yelling anymore. Like a tortoise
slowly emerging from its shell, I cautiously poke my
head out and hear . . .

Silence.

No, it's not entirely silent. Footsteps move closer. From beneath the earthmover, I see a pair of shoes halt right beside where I am hiding. Black ankle boots, narrow and scuffed and strangely familiar.

"Mom?"

Jane's face suddenly peers at me beneath the earthmover. We stare at each other and for a moment I think I am hallucinating. How is this possible? My brilliant, relentless daughter has magically arrived. She's come to rescue me.

"Hey, are you okay?" she says.

I crawl out from beneath the earthmover and haul her into my arms. I can't remember the last time I hugged my daughter this hard. Not since years and years ago, when she was still a little girl, when I could sweep her up off her feet into my arms. She is too big for that now, but I can still try, and as her heels lift off the floor, I hear her laugh. "Whoa, Ma!"

I used to be the one who came to her rescue, who patched up skinned knees and brought down fevers. Now she's the one who rescues me, and I have never been so grateful to have this girl, this daughter.

"Ma." She pulls away and stares at my battered face. "What the fuck did they *do* to you?"

"Knocked me around a little. But I'm okay."

She turns and yells: "Greeley! I found her!"

"Who's Greeley?" I ask.

Then I see him striding toward us, the man I once knew as Matthew Green. He looks me up and down, coolly tallying up my damage. "You think you need an ambulance, Mrs. Rizzoli?" he asks.

"I just want to go home," I say.

"That's what I thought you'd say. Let's have your

daughter take you home and get you cleaned up. And then you and I need to have a chat." He turns to leave.

"About Nina?" I ask.

He halts. Turns back to face me. "What do you know about her?"

"I know she's going to testify against him. I know that if he ever finds her, she's a dead woman. I know he has a snitch inside Revere PD feeding him information, so you better check into that. And one of his men is over at the Colonnade right now, looking for her."

He regards me for a moment, as if seeing me—really seeing me—for the first time. The corner of his mouth tilts up. "I guess there's more to you than meets the eye." He turns to Jane. "Please take her home, Detective. And keep her out of my hair. If you can."

"What about Nina?" I call out as he turns away.

"She'll be fine now."

"How do you know that?"

"Trust me."

"Why should I? And is Greeley even your real name?"

He raises his hand in a careless wave and just keeps walking away.

"Come on, Ma," says Jane. "I'll take you home."

Now that I'm no longer terrified, my cheekbone is really starting to ache. Maybe I do need an ambulance, but I'm too proud to admit it, so I just let Jane lead me away from the earthmover, toward the bay door, where a dozen officers wearing vests labeled *U.S. Marshal* are milling around.

"Don't look, Ma," Jane warns me.

So of course I have to look. At the blood spattering the concrete floor. At the two bodies lying at the officers' feet. So this is why Greeley said Nina will be fine. Because the man who's been hunting her now lies dead, shot to death in a gun battle with U.S. Marshals. I can still smell his stinky aftershave.

I pause, staring down at the man who'd battered my face, who'd breezily ordered me killed, and I want to give that corpse a good, hard kick. But I have my dignity, and all these officers are watching. So I just keep walking out of the warehouse and climb into my daughter's car.

A FEW HOURS LATER, AFTER A HEFTY DOSE of Advil and with a bag of frozen peas pressed to my cheek, I'm feeling much better. Jane and I sit in the living room, and this alone is a treat because my daughter doesn't often take the time to just be with me. Usually she's distracted by her job or by Regina or by the thousand other things she really ought to be doing instead of hanging out with her mother. But this afternoon she seems content to drink tea and just . . . talk. About what happened today. About the people formerly known as Matthew and Carrie Green.

"So that's why their blinds were always down," I say. "Why he was carrying a weapon. Why he installed bars on the windows. Why he never mixed with the rest of the neighborhood."

"She was their star witness, Ma, and they had to keep her alive. They'd moved her twice before, but somehow he always tracked her down."

"Because he had someone in Revere PD tipping him off."

Jane nods. "They know that now, thanks to you. And they'll find out who the hell it is."

I feel a nice little rush, hearing praise from my daughter, the cop.

"Greeley got alarmed when he saw the van two weeks ago," she says. "So they moved her to another safe house."

"But *someone* was still living across the street. I saw the lights."

"He stayed behind, to make it look occupied. To keep an eye out for that van. Then you walked into the operation."

"And screwed things up, I guess."

"No, Ma. You gave them a reason to finally move in and arrest him. They just needed to nail their target with a charge he couldn't wriggle out of, and now they had a charge of kidnapping. They'd already put a tracker on his Escalade, so they followed it straight to you. When he started shooting, he left them with only one option. To shoot back. No trial necessary now."

"Remember what I said when you were a kid? About making bad choices?"

Jane laughs. "Yeah, that was a bad choice. Kidnapping *you*."

I look out the window at the house across the street. No one lives there now, and I have to admit I miss the Greens. I miss all the mystery, all the tantalizing possibilities. Now it's just my boring old neighborhood where the only mystery I've managed to solve is who was schtupping whom.

"Speaking of people who make bad choices," I say, "I finally got the whole story about why Rick Talley shot Larry Leopold. All this time, I thought Rick hired a PI and that's how he found out about the affair. But it was Tricia who told him."

"*Tricia* knew?"

"She came here to thank me for stopping her dad from killing Larry."

"How did Tricia find out about the affair?"

"Biology class. They were learning about genetics and they had to type their own blood. Tricia's a B positive and her mom's an A positive. The problem is, Rick's an O positive, which means he couldn't be her biological dad. That's why she was so pissed off at her mother. She told Rick, then Rick found out who it was, and that's why he showed up at Larry's house."

For a long time Jane is silent and I can see she's thinking about something else. That's how it always goes. I talk and her mind wanders to other things. Things that are more important than what her mother's saying. Any minute now, she'll find an excuse to end this boring conversation and get away.

"Jesus, Ma," she says and suddenly jumps up from her chair.

"I know," I sigh. "You have to leave."

"You just cracked it! Thank you!"

"What? What did I say?"

"Blood types! I should have realized this was all about *blood types*." She heads to the door. "I've got a lot of work to do."

"What are you talking about?"

"Sofia Suarez. I had it all wrong."

THIRTY-EIGHT

AMY

DETECTIVE RIZZOLI WAS BACK. THROUGH THE FOYER window, Amy could see her standing at the front door and she wondered why, weeks after they last spoke, she had returned. Perhaps there were some final details to clear up before the case was officially closed, a few last *T*s to cross and *I*s to dot.

Amy opened the door and greeted Jane with a smile. "I didn't know you'd be coming by today. It's so nice to see you again."

"I thought I'd check in to see how you and your mom are doing."

"We're fine, thanks to you. We're both sleeping a lot better now that it's all over. Please, come in."

"Your mom around?" Rizzoli asked as she stepped inside.

"She just ran out to get some groceries, but she'll be back soon. Did you want to talk to her?"

"Yes. And to you too."

"Let's go into the kitchen. I was about to make a pot of tea. Would you like some?"

"That'd be great, thanks."

They went into the kitchen, where Amy put the kettle on. It was something her mother taught her long ago: In the morning you offer your guest coffee, in the afternoon you offer tea. Either way, you must always offer your visitor something to drink. As Amy waited for the water to boil, she saw Detective Rizzoli type out a text and then take a thoughtful look around the kitchen. It was as if she were seeing it for the first time, although this was certainly not Rizzoli's first visit to their house. Maybe she was just admiring the stainless steel Sub-Zero refrigerator or the six-burner Viking stove, appliances that her mother was very proud of.

"She's quite a cook, isn't she? Your mom."

"She makes everything from scratch. It's a point of pride for her," said Amy, opening up a plastic container of Julianne's lemon bars.

"How did she learn to cook?"

"I don't know. She's just always done it. It's how she paid the bills when I was a kid. Worked in restaurants, coffee shops."

"I heard that's how she met Dr. Antrim. At the café across from the hospital."

Amy laughed. "I've heard that story a thousand times."

"That was right after you moved to Boston?"

"I was nine years old. We lived in this horrible little apartment in Dorchester back then. Then Mom met Dad and everything changed." Amy arranged the lemon bars on a pretty china plate and placed them on the table. *Presentation is half the appeal,* her mother always said.

"Where did you and your mom live before that? Before Boston?"

"A lot of different places. Worcester. Upstate New York."

"And Vermont. That's where you were born, isn't it?"

"Well, I don't remember *that* far back."

"Do you remember living in Maine?"

"We never lived there." Amy spooned oolong leaves into a teapot, poured in hot water, and left it to steep.

"But you have been there."

"Once, on vacation. Dad wanted to tour the lighthouses and it rained all week. We've never been back."

They sat at the table for a moment as the kitchen clock ticked and the tea steeped. With all this small talk, it seemed they were just killing time and Detective Rizzoli must really be here to see Julianne. The tea wasn't quite ready, but she poured it into two cups anyway, slid one to her visitor, and lifted her cup to her lips.

"Before you take a sip of that tea, I need to get a mouth swab from you," Rizzoli said.

Amy set down her cup and frowned as Rizzoli pulled a swab out of her pocket and uncapped it. "Why? What is that for?"

"It's just for exclusionary purposes. The knife had blood from more than one individual on it and the lab needs DNA from everyone who was in the cabin."

"But you know my mom cut herself that night. So her blood *would* be on the knife."

"We need DNA from you as well. Just to close out the case. It's routine."

"Okay," Amy finally said.

Rizzoli collected the sample, recapped the swab, and slipped it into her pocket. "Now, tell me how you're doing, Amy. It must have been a rough few weeks for you. Being stalked by that man."

Amy cradled the warmth of her teacup. "I'm fine."

"Are you, really? Because it would be normal to have some measure of PTSD."

"I've had nightmares," Amy admitted. "Dad says the best thing I can do is to stay busy. Go back to school, finish my degree." She gave a rueful laugh. "Even if Mom wants me to stay home with her forever."

"Has she always been this protective?"

"Always." Amy smiled. "Before she met Dad, it was just her and me. I remember we used to sing this song in the car: *You and me against the world*."

"How far back *do* you remember?"

The question made Amy pause. The conversation had suddenly changed, taking a new direction that puzzled her. She felt unsettled by Rizzoli's intent look, as if she was hanging on Amy's every word. This no longer felt like a casual conversation over tea; it was starting to feel like an interrogation.

"Why are you asking all these questions?"

"Because I'm still trying to understand James Creighton's motives. Why did he stalk *you*? What made *you* so special to him, and when did he first see you?"

"At the cemetery."

"Or was it earlier? Is it possible, when you were very young, that James Creighton knew your mother?"

"No, she would have told me." Amy took a sip of tea, but it was already going cold. She noticed that Rizzoli had not touched her tea, but was simply sitting there, watching her.

"Tell me about your father, Amy. Not Dr. Antrim, but your real father."

"Why?"

"It's important."

"I try not to think of him. Ever."

"But you must remember him. When your mother married Mike Antrim, you were already ten years old. I saw the wedding photo in Dr. Antrim's study. You were the flower girl."

Amy nodded. "They got married at Lantern Lake."

"And your real father?"

"As far as I'm concerned, Mike Antrim is my *only* father."

"But there *was* another man, named Bruce Flagler. A carpenter who worked odd jobs, moving from town to town, repairing decks, renovating kitchens."

"What does Bruce have to do with this?"

"So you do remember his name."

"I try not to." Abruptly Amy rose to her feet and picked up her cell phone from the kitchen counter. "I'm going to text my mom to come home right now. She's the one who can answer your questions."

"I need to know what *you* remember."

"I don't *want* to! He was horrible."

"Your mother said you were eight years old when she split up with him. That's old enough for you to remember a lot of details."

"Yes, I was old enough to remember him hitting her. I remember her pushing me into my bedroom to keep me away from him."

"What happened to Bruce Flagler?"

"Ask my mother."

"Don't you know?"

Amy sat down and looked across the table at Jane. "What I do remember is the day we left him. The day we threw our clothes into a suitcase and jumped into the car. Mom told me everything would be okay, that we were going on a big adventure, just the two of us. Far enough away that he'd never find us, and we'd never be scared again."

"Where is he now?"

"I don't care. Why do you?"

"I need to find him, Amy."

"Why?"

"Because I believe he killed a woman nineteen years ago. He strangled her in her home and he took her three-year-old daughter. He needs to be in prison."

Amy's phone dinged. She looked down to see a text from her mother.

"Did your mother know what Bruce did? Is that why she left him?"

Amy tapped out a reply and put down her phone.

"Did she know the man she was living with was a murderer?" asked Jane.

They both heard the sound of a key in the front door and Amy jumped up. "She's home. Why don't you ask her?"

Julianne walked into the kitchen carrying a grocery sack and the scent of fresh basil wafted in with her. Glass bottles clinked as she set the sack down on the countertop and she flashed Jane a smile. "Detective Rizzoli, if I'd known you were coming to visit, I would've rushed home earlier."

"Amy and I were just catching up," said Rizzoli.

"She took a swab of my mouth, Mom," said Amy.

"From Amy?" Julianne frowned. "Whatever for? Now that this nightmare's all over—"

"Is that what you think? That it's all over?"

Julianne regarded Rizzoli for a moment and Amy did not like the long silence that followed. She didn't like how her mother's smile had vanished. Julianne's face was now unreadable, a blank mask that Amy had seen before, and she knew what it meant.

"I'm going to need a swab of your mouth too, Mrs. Antrim."

"But you already know my blood's on that knife. You saw the cut on my hand that night. I got it defending my daughter. Fighting off that man."

"His name was James Creighton."

"Whatever his name was!"

"I'm sure you knew his name, Mrs. Antrim. You also knew why he was so interested in your daughter. He had every reason to be."

"I don't know what you're talking about."

"Tell me about Amy's biological father. I believe his name was Bruce Flagler."

"We don't say that name. Not ever."

"Why not?"

"Because he was a mistake. The biggest mistake of my life. I was seventeen years old when I met him. It took me ten long years to finally get away."

"Where is Bruce now?"

"I have no idea. Probably beating up some other poor woman. If I hadn't left him when I did, I'd be dead. Maybe Amy would be too."

"You'd do anything for Amy, wouldn't you?"

"Of course." Julianne looked at Amy. "She's my daughter."

"But I don't think she is, Mrs. Antrim."

Amy looked back and forth at the two women, uncertain what to do. What to say. Her mother had gone very still, but there was no hint of panic in her face. "Amy," Julianne said calmly, "please go upstairs to my bedroom. Bring down our old photo album. The one with your baby pictures and your birth certificate. It's in the closet, up on the shelf. And bring me the passport. It's in my scarf drawer."

"Mom?" Amy said.

"Go, sweetheart. It's just a mix-up. Everything's going to be fine."

Amy's legs were trembling as she walked out of the kitchen and climbed the stairs to her parents' bedroom. She went straight to her mother's closet and reached up for the stack of photo albums on the shelf. She set them on the bed and found the album her mother wanted. She knew this was the right one because it was decades old and the binding had started to crumble, but she opened the cover just to be sure. On the first page was a picture of a young Julianne standing beneath an oak tree, cradling her black-haired infant in her arms. Facing that photo, on the inside front cover, was a certificate of live birth for Amy Wellman, born in the state of Vermont, weighing five pounds, six ounces. The line for the father's name was blank. She closed the album and sat on the bed for a moment, thinking about what would happen next. What her mother would do, what she must do.

She crossed the room to her mother's dresser and slid open the top drawer. Pushed aside the neatly folded silk scarves and reached in for what her mother had asked her to fetch.

THIRTY-NINE

JANE

"SHE DOESN'T KNOW, DOES SHE?" said Jane. "Who her real father was."

The two women sat facing each other across the kitchen table, the teapot and cups and the plate of lemon bars spread out between them. Such a calm and domestic setting for an interrogation.

"I'll show you her birth certificate," said Julianne. "I can show you photos of me holding her, right after she was born, and photos don't lie. I can prove I'm Amy's mother."

"I'm sure the photos are real, Mrs. Antrim. I'm sure you really are Amy's mother." Jane paused, her gaze fixed on Julianne. "But the real Amy's dead. Isn't she?"

Julianne went very still. Jane could almost see tiny cracks starting to form in that mask she had so carefully maintained.

"How did your real daughter die?" Jane asked quietly.

"She *is* my daughter."

"But she's not Amy. The remains of your daughter—the real Amy—were found two years ago, in a state park in Maine. They were just a short distance from where you once lived with your boyfriend, Bruce Flagler. A carpenter who helped renovate the kitchen of Professor Eloise Creighton. Bruce had a record of domestic abuse and we know he assaulted *you*. Is that how little Amy died? Did he kill her?"

Julianne said nothing.

"The police didn't know who those bones belonged to. To them, she was just Baby Girl Doe, left in a shallow grave in the woods. But now we know she did have a name: Amy. I can't imagine how horrible it must have been for you, losing that little girl. Knowing you were never going to hold her in your arms again. After something like that, I can't imagine even wanting to be alive."

"He said it was an accident," Julianne whispered. "He said she fell down the stairs. I could never be sure what the truth was . . ." She took a deep breath and stared out the window, as if looking back to that day. To that moment of loss. "I did want to die. I *tried* to die."

"Why didn't you go to the police?"

"I *would* have. But then that night, he brought her home. She was so small, so scared. She *needed* me."

"He brought you another little Amy, to keep you quiet. A replacement Amy for the one he broke. That's why you never told the police. Why you gave him an alibi for the night he kidnapped her, all so you could keep your new little girl. But she wasn't yours. Did Bruce ever tell you how he killed the mother? How he wrapped his hands around her throat?"

"He said he panicked. He said when the child screamed, the mother woke up, and all he could do was—"

"Strangle her, with the only weapon he had. His hands."

"I don't know how it happened! All I knew was this

little girl needed me to love her. Take care of her. It took time for her to forget the other woman, but she finally did. She learned to love *me*. She learned *I* was her mother."

"She also had a father, Julianne. A father who loved her too, and would never stop looking for her. So you and Bruce packed up and left Maine. You changed your names, moved on to Massachusetts, to New Hampshire, and finally to upstate New York. That's where you finally managed to leave him. You took your little girl and you moved to Boston, and here, for the first time in your life, everything finally goes right for you. You marry a decent man. You live in this nice house. It's all perfect—until Amy has her accident. It's a completely random bit of bad luck that put her in the hospital. But it changed everything."

Julianne's face revealed no nervous twitch, no glint of panic in her eyes, and Jane suddenly wondered if she'd gotten this all wrong. If Julianne would somehow pull out the proof of her own innocence.

No, I've got it right. I know I have.

"Amy ends up in the intensive care unit, where Sofia Suarez is her nurse. Sofia sees the scar on Amy's chest from a childhood heart operation. She sees that Amy has a rare blood type, AB negative. And she remembers a patient she took care of nineteen years ago. A three-year-old girl with AB negative blood who had heart surgery. She remembers that girl very clearly because of the shocking thing that happened to her. Little Lily Creighton was abducted from her home and never found. Now, nineteen years later, Sofia sees Amy's surgical scar, from an operation that's nowhere in her medical record. She notes her rare blood type."

"How can you possibly know all this?"

"Because Sofia Suarez left the clues I needed to put it all together: Her online search for blood types. Her search for James Creighton. Her call to an old nursing colleague in California, who also remembers the kidnapping of Lily very well. But Dr. Antrim was Sofia's friend, and she couldn't raise her suspicions with him. So she asked her questions quietly, questions that must have alarmed you. About why Amy's heart surgery wasn't mentioned in her medical record."

"It's because we moved so many times! Amy and I lived in different places, different states. Records get lost."

"And why didn't you donate blood to your own daughter, when she clearly needed it? Sofia must have wondered that too. I don't know what excuse you gave, but I do know the real reason. You couldn't give her blood because you're O positive, Julianne. Something Sofia found out when she called a friend in medical records to look in your chart. If you're not her mother, then who are Amy's *real* parents? Sofia knew the only way to find out is with DNA.

"So she searched for James Creighton. She tracked down his old address and sent a letter that was eventually forwarded to him. That's how he learned his daughter, Lily, might be alive. The man wasn't stalking a random woman. He was trying to find out if Amy was *his own daughter.*"

"Mom, I've got it," said Amy. She'd come back downstairs and she walked into the kitchen holding a photo album, which she set down on the table.

"There," said Julianne, pushing the album to Jane. "Open it. *Look* at it."

The binding was about to fall apart and the pages were brittle. Gently, Jane opened the album cover and saw a faded photo of a young Julianne cradling a black-haired infant in her arms.

"You see?" said Julianne. "That's me and Amy. She's only a few months old there, but she already has a head full of hair. Beautiful black hair." She looked at her daughter. "Just like she has now."

"Courtesy of Clairol," said Jane.

Julianne frowned at her. "What?"

"I saw a box of Clairol hair coloring in your lake house. At the time I assumed it was yours, to touch up gray roots. But it was really for your daughter, wasn't it? To keep her hair black." Jane looked at Amy, who stood mute and frozen. "Another detail I missed, but a nurse would have seen it. A nurse who bathed her, washed her hair, and noticed that blond roots were starting to grow out." She looked back at Julianne. "When did Sofia finally confront you? When did she tell you that she knew Amy wasn't really your daughter?"

Julianne's hands were trembling. She clasped them together to steady them, her fingers bunched so tightly that her knuckles jutted out, white as bone.

"Is that why you went to Sofia's house, to plead with her to keep the secret? Maybe you didn't *plan* to kill her. For that I'll give you the benefit of the doubt. But you brought a hammer with you that night. Just in case."

"She wouldn't *listen*!" Julianne sobbed. "All I asked her to do was keep quiet. To let us go on with our lives . . ."

"But she wouldn't, would she? She refused because she knew it was wrong. So you pulled out the hammer and took care of the problem. Then you broke the window in the kitchen door, stole a few items to make it look like a burglary. You must have thought you'd covered every detail. Until James Creighton showed up looking for his daughter. And you had to take care of *that* problem as well."

"That was self-defense! He *attacked* us."

"No, he didn't. You staged that attack. You called his burner phone and invited him to meet you at the lake house."

Julianne snatched up her cell phone and thrust it toward Jane. "Here. Look at my phone log. You can see I never called him."

"Not from your cell phone. You're not that careless. We have the records from Creighton's burner phone, and you called him from a pay phone. It's not easy to find pay phones these days, but you found one at a turnpike rest stop. Unfortunately for you, rest stops also have surveillance cameras, and there you are. Standing at that pay phone at precisely the time the call was made to Creighton's burner phone. Did you promise him he could talk to his daughter? He was dying of cancer and he had less than a year to live. He must have been desperate to see the little girl he thought he'd lost, so of course he showed up at the lake. Because you invited him there. Except it was a trap. You lured him, stabbed him to death, planted the hammer in his car. You even bruised your own daughter's neck, to make us believe he attacked her. You tied up all the loose ends."

"I did it for *us*. I did it for *Amy*." Julianne took a deep breath and said softly: "Everything I've done was for her."

Which Jane did not doubt. There was no more powerful force in the world than a parent's love for a child. A beautiful, terrible love that had led to the murders of two innocent people.

"Mom," said Amy. "What do you want me to do?"

Jane turned and for the first time she saw the gun in Amy's hands. Her finger was already on the trigger and her grip was unsteady, the barrel wavering. A frightened young woman on the edge of making a terrible mistake.

"We'll do what we always do," said Julianne. "We'll get past this, darling, and we'll move on." She stood up, took the gun from her daughter, and pointed it at Jane. "Stand up," she ordered. "Amy, get her weapon."

Calmly Jane rose to her feet and held up her arms as Amy pulled the gun from Jane's holster. "I take it we're going for a drive?" said Jane.

"I won't have blood in my kitchen."

"Julianne, you're only making things worse. For both of you."

"I'm just fixing things. The way I've always done."

"Do you really want to pull your daughter deeper into this? You've already made her an accomplice in James Creighton's murder."

"Go," Julianne ordered her. "Walk to the front door."

Jane looked at Amy. "You can stop this. You can stop *her*."

"*Go.*" Julianne's hands tightened on the weapon and unlike Amy, she had a steady grip and unwavering aim. She had killed before; she certainly wouldn't hesitate to kill again.

Jane could feel that gun aimed at her back as she walked out of the kitchen and up the hallway toward the foyer. She could not outrun a bullet; she had no choice but to comply. She reached the front door and paused. Turned to look once again at Julianne and Amy. Though they weren't related by blood, these two women were mother and daughter all the same, and they would protect each other.

"One last chance, Amy," said Jane.

"Just do what my mother says."

So this is how it's going to be, Jane thought. She opened the door and stepped outside. Heard Julianne suck in a gasp as she saw who was in the front yard: Barry Frost and two Boston PD patrol officers, who'd been poised to move in upon Julianne's arrival.

"It's over, Mrs. Antrim," said Jane.

"No." Julianne swung the gun toward Frost, then back to Jane. *"No."*

Both patrol officers had their weapons drawn and aimed at Julianne, but Jane raised her hand in a command to hold their fire. There'd been enough bloodshed; let this end without more.

"Give me the gun," Jane said.

"I had to do it, don't you see? I had no choice."

"You have a choice now."

"It would have torn apart my family. After all I did to protect her—"

"You're a good mother. No one doubts that."

"A good mother," Julianne whispered. She stared down at the gun in her hands, its barrel still pointed toward Jane. "A good mother does what has to be done."

No, thought Jane.

But Julianne was already raising the gun to her own head. Finger on the trigger, she pressed the barrel to her temple.

"Mom, don't!" cried Amy. "Please, Mommy."

Julianne went utterly still.

"I love you," Amy sobbed. "I need you." Slowly she moved toward her mother.

As much as Jane wanted to lunge between them and push Amy out of harm's way, she knew that Amy was the only one who could reach Julianne. Who could end this.

"Mommy," whimpered Amy. She wrapped her arms around Julianne and dropped her head on her mother's shoulder. "Mommy, don't leave me. Please."

Slowly Julianne lowered the gun. She offered no resistance when Jane took it from her grasp. Nor did she resist when Frost pulled her wrists behind her and slipped on handcuffs. He grasped her arm, pulled her away from her daughter.

"No, don't take her," Amy said as Frost led Julianne toward the patrol car.

Jane snapped handcuffs over Amy's wrists and led her toward a different vehicle. Only then, as the two women were pulled in different directions, did Julianne start struggling. She tried to twist away from Frost.

"Amy!" she screamed as Frost wrestled her into the cruiser. Her unearthly wail rose to a shriek as the car door slammed shut, locking her inside, separating her from her daughter.

"Amy!"

Even as the cruiser drove away, Jane could still hear that shriek, an echo of despair that lingered in the air long after Julianne was gone.

FORTY

ANGELA

I FEEL EVERYONE STARING AT ME as I stand at the bottom of the airport escalator, waiting for Vince to arrive. No wonder they're looking; I am a terrifying sight. My face is even more purple than it was four days ago, after my escape from the warehouse, and my cheek is so swollen it looks like an inflated balloon. These are the bruises of a warrior woman and I'm not embarrassed by them. I wear them proudly because I want Vince to see just how tough a cookie I am. Among all these people bustling around me in baggage claim, how many of them can say that they survived a kidnapping and *also* disarmed a neighbor?

That's how we Rizzoli women roll. No wonder my daughter's so good at what she does.

A hand gently settles on my arm and I turn to see a young woman with kind eyes frowning at me in concern.

"Excuse me for asking," she says softly, "but are you okay? Are you safe?"

"Oh, you mean this?" I point to my face.

"Did someone hurt you?"

"Yeah. He smacked me around pretty good."

"Oh honey, I hope you called the police. I hope you're pressing charges."

"I don't need to. He's dead."

My grin seems to startle her and she slowly backs away.

"But thanks for asking!" I call out as she retreats. What a nice lady, inquiring about my welfare. We should all be like her, watching out for one another, keeping one another safe. Something I already do because it comes naturally to me, even if too often it seems like I'm just meddling. I got these bruises from asking too many questions and poking my nose into other people's business, but that's why Larry Leopold's still alive, why Rick Talley won't be spending the rest of his life in jail, and why Nina Whatever-her-real-name-is no longer has to be afraid for her life.

"*Angie?* Oh my god, baby!"

I turn to see Vince stepping off the escalator. He drops his carry-on, grabs me by the shoulders, and stares at me.

"Oh, honey," he says. "It's so much worse than Jane told me."

"You talked to her?"

"Yesterday. She called to warn me about the black eye but she never said he beat the crap outta you. I swear, if that son of a bitch wasn't already dead I'd kill him myself!"

I take his face in my hands and gingerly lean in to kiss him. "I know you would, sweetie."

"I shouldn't have been in California. I should've been here to take care of you."

"I think I did a pretty good job of it myself."

"Not according to your daughter. She says you've turned into some kind of neighborhood watch lady. She says I should give you a good talking-to about the dangers of getting involved where you shouldn't."

"We'll discuss this when we get home."

But when we do get home, when we walk through the front door, I don't feel like talking about any of that. So we don't. Instead I bring a bottle of Chianti into the living room and I fill two glasses. I kiss him and he kisses me back. Being away in California for a month has not been good for him. His belly pokes out from all the fast food he's been eating and from being cooped up indoors with his sister. And he looks tired, so tired, from the flight. We wrap our arms around each other and it's as if my world has suddenly righted itself again and all the craziness of the past few weeks never happened. This is the way things should be: Vince and me, sipping wine, with dinner in the oven.

Through the window a movement catches my eye. I look across the street and see Jonas, who's once again pumping iron. He doesn't look my way because he knows that I know his secret. He's not who he claimed to be. There are so many secrets I've discovered about my neighbors. I know who had an affair with whom. I know who is not really a Navy SEAL. I know which one was terrified for her life. And most important, I know who I can count on to gamely rush into battle at my side, even if she has to do it wheezing and coughing.

Yes, I've come to know them all a little better and they've come to know me, and even though we don't always see eye-to-eye, and we sometimes stop talking to one another and occasionally even try to kill one another, this is my neighborhood. Someone has to keep an eye on it.

It might as well be me.

FORTY-ONE

AMY

Six Months Later

HER BLOND ROOTS WERE GROWING OUT. Every time she looked in the mirror she could see the hairs sprouting like a golden crown bursting free from her scalp. As long as she could remember, her hair had been black, her pale roots obsessively painted over every few weeks by her mother. *It's what we have to do to stay safe,* Julianne would say. And staying safe was the reason why they did what they did. The dyed hair. The moves from town to town. The repeated warnings: *Never trust anyone, Amy. You never know who will betray us.*

But then they moved to Boston and her mother found a job in the café across the street from the hospital and she met Dr. Michael Antrim. They fell in love and Julianne cast aside her own advice. They became a family. They had a home, a permanent home, one they would never have to leave. They were finally safe.

Until a completely random hit-and-run accident sent Amy to the hospital, where a nurse named Sofia saw the scar on Amy's chest and the rare blood type listed in her chart and the blond roots peeking out beneath her dark hair.

And their safe little world imploded.

Now her blond roots were longer than they'd ever been, longer than they'd been allowed to grow. Amy dipped her head, ran her fingers through the bicolor strands. This time she would not bother to darken them. She would let them grow; it was part of her transformation, back to the girl she used to be, a girl who was still a stranger to her. Every week she will surrender a little more of herself, a little more of Amy, until the real girl reclaimed it all.

There was no longer any reason for Lily to hide; everyone knew the truth now. Or part of the truth.

No one would ever know all of it.

Julianne had confessed to killing both Sofia Suarez and James Creighton. She had little choice but to confess; the evidence was there, in the record of the phone call she made to Creighton, a call in which she promised he would finally spend time with his long-lost daughter, Lily. He did not stalk them to Lantern Lake. He was invited there.

DNA had proved he was Amy's real father, but that only meant it was his sperm that fertilized the egg. He did not watch her grow up. It was Julianne who fed her and clothed her and sang to her. Julianne who protected her.

And who, in the end, sacrificed herself for her. Julianne pleaded guilty to both murders so Amy could walk free, all charges against her dropped. Amy, after all, was merely a victim, an abducted child who over the years bonded so thoroughly with her caregiver that loyalty clouded her judgment. She loved her mother; of course she would fetch her mother the gun. Of course she would lie about the death of James Creighton. Of course she would protect Julianne.

The way I protected her before.

She thought of the ugly rental house on Smith Hill Road where she lived with her mother and Bruce when she was eight years old. She remembered the hillside looming outside her window and the smell of ancient cigarette smoke that clung to the walls. She remembered all of this, right down to the stained wallpaper in her little closet of a bedroom. Faded blue cornflowers. She would huddle in bed, listening to the shouts in her mother's room, and she'd trace those blossoms on the wall, her finger skipping across the rip in the paper, where the old wallpaper showed through. Something tatty and green. Beneath the prettiest surfaces, there was always something ugly waiting to show itself. How many hours did she poke at that wallpaper, longing to be somewhere else, listening to Julianne's sobs and the thud of Bruce's fists on her mother's flesh? And the words he always used to make Julianne obey him: *If I lose, you lose. If you tell them what I did, they'll take your little girl away.*

Then one day, it all stopped. One day Amy could no longer stand the screaming. That was the day she finally found the courage to creep out of her bedroom, to walk into the kitchen and pull a knife from the drawer. When you are desperate enough, you find the strength to plunge a knife into a man's back. Even if you are only eight years old.

But the knife didn't go in deep enough to kill Bruce, only enrage him. He howled in pain and turned to face her, and at that moment it was not a man she saw standing over her, but a monster whose rage was now focused on her.

She remembered the alcohol on his breath as his hands closed over her throat, as he pressed the life out of her. And then it all went black and she did not remember anything else. She did not see Julianne snatch up the knife and plunge it into his body, again and again.

But she remembered what she saw when her vision cleared. Bruce, lying on the floor, his eyes frantic, his breath gurgling. And there was blood. So much blood.

"Go to your room, darling," her mother said. "Shut the door and don't come out until I tell you to. Everything will be fine, I promise."

And everything did turn out fine, in the end. Amy went to her room and waited for what seemed like forever. Through the closed door she heard the sound of something being dragged, then thumps on the porch steps, followed by a very long silence. Much later, water running in the sink and the washing machine rumbling and spinning.

When at last her mother told her to come out, Bruce was gone and the kitchen floor was damp and so clean, the linoleum was gleaming. "Where is he?" she asked.

"He left" was all her mother said.

"Where did he go?"

"It doesn't matter, sweetheart. All that matters is he won't hurt us again. But you have to promise me you won't tell anyone what happened today. It's the only way we'll be safe. Promise me."

Amy did.

A week later, they were on the road, just the two of them. *You and me against the world,* they sang as they drove away from the shack. Amy never knew what her mother did with Bruce's body and she never asked. Buried him in the field, perhaps, or dropped him down the abandoned well. Julianne had always been good with details; she'd surely disposed of him someplace where he'd never be found and she'd scrubbed that kitchen so clean that the landlord never knew the linoleum hid microscopic traces of a dead man's blood.

They had lived so long under the radar, moving from place to place, that they made few friends and developed few attachments. No one ever asked about Bruce Flagler's disappearance. No one cared. Only Amy and her mother knew what happened in that kitchen, in that sad shack under the hill, and neither of them would ever tell because along with courage, love sometimes demanded silence.

A knock on the bathroom door abruptly brought her back to the present. To the house in Boston where she now lived.

"Amy?" her father called through the door. "It's getting late."

"I'll be right out."

"Are you—are you sure you want to visit her?"

She could hear the doubt in his voice. And the pain. Although Amy insisted on visiting her mother every two weeks, Mike Antrim still could not bear to lay eyes on Julianne. In time, perhaps, he'd come to understand why she had done it. He'd understand the desperation that made her drive to Sofia's house that night and plead for her silence. He'd understand why, when her pleadings failed, she'd pulled the hammer from her purse.

Amy understood.

She looked once again at the mirror and wondered if her mother would disapprove of the blond roots. After so many years of keeping herself hidden, this new girl was emerging from her chrysalis, every day a bit blonder, a bit more Lily. She hadn't decided yet if this was a good thing; she would have to ask Julianne. Julianne would have the answer.

Mothers always do.

ACKNOWLEDGMENTS

A MANUSCRIPT IS JUST THE BEGINNING. I'm grateful for the hard work and expertise of everyone who turned my mere words into a finished book. A big thanks to my editors Jenny Chen (U.S.) and Sarah Adams (U.K.) for helping make this story shine, to my copy editor for rescuing me from countless embarrassments, and to my publishing teams at Ballantine and Transworld for their enthusiastic support through the years. Thanks also to my tireless literary agent Meg Ruley and the incomparable Jane Rotrosen Literary Agency. Go Team JRA!

And to my husband, Jacob, thank you for hanging in there. It's not easy being married to a writer, but you do it better than anyone.